Remembrance Man

Fear and despair during
the 1832 cholera epidemic

BY

NICHOLAS KINSEY

Printed on acid-free paper

Second Edition, October 2023
ISBN 978-1-7389911-9-8

Cinegrafica Films & Publishing
820 Rougemont
Quebec, QC G1X 2M5
Canada
Tel. 418-652-3345

In memory of my mother
Winifred Mary Pryce

FOREWORD

I am a Canadian and British writer and director of film and television drama. I started work on a film version of this story back in 2003 and so it has been some 17 years now that I have been drawn to this fascinating story. This is a novel, not a work of history. Whenever the demands of the two have clashed, I have chosen to go with the former. I have nevertheless tried to make the fiction accord with the facts about the extraordinary events of the summer of 1832 when the cholera epidemic hit Western Ontario.

PROLOGUE

"...From the south to the north hath the Cholera come,
He came like a despot king;
He hath swept the earth with a conqueror's step,
And the air with a spirit's wing.
We shut him out with a girdle of ships,
And a guarded quarantine;
What ho! Now which of your watchers slept?
The Cholera's past your line!
There's a curse on the blessed sun and air,
What will ye do for breath?
For breath, which was once, but a word for life,
Is now but a word for death.
Wo for affection! when love must look
On each face, it loves with dread—
Kindred and friends—when a few brief hours
And the dearest may be the dead!
The months pass on, and the circle spreads
And the time is drawing nigh
When each street may have a darkened house
Or a coffin passing by..."
"Christmas" by Letitia Elizabeth Landon,
Literary Gazette, January 27, 1832

Cholera was an ancient disease that had spread from the Indian subcontinent to Europe. 'Cholera morbus' was first described during an outbreak among British soldiers and their camp followers in Jessore, India, in 1817. It appeared suddenly and spread rapidly. It had many nicknames: 'King Cholera' and the 'Blue Death' due to the bluish pallor of its victims. The disease swept through the cities of Europe, claiming the lives of some 6,500 people in London and 20,000 in Paris during the summer of 1832. People were deathly afraid of cholera and fear spread faster than the disease itself.

The German poet Heinrich Heine described the arrival of cholera in Paris: "On March 29th, the night of mi-careme, a masked ball was in progress. Suddenly, the merriest of the harlequins felt a chill in his legs, took off his mask, and to the amazement of all, revealed a violet-blue face. Laughter died out, dancing ceased, and in a short while several carriage loads of people were driven directly from the ball to the Hotel-Dieu, the main hospital, where they arrived in their fancy dress and promptly died. To prevent a panic among the patients, they were thrust into rude graves in their gaudy costumes... Soon the public halls were filled with dead bodies, sewed in sacks for want of coffins. Long lines of hearses stood in a queue outside Pere Lachaise. Everybody wore flannel bandages. The rich gathered up their belongings and fled the town."

The word cholera came from the Latin word 'choler' meaning diarrhea and from Greek word 'kholera' meaning 'bile'. The bacterium *Vibrio comma* is a comma-shaped, one-celled organism that is found in drinking water contaminated by the feces of an infected person or from contaminated fish and shellfish. It produces a toxin in the small intestine, which renders the wall of the stomach porous to water. Vomiting and massive purging of liquids result in de-hydration. Cholera can drain up to a litre of fluid from its victims every hour, mostly in the form of diarrhea. The victim suffers severe spasms and cramps, great thirst, and eventually kidney failure. A person in good health at daybreak can suddenly become violently ill, have their skin turn a ghastly bluish tint, become severely dehydrated, and die within hours.

The movement of the disease across continents and countries was a mystery. It would not be until the late 19th century that scientists knew that cholera was caused by a bacillus carried in water and that proper sanitation could prevent the spread of the deadly disease. People were terrified by the horrific symptoms, which seemed to afflict victims instantly. There was no known cure, and the sense of panic among the population was palpable. A description in the London Gazette described the symptoms: "Sufferers appeared sharp and contracted, the eye sinks, the look is expressive of terror and wildness. The skin is deadly cold and often damp, the tongue always moist, often white and loaded, but flabby and chilled like a piece of dead flesh."

During those dark days, stories spread about reopening coffins in which the dead had apparently come back to life only to die from suffocation. No one wanted to bury a loved one who might still be alive. Corpses were often placed in public viewing mortuaries to avoid premature burial and to provide morbid entertainment for onlookers. The fear of being buried alive was so great in the 19th century that families would install 'burial reeds' in coffins with long tubes to the surface, allowing the dead to call for help. Safety coffins were invented with bells installed at the surface so that the dead person could pull on a string to ring the bell to call for help. Cemeteries hired *remembrance men* to watch over graves to reassure families that their loved ones had stayed peacefully dead and to rescue them if they ever came back to life.

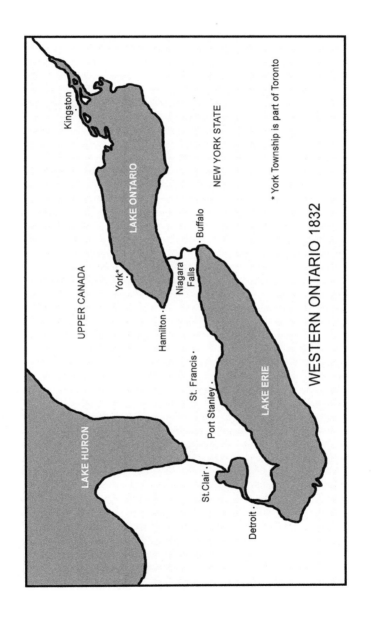

WESTERN ONTARIO 1832

UPPER CANADA

LAKE HURON

LAKE ONTARIO

LAKE ERIE

NEW YORK STATE

Kingston

York*

Hamilton

Niagara
Falls

Buffalo

St. Francis

Port Stanley

St. Clair

Detroit

* York Township is part of Toronto

One

August 1832

I'm coming, I'm coming the scourge of mankind,
I float on the waters, I ride on the wind,
Great hunger and squalor prepare my dread way,
In the homes of the wretched my sceptre I sway,
In filthy, damp alleys and courts I reign,
O'er the dark stagnant pool and putrid drain.
"Cholera" by James Withers, 1853

A two-wheel buggy rolled across the long grassy prairie near a large manor house in St. Francis in Western Ontario. A man in a buckskin coat and cap approached the estate, driving along the rutted track that joined the hedgerow perimeter. The manor sat at the centre of a vast estate belonging to the Grenville family. Loyalists after the American War of Independence, the family had acquired the manor and land some fifty years earlier and it had been passed down from father to son. The rich loamy soil was perfect for farming and, with a creek running through it, the Grenville estate had flourished ever since.

The man spied a young woman in a bonnet and a dirty white apron picking beans in the vegetable garden on the other side of the hedgerow. He stopped the buggy and stepped down, carefully picking up a baby boy wrapped in a blue blanket. He slipped through the hedgerow with the child under his arm and laid him down gently in a row of cabbages. He kissed the child's forehead and wiped away his tears before returning to the buggy.

With her back to the road, Gerty never noticed the man and the buggy disappearing in the distance. As she collected her basket of green beans for the return to the manor house, she spotted the child in the row of cabbages. She approached warily, looking around for a parent, but seeing no one. She peered down at the boy with his pale bluish complexion, and his eyes lit up at the sight of her.

"What are you doing here, little man?"

Gerty was an eighteen-year-old scullery maid and servant in the Grenville kitchen. She smiled at the baby, who looked dehydrated and feverish. She leaned down and picked him up in his blanket.

"You poor thing. Where's your mama, child?"

She looked at the empty track beyond the hedgerow before turning around and heading back to the main house.

In the summer kitchen, the sight of the sick child created alarm among the cooking staff. Gerty had laid the baby on a bench near the entrance and was surrounded by several servant girls eager to get a look at the child. She touched the lips of the boy with the ladle from the water bucket just as the cook arrived, holding a kitchen knife. The cook shrieked at the sight of the baby.

"That child's sick. Get him out of here," she yelled. "He's carrying something."

"But matron, I couldn't leave him in the field," Gerty replied. "We must look after him."

"No, you don't. If Missus Grenville gets wind of this, we'll all be sent home."

"We can hide 'im in the barn. No one will be the wiser. Please, matron."

"Get him outta here, Gerty, 'fore Baxter or the girls come waltzing into my kitchen."

Gerty wrapped the child in the blue blanket and ran out the back door. The cook collected the ladle and dumped it into the pail of fresh water before returning to the stove.

Two

The following morning, Gerty collected the pail of slops and carried it out to the pigs. She looked sad and exhausted after a long night. She returned to the kitchenm where the butler and the lady's maid were waiting for her. The kitchen staff looked sheepish as they assembled in front of Baxter and Miss Millie.

"Gerty, what were you thinking?" asked Miss Millie.

"I'm sorry, miss," Gerty said as she tried to fight back tears and failed. "What else could I do?"

"You should have warned us, my dear, and not taken it upon yourself to bring the blue death into this house."

The little boy had died during the night. Gerty and the other scullery maids had worked feverishly to save the child, but the truth of it was they'd had no idea how to save him.

"The child is dead, so we must bury it as soon as possible," said Baxter. "I don't want Madam Lucille and the girls to know about this, so please keep your mouths shut."

"How could they leave a child like that in the field, sir?" asked Gerty. "He was just a baby. I don't understand."

"Fear, Gerty. People are fleeing the cholera. They are abandoning the sick everywhere," said Baxter.

"Where's the cook?" asked Miss Millie. "We need to get on with the breakfast serving."

"I haven't seen her, miss," Gerty replied.

Miss Millie turned to the other maids, but they were already shaking their heads. Miss Millie fixed one of them with an imperious stare.

"Go down and knock on her door," she ordered.

The girl ran off, clattering down the stairs.

"Gerty, go fetch the child and bring it to the back pasture," said Baxter. "I'll have Smiley join you there and dig the grave."

"Will we have a ceremony, sir?" Gerty asked.

"No, we must keep this quiet. We must forget this ever happened."

"But sir, every child deserves a Christian burial," said Miss Millie, who was a very religious woman.

Baxter shot her a sidelong glance but said nothing. They all waited in an uncomfortable silence until the maid returned and breathlessly announced that the cook was not feeling well.

"She was fine yesterday, sir," said Miss Millie. "Maybe she's just starting a cold."

"How is she?" Baxter asked the maid.

"She's vomiting, sir. She looks very pale."

There was a collective gasp in the room. The kitchen staff were fearful of any symptoms that might lead to a cholera death. It was happening all around the country, and word travelled fast. A seemingly healthy person could suddenly fall ill and die from the blue death within hours.

Baxter noticed the furtive glances around the room and knew that the young and impressionable maids, flighty at best, were already gauging the others for signs of illness. Baxter tried to quell the fear with a few words of comfort.

"Look," he said, trying to convey an assurance he did not feel, "it may be nothing at all. Let's get on with the breakfast schedule. We'll talk later."

Lucille Grenville, the matriarch of the family, had to be told immediately. There was no way to hide a sick cook from her eagle eye. A flustered servant girl was about to enter the dining room with Lucille's hard-boiled egg and toast when Baxter stopped her in the hall with a stern look and took the breakfast tray from her.

Lucille was seated alone in the room at the head of a long table. She was a small, thin woman with grey hair who had lost her husband to the typhus epidemic four years earlier. She had run the farm and estate alone since her husband's death. She was an energetic forty-year-old with an imposing presence, who would not tolerate disrespect, real or imagined.

"Well?" she asked, raising an eyebrow when she saw Baxter enter with the tray. He went to the head of the table and whispered in her deaf ear.

"We have a problem, ma'am."

"Please repeat that, Baxter," said Lucille, as she picked up a spoon to crack the egg. "I didn't catch it."

"The cook, ma'am. She's sick."

"What do you mean, sick?"

"She's vomiting, ma'am."

Lucille jerked upright in her chair, dropping the spoon and the sudden motion caused the egg to roll off the table and hit the floor.

"You don't mean?"

"We don't know for sure, ma'am," Baxter said hastily as he leaned down to pick up the egg. "She was fine yesterday."

"We can't have this, Baxter," said Lucille with a trace of fear crossing her face. "We need to get her out of the house immediately and send her home."

"Yes, ma'am."

"Put her in a wagon and get someone to drive her back to the town."

Baxter bowed silently, wiped the egg clean and deposited it in the silver cup in front of Lucille.

"Thank you," said Lucille as Baxter hurried out of the room.

"Why so glum, mother?"

Lucille started at the sound of her daughter's voice. She hadn't heard Emily come into the room. Her daughter was a lively blonde with blue eyes and a ready smile, who had just turned twenty.

"The cook is sick. She's vomiting," Lucille told her.

The seriousness suddenly dawned on the young woman who looked stricken with fear, whether it was for her own family or the cook, or both, it was hard to tell. Emily took after her mother. She was a bright girl, a quick study, whose only fault, in her mother's view, was to wear her heart on her sleeve.

"Are you sure, mother?" Emily could hardly bring herself to ask. "Are you sure it's cholera?"

"It doesn't matter. We can't take the chance."

"But mother, if she's sick, we can't send her home."

"We can and we will," said Lucille, her voice brooking no argument. She saw the look in her daughter's eyes and gently patted her hand. "Emily, her family can look after her. We cannot have the sickness in this house. Do you understand me?"

"Yes, mother."

In the oppressive silence that followed, the servant girl brought in a breakfast tray for Emily with a bowl of porridge, toast and juice. She put it down in front of Emily and started to fill the water glasses on the table.

Three

The rolling prairies extended as far as the eye could see. On a hill to the east, a man on a white horse appeared in the midday sun. He was followed by two men in a wagon that rattled over the rough track, rolling down the hill towards a sharecropper's sod house near a creek hidden in a copse of pine trees. The house appeared to be folded into the prairie grassland, its back wall dug into the ground and its roof covered with grass.

A woman appeared in the doorway holding an old flintlock musket. Her short hair was uncombed and dirty, as was her ill-fitting brown shirt and skirt. She crossed her arms as she watched the men make their approach.

Constable John Riley led the way. He sat his horse well, with the assurance of a man who had spent a lifetime in the saddle. He looked like a wizened old cowboy in a John Bull hat and brown waistcoat with a collarless shirt. Young Paolo Morelli, in a brown tweed cap, drove the wagon sitting next to his uncle Vito in shirtsleeves, smoking a clay pipe.

A naked five-year-old boy with a runny nose grabbed his distraught mother's hand as they watched the men approach. The woman ignored the boy's hand and raised the musket to her shoulder. She would need both hands to shoot. She cocked the hammer and looked down the sights. She held her breath and carefully pulled the trigger. The boom and crack of the ball as it whizzed over the heads of the men in the wagon caused instant panic. The constable struggled to calm his mount, and Paolo had to lean back hard to stop the team of horses from bolting. The men were taken by surprise and had not expected to be shot at. The constable ordered the men in the wagon to stay put.

"Ma'am, don't shoot. We've come for the body," yelled Riley, advancing on his horse.

The boy whimpered in fear, but his mother ignored him. She busied herself reloading the musket, opening the flash pan and reaching into her shirt pocket for another paper cartridge containing powder and ball.

"You ain't comin' in 'ere," she yelled at the constable. "He ain't dead yet."

"Not what we've been hearing, ma'am."

"You comin' any closer. I'm gonna shoot you."

"Please, ma'am. Put down that gun right this minute or I'll have to take it away from you."

The little boy in the doorway started to cry as the constable negotiated with the woman.

"Go back inside, child."

The boy continued to whimper as the woman finished loading the musket and raised it to her shoulder.

"You go on outta 'ere. You ain't got no bizness 'round 'ere."

"We've come for the body, ma'am."

"You go on home now or I be shootin'."

"Your man is dead, ma'am. Nothing's gonna change that. Are you going to let us see him?"

The woman fired a second round above the head of the constable, who had lost all patience and charged forward on his horse, pushing the woman to the ground and causing the little boy to run into the hut, wailing. He quickly dismounted and grabbed the musket away from the woman.

All the fight had gone out of her. She was waif-thin with dark hair and fine features. She wrapped her arms around herself and glared at the constable. There was something dignified and refined in the woman's defiance, in spite of her dire circumstances.

The Morellis entered the hut, pulling bandanas over their noses. They found the dead husband lying on a bedsheet in a dark corner of the one-room hut as the boy continued to sob nearby.

"Your sister Rebecca came by, ma'am. She's worried about you."

"My sister, she don't know nothin'."

"You're putting your child at risk, ma'am, keeping a blue death in here."

The constable entered the hut and picked up the little boy, trying to distract him as the men collected his father's body. The smell of putrefaction was overpowering as Vito and Paolo quickly hauled the man in the sheet out the door while the distraught woman looked on. They carried the body over to the wagon and dumped it unceremoniously in the back.

In the doorway, the child grasped the constable's moustache and pulled on it, eliciting a smile from the lawman.

"You have a wonderful boy here, ma'am. Why don't you collect your things and come with us? Your sister is asking for you."

"I ain't goin' nowhere," said the woman, glaring at the constable. "This is my land. Now get the hell off my property."

"I'm sorry you feel that way, ma'am."

Constable Riley put down the child and realized that he had just removed any hope of survival on the prairie for this woman. Without her man, there was no way she could farm this land alone. She was just too stubborn to listen to reason, thought the constable. He would certainly have a talk later with the sister about bringing them both to town.

"My condolences, ma'am. He'll be buried in the cemetery in St. Francis. Good day."

He donned his hat to the woman and climbed on his horse. The woman and boy watched in silence as the men departed.

Four

In the pasture, the black houseman took off his frock coat and rolled up his sleeves. Smiley Webb was going grey around the temples and looked tired. With the lack of farm workers on the estate because of the epidemic, Smiley had been recruited for all kinds of physically demanding jobs around the manor. He didn't mind the hard work and was happy to help, but he didn't like his present task.

He picked up a spade and began to dig a shallow grave near an oak tree for the body of the child. Gerty sat nearby, looking on disconsolately as Smiley worked the spade in the hole.

"He was such a nice boy. I found him in the vegetable garden only yesterday and now he's dead," she said, wiping tears from her eyes.

"It's a shame, Miss Gerty. A real shame, a child so young."

"We tried to save him, but it happened so fast."

"A few years back, I had a child die on me from typhus. His mother couldn't face the death of her son, so I was sent in to hold his hand in the last moments. It seemed the Christian thing to do. The little boy looked me in the eye and asked me how his Soul was ever gonna get to Heaven,..."

Smiley thrust the spade deeper into the hole as Gerty hung on his words.

"... 'cause his legs would no longer carry 'im, seeing as they'd be full of worms."

Smiley grunted as he flung the dirt aside.

"How does a grown man comfort a dying child?"

"I wouldn't know, Mr Webb."

"Well, I'd never done this before, so I took his hand in mine and told him something like what the pastor of my church might have said."

"What did you say?"

"I tole 'im not to worry that God would send his angels down to earth and they'd carry his Soul to Heaven. He looked happy to hear it, 'cause it had been bothering him for a long time. Then moments later, he died."

"Mr Webb, you know you are a good man," said Gerty tearfully.

"I was sitting there on the child's bed and, as I looked up, I saw this rustling in the drapes and his Soul gone out through that there window. I ain't never seen nothin' like that before."

With wide eyes, Gerty watched Smiley finish digging the hole in the ground.

After supper, a wagon was prepared and Baxter called to Miss Millie and the kitchen staff to help prepare the cook for her trip to town. The scullery maids had visited the poor woman several times during the day, but she was no better. She was dehydrated, and her skin had turned a bluish tint. There seemed to be little doubt that cholera had found its first victim among the staff.

Baxter planned to send Gerty along with the cook to give her water and make her as comfortable as possible. He sent two men downstairs to collect the woman and bring her out to the wagon for the trip. When they finally came out, they were carrying the cook on a makeshift litter, one at her head and the other at her feet. A bedsheet covered her face.

"How is she?" asked Gerty.

"She's dead," said a man.

"She ain't breathin'," said the other.

The men didn't slacken their pace as they carried the body out to the wagon. It took a moment for Gerty and the others to take it in. She had been as strong as an ox and, in less than twenty-four hours, she had been struck down by the blue death. It seemed like the act of the devil. She had been such a good-natured, happy person and was loved by everyone in the kitchen. Their shock gave way to tears as they realized she was gone for good.

"I'm sorry, Gerty," said Baxter, looking shaken. "She's dead, so you won't be making the journey."

Miss Millie was crying when she came upstairs with the cook's battered suitcase, everything the woman had once owned inside it. She wordlessly handed it to Baxter, who went outside to see the driver. He gave the suitcase to the man, who placed it carefully in the bed of the wagon. Baxter said a final word to the driver, who nodded and then climbed on the wagon and took the reins. Gerty and the kitchen staff watched as the wagon moved off in the failing light.

Five

It was hard work, digging graves in the heat of the summer. Vito was down in a hole some four feet deep, digging a new grave. Wearing suspenders and a dirty white shirt with sweat rings, his head bobbed up and down, wet with perspiration.

Nearby Paolo and partner Joey, naked to the waist, were busy digging similar graves with shovels and picks. Paolo stopped to wipe his brow as he watched a horse-drawn wagon arrive at the far side of the cemetery. Two cholera men with bandanas covering their faces jumped down from the wagon and started to unload. They grabbed the nearest body and threw it into the cholera pit. The pit was about twenty feet long and six feet wide, located as far away as possible from the richer plots belonging to the wealthier citizens of St. Francis. Anonymous bodies in rags and bedsheets were laid out in rows, one on top of another, with a coating of lime between them. Cholera men were paid a pittance by the town council to remove unclaimed bodies on the public roads around the town.

The good citizens of St. Francis were quick to abandon their friends and loved ones as soon as they fell ill. Sisters and brothers, fathers and mothers were shunned and isolated as quickly as possible. The townspeople felt that they had to maintain a minimum appearance of normality and couldn't afford the stigmatization of being labelled a 'cholera town'.

Paolo stepped out of the grave and collected a water bottle from his kit. He drank greedily as he watched a fancy wagon enter the cemetery carrying a simple pine coffin. Paolo watched as it drove over to the grave where his Uncle Vito was working. A man wearing a straggly Van Dyke beard and dressed in a black frock coat and top hat stepped down from the wagon. Paolo recognized him as Maloney, the funeral director.

The director was proud of his gold medal of Our Lady of Grace fixed to his buttonhole, which gave him a certain prestige among both Catholic and Protestant churchgoers in St. Francis. The engraving showed Mary with her open arms, standing on a globe crushing a serpent beneath her feet. The Miraculous Medal was highly coveted and inspired by the vision of Saint Catherine Labouré in 1830 in the *Chapelle des Soeurs de la Charité* in Paris. Maloney had gone to enormous trouble to procure the medal from a rich merchant in Hamilton. From experience, he had discovered that it paid for a funeral director to flaunt his religious convictions and show piety and respect on all occasions.

Vito mopped his face and climbed out of the grave, cap in hand, to greet Maloney as the driver and another man went to the back of the wagon and hauled the coffin out of the back. They laid it on the grass a short distance away, near some large headstones. Maloney stepped away from Vito, holding a handkerchief over his nose.

"Keep your distance, Morelli," said Maloney. "This one goes in the Elliott plot."

He slipped some coins into Vito's hand and withdrew quickly.

"It's ready, sir," Vito said.

"Good. The blue death will get us all."

"Yes, sir."

"My instructions are to watch this one real close," said Maloney, as he looked over at young Paolo digging a grave nearby. "Who is the young man?"

"My nephew, sir. He arrived from Detroit a week ago."

"And is he pulling his weight?"

"He will, sir. He just started."

"Well, good day to you."

Vito gave a slight bow, but Maloney had already turned away. He and his underlings hurried back to their wagon and beat a hasty retreat, whipping the horse as they trotted off towards the entrance.

Late that afternoon, Vito, Paolo, and Joey used straps to lower the coffin of the Elliott family member into the ground. Vito jumped down into the grave with a hand drill and quickly bored a hole into the pine box. He carefully hammered a burial reed into the box using a brass sleeve. He crossed himself and climbed out as Paolo and Joey threw dirt down on the coffin.

A wagon approached slowly from the south, driven by a short, wiry forty-year-old woman in a wide-brimmed straw hat. The men watched Nelly, Vito's wife, as she wound her way through the woods towards them. Paolo and Joey gathered up their things as Nelly arrived in the wagon.

"Did you have a nice day?"

"Yes, ma'am," said Paolo, putting his things in the back of the wagon as Vito removed his lunch basket.

"Maloney came by," said Vito.

"So you got a new one to watch," said Nelly. "There's a puddin' in that basket for your sweet tooth, honey."

"*Grazie, tesoro.* I love you."

REMEMBRANCE MAN

Paolo and Joey climbed on board for the return trip to the cabin and waved to Vito on their way out of the cemetery. While Joey joked with Nelly upfront, Paolo fell asleep in the back of the wagon.

I'm so tired after a long day's work, I often fall asleep in the wagon on our way home. Poor Uncle Vito will be up most of the night watching over the graves. He's a 'remembrance man' hired by the families of the deceased to watch over their graves. If someone calls for help, he's supposed to dig out the graves and save them. I asked him how this can work. Dead people don't resurrect from the grave. They are dead and can't come back to life. Uncle Vito says that no one has been lucky enough to do this yet under his watch.

I was delivering groceries in Detroit when cholera struck the town. People disappeared from our street every day. One day they were smiling at you, and the next day they were gone. My mamma and papa locked up the shop and stayed home. They sent me to join Uncle Vito because business was bad in the city and I could earn more here working in the cemetery. They say that the air is better for one's health out in the country. I don't know about that. The air may be good, but you could always die from exhaustion digging graves.

Six

Constable Riley crossed the street from the jail and entered the hotel bar. The bartender had his whisky ready by the time he sat down.

"Long day, Constable."

"Yeah," sighed Riley. "You ain't seen Rebecca around, have you, Eddy?"

"Nope, she took off with that whisky trader a few days ago."

"Damn."

He'd hoped to take Rebecca out to see her sister, get her to talk some sense into the woman. I should have done that in the first place, thought Riley. He drained the whisky in one go and waited for Eddy to pour him a refill.

"She sent me out to her sister's place when she heard that Ross had died."

"I hadn't heard."

"Dead and buried now," Riley told him. "She wouldn't come back with me."

"What are you gonna do?" asked Eddy. "You can't leave no woman and child alone out on the prairie. There are wolves and Indians out there."

"I know, Eddy," Riley said drily, remembering the musket and the woman's angry defiance. "She can defend herself all right. She fired her musket at me."

"She did?" asked Eddy. "Well, well. That's Eleanor Ross. She's got quite a reputation, just like her sister."

It was after midnight when Baxter knocked on Emily's door in the silent house.

"Miss Emily, please get up. Your mother is not feeling well. She's asking for you."

"I'm coming," called Emily from her bed, still drowsy from sleep. She put on a shawl over her nightdress and hurried to the door. Baxter held up an oil lamp and led the way. Lucille Grenville slept in the master bedroom on the floor below Emily. They hurried down the stairs and joined a housemaid with a bucket of water and a washcloth. As soon as Emily appeared in the doorway, her mother called to her.

"Emily, come here, my dear."

Lucille was lying in bed. She looked haggard, with a pale bluish tint to her translucent skin. She had started vomiting after the family had gone to bed and had called Baxter.

"Mother, are you all right?"

"No, dear, I'm not all right. I believe I've caught the blue death just like the cook. Come closer, dear. I want to talk to you about your future."

"But mother, we can save you. We must save you."

"Don't talk nonsense, my dear. I may not last the night. I don't have much time. Please sit down and listen to me."

Emily sat on the edge of the bed after pushing the bedpan away. She reached out a hand and touched her mother's forehead. Her skin was cold and clammy.

"Mother, you cannot die. I need you. You have to get better."

"Tomorrow, I want you to send a letter to your cousin Lionel and have him come out here. He'll handle everything. My will is in the desk drawer. Lionel will take it to the court."

"But mother, you cannot die on us. What are we to do?"

"Child, you are the strong one. All your life, you have been preparing to take on the task of running the estate. You can do it with Lionel's help. And don't forget Smiley. That man is an angel and devoted to our family."

Emily wiped her tears away.

"Now listen, it was your father's wish that Daphne be locked up. I was against it in the beginning, but now that I'm dying, I want you to respect his decision. Daphne's condition has not improved."

"Mother, you can't leave us."

"Now go wake Jimmy and Tommy. I want to say goodbye to my boys."

Emily stood up with tears in her eyes and stumbled out of the room. Lucille watched her go and then summoned Baxter from his post just outside the door. There was a brief pause before he came and stood by the bed with his eyes lowered.

"I want you to keep an eye on Emily and the boys. They will need help in their new life."

"Yes, ma'am."

"Look at me, Baxter."

He reluctantly raised his head. She thought she could see a tear in the corner of his eye, but dismissed it as a trick of her failing sight.

"Will you do it?" she asked.

"I will, ma'am."

Seven

Emily had managed only a few hours of fitful sleep, curled up in an armchair beside Lucille's bed. The chirping of the birds woke her an hour before dawn. She looked at her mother, who was lying very still in the bed. Finally, she noticed the slight rise and fall of her chest. Emily went to the door. A maid had been on watch all night.

"Some water, please. She's parched."

The maid stood up and poured water into a glass from the pitcher on the sideboard. She gave it to Emily, who returned to the bedroom. Baxter arrived as Emily dripped water from the glass into her mother's mouth.

"Would you like a cup of tea, Miss Emily?" Baxter asked.

"Yes, please."

Baxter went downstairs to get the tea. In the kitchen, Gerty and Miss Millie were wide awake, waiting for news.

"How is she, sir?" asked Gerty, putting the water on the boil.

"Not good, I think," said Baxter, shaking his head. "Let's see whether she'll drink some tea."

Baxter looked out the window as the light came up. Two scullery maids had been sent home the previous week, and both had died. He had never seen anything like it. He feared for his job and the future of the Grenville estate.

Light was coming through the bedroom window when Baxter returned with the tea tray. He stopped for a moment in the doorway. Emily was slumped over Lucille. He put the tray down on the bedside table and gently touched Emily's shoulder.

"She's gone, Baxter," she sobbed. "She's gone."

At first, he thought it was a large dog lying on the grassy roof. He couldn't remember a dog from the day before. As he rode closer amid the profusion of wildflowers, the animal raised itself and took one look in his direction before loping off toward the creek. It wasn't a dog.

It was a big grey wolf. At that moment, he knew he had done the right thing. At the risk of making a fool of himself, he had returned to the sod house on his white gelding, leading a second mount for Eleanor Ross and her child in the hope that he could persuade them to leave. The sod house looked deserted, and between that and the sight of the wolf, Riley felt a growing sense of alarm. He dismounted near the front door.

"Ma'am, it's Constable Riley. Are you in there?"

He pushed the door open and stepped inside. In the dark interior, it looked like Eleanor Ross had left in a hurry. The cooking pots and clothes were gone, but the bedsheets and the stink of cholera remained.

Riley thought she must have had the help of a friend or a neighbour to get to town. He stepped out of the house and walked around the perimeter. One wall was folded into the prairie grassland, so he stood on the roof and looked down on the creek behind the trees. The wolf was still there, lurking near the water's edge. Maybe the Ross family had succeeded in domesticating the animal. Now, the wolf would have to return to nature and hunt for its own food. There weren't any other families living in the vicinity to throw it scraps from the dinner table.

Riley looked at the promising corn crop with no one to care for or harvest it. This was the end of a dream for the Ross family. All their efforts over the years had come to nought.

Eight

With the cholera epidemic raging, families preferred to avoid public gatherings, especially funeral masses where they might be exposed to the disease. They favoured prayer services or vigils at home with family and friends, followed by the rite of committal at the interment.

At the wake for Lucille Grenville, her body was laid out on a table in the parlour, facing a row of hard-backed chairs. She was dressed in a white nightgown and a handkerchief was tied under her chin to keep her mouth closed. Rosary beads were wrapped around her hands. Emily sat with her brothers, five-year-old Tommy and eight-year-old Jimmy, who fidgeted constantly near several housemaids who were busy catching up on their knitting. Emily looked up at the clock on the wall, which was stopped at the hour of her mother's death. The windows were kept open to allow the spirit of the departed to leave the house, but also to air out the room, what with the smell coming off the dead woman's body.

From time to time, friends of the family would enter the room to pay their respects to the departed. They would whisper a few words to Emily and silently view the corpse, crossing themselves, before leaving the room. The tradition was that the body should never be left alone without the presence of a family member and, if that were not possible, a woman must at all times be in the room.

The wake went on for two full days and nights. Emily remained there through the nights, except when Miss Millie or Gerty replaced her so she could catch a wink of sleep. The boys quickly lost interest and only joined their sister from time to time to keep her company.

It was during the waning hours of the second night when Emily became aware of another presence in the room. She'd been dozing in a chair when she opened her eyes to see Smiley praying silently over her mother's body. He was wearing his best clothes, threadbare as they were. There was a solemn dignity about the man that Emily had recognized from an early age.

"Smiley, you came," said Emily. "I'm sure mother would be happy to see you."

"Your mother was a wonderful woman, Miss Emily. We will miss her terribly."

"Come and sit with me," said Emily. "It's been a long night."

"It's not my place. The wake is for family and friends, but thank you."

Smiley retreated quietly, going to the door. He turned around to look out the window at the first rays of light coming up in the east. He made the sign of the cross and then looked back at Lucille's exhausted daughter.

"Her spirit has departed the body, Miss Emily. Lucille is free. Let me get you a cup of tea to welcome in the new day."

"I would love that, Smiley."

Maloney's fancy wagon was loaded with Lucille Grenville's coffin and draped in black. Two men in top hats and dark cloaks sat up front, waiting for an order to leave the manor for the cemetery. Miss Millie, Gerty and a dozen kitchen and house staff stood in two rows flanking the entrance to the manor house. Smiley sat at the reins of the waiting calash as Baxter opened the door from within the house and stood ramrod straight against it as Emily emerged with the two boys. The distress was visible on their faces, and they seemed unsure as to what was expected of them. Emily was veiled and dressed in black. The boys waited quietly as Baxter walked past them to help Emily into the calash.

The driver of the funeral carriage paused a respectful moment before setting off toward the front gates. Smiley followed with the calash, Baxter and the rest of the staff falling in behind. It was a sad, slow-moving procession as it emerged from the estate. Many more mourners joined the cortege as it wound its way through the countryside. It was a measure of the regard in which they held Lucille Grenville that their fear of the blue death did not stop them.

Nine

Vito and Paolo leaned on their shovels as they watched the funeral wagon wind its way over to the Grenville plot on the far side of the cemetery. A priest was already waiting at the head of the grave, ready to provide the funeral rites.

The funeral procession was a large one, and it took time for the mourners to assemble themselves around the grave. A man detached himself from the group and helped a young woman in a veil step down from the calash. She stood near the calash and waited for two young boys to descend, then shepherded them close to where the priest was standing. Maloney's men had already removed the coffin from the funeral carriage and were carrying it to the gravesite. They were a long way off, but Paolo could see that the coffin was much more elaborate than the pine boxes and rude coverings he and his uncle dealt with daily.

The ceremony itself was short, lasting only a few minutes. The crowd dwindled rapidly as people turned away to walk home. Various friends of the family came forward to speak to the young woman and wish her well. Finally, they were left alone, except for a handful of servants and the priest.

Paolo and Vito watched as the boys knelt down and then straightened up again. One of them handed something to the woman and then all three gently tossed dirt on the coffin and hurried away.

Paolo felt a nudge at his shoulder and realized he had been daydreaming. The calash bearing the young woman and boys was already on its way out of the cemetery.

"Let's get back to work," said Vito.

On the road back to the manor house, Smiley nearly ran into a cholera wagon coming his way. The cholera men in their ragged clothes and bandanas were racing along the narrow track and pulled over in the nick of time to let the calash pass. They nodded to Smiley in respect for the deceased as they passed them by. The boys held their noses as they tried to get a glimpse of the bodies in the wagon.

"Are they carrying dead people, Emily?" asked Tommy, the youngest.

"I'm afraid so. They collect the bodies of people who have been abandoned by their families," said Emily, smiling at the boys and patting Tommy on the knee.

"They stink," remarked Jimmy with a smirk. He was trying to downplay the seriousness of the day's events.

"They are the unfortunate victims of the cholera, Jimmy," Emily replied. "It is not their fault."

"It's the smell of death, young man," said Smiley. "We all smell that way when we're dead."

Jimmy looked chastened by Smiley's words, as did his younger brother.

The Provincial Lunatic Asylum in York (present-day Toronto) did not get many visitors at this time of day. The clerk at the front desk put aside his newspaper as a short man in a black frock coat and top hat entered the reception area. He paused for a moment to remove his hat, revealing a bald pate that gleamed in the bright light. The man had an air of authority about him, reinforced by dark penetrating eyes and a muff of side whiskers. The clerk asked if he could be of assistance.

"My name is Burke," said the man, speaking with a slight lisp. I'm here to see Dr Noble."

"Yes, sir," said the clerk, indicating the door behind him. "Go through there and straight down the corridor. Dr Noble's office is the last door at the end."

Burke nodded curtly to the clerk and walked past him, opening the door. The corridor was long and crossed at intervals by other hallways. He passed men in white coats who he presumed to be doctors and burly men wearing tunics who must be attendants. He arrived at the end of the corridor and knocked on the last door.

"Enter!"

He opened the door, wondering if he would find the office as impressive this time as he had the first. These doctors had a nice life with their elegant offices and fat pay packets. Dr Noble had been expecting someone else, an underling of some kind, and, when he finally looked up from the papers on his desk, his face flushed with embarrassment and he stood up.

"Mr Burke!" He stammered. "Please come in and have a seat. I did not expect you so soon. I only sent out the letter yesterday morning."

The doctor waited for Burke to settle in the chair before he sat down at his desk.

"I'm so sorry about your niece, Mr Burke."

Burke inclined his head in acknowledgement, but said nothing.

"She was making progress, but I'm afraid she has succumbed to the epidemic like so many of our patients."

"When did she become ill, doctor?"

"A few days ago, sir."

"And you did not see fit to notify me of this at once?"

The doctor was not used to being challenged in this way. He shifted uncomfortably in his chair.

"We had hoped," he said weakly, "that it was not cholera but something less serious. I can assure you we did everything we could to save her. I'm sorry for your loss, Mr Burke, but the epidemic respects no one."

There was a silence between them, but when Burke spoke again, his manner was businesslike, almost brisk.

"When can I collect the body? I have to take her home."

"We can have her ready by tomorrow."

"Can you arrange her transport?"

"Of course, sir. When is the funeral service?"

"The funeral service? Don't worry about that, we'll handle it. Just put her body in a pine box and send it off."

"There will be an extra charge for the coffin and the transport by wagon, sir. Why not simply bury her here in town?"

"Can't do that, wouldn't be right."

"You do know that we have our own cemetery behind the building and the cost of the funeral and burial aren't too dear. A lot of families don't want the fuss of a large public gathering."

"Put her on a wagon and send me the bill, sir. The family will pay. I'll write the address out for you."

Lionel Burke picked up a steel dip pen from the desk and wrote something on a piece of paper. He handed it to the doctor and stood up to go as the doctor glanced at the address.

"This is the address of the cemetery, sir?"

"Yes, they'll be expecting her."

"Thank you, Mr Burke."

Lionel Burke shook the doctor's hand and left the room.

Ten

Lionel descended from the mail coach in St. Francis, feeling stiff and thirsty after the long dusty drive in the heat from York. The team of four horses were all lathered up, snorting and stamping their hooves as a young man gave them water from a wooden bucket. The passengers waited as the driver unloaded their baggage from the roof of the coach. Lionel wiped the sweat from his brow before putting on his hat and pointing to a small suitcase. The driver leaned down to hand it to him.

Lionel thanked the man and set off for the hotel. The town looked busier and bigger than it had on his last visit. He went up the steps into the hotel bar for a drink. It was dark and cool inside, with Moosehead wall hangings on rough knotty pine walls. Lionel spotted Maloney right away. He was playing poker with several patrons in a booth in the back. Lionel sat down at the bar and ordered a large whisky.

"Hey, bookkeeper," Maloney called to him as he pushed into a seat at the bar. "I ain't seen you in years. You just get in?"

"I'm handling a few things for Lucille. I sent you the payment for the burial. Didn't you get it?"

"Yep, I got it. That's for the loony daughter, right?"

"Yeah, that girl caused a lot of trouble for the family, so they'll be right happy to be rid of her."

Maloney leaned in closer with a sly grin.

"So you don't know?"

"Know what?" Lionel pulled away from him, annoyed. The man stank of sweat and his breath was no better.

"Lucille's dead. She died a few days ago."

Lionel stared at him in shock.

"My God, that's terrible," he said finally. "Daphne, now Lucille."

"The family has had its share of misfortune."

"That leaves only Emily to run the estate."

"I suggest you get your arse over there, see what's what."

Maloney reached across and clinked glasses with Lionel.

"If they wanna sell up, I can make it happen, old chum."

"Fuck you, Maloney. I wouldn't touch your dirty money with a ten-foot pole."

Maloney gave up and returned to the poker game.

Several days later, a bearded man in a flat cap and overalls drove a wagon into the cemetery. He pulled up near Vito and Paolo, who were digging new graves in a new part of the cemetery. Joey was sitting at the base of a tree having lunch.

"Hey fellas, you know where the Grenville plot is?"

"Over there," said Joey, "on the other side."

"Mr Maloney said you'd be ready for the new one."

"Yes, sir," said Vito. "Paolo, go over there with the man and help him unload."

Paolo climbed out of the hole and took a drink of water before following the wagon to the other side. He helped the man remove the pine box from the wagon and carry it over to a new grave near the marble headstone of Lucille Grenville. She had been interred next to her husband, Marcus. There were fresh flowers on Lucille's grave and a burial reed sticking out of the ground. The inscription read:

Here lyes buried
the Body of Lucille Grenville,
who was formerly the wife of
Marcus Grenville late deceased
Born June 5, 1775
Dyed August 10, 1832

Life is Uncertain
Death is ſure
ſin is the wound
& Chriſt the cure
St. Francis, Upper Canada

"Who is it?" asked Paolo.

"I don't know," replied the man. "I just deliver the coffins. Must be a family member."

"We buried the mother not long ago. Maybe a child?"

The man shrugged and climbed back on the wagon. He whipped the horse and drove out of the cemetery. Vito came over with a shovel, a hand drill, and straps.

"That the body we're waitin' on?"

"Yes, sir. Another Grenville."

"Well, let's get it done, time's a-wasting."

Vito handed the straps to Paolo, who attached them, one at each end. Then together they lifted the coffin and lowered it into the grave.

"You want to do the honours, Paolo?"

"*Grazie, caro zio.*"

"This one will be yours."

Paolo took the hand drill and carefully bored a hole into the pine box. He then hammered the burial reed into place using the brass sleeve. After Vito had left, Paolo started to fill the grave with dirt.

I've gotten good at putting in burial reeds. The reeds come from a place in Chicago. People are in fear being buried alive so their families hire us to watch over the graves at night.

Mamma says it all started with that English woman, Mary Shelley. She was living in a house on Lake Geneva with her friends and wrote this ghost story. She had seen the work of Giovanni Aldini, a professor of physics at the University of Bologna, who thought electricity could be used to bring dead people back. Aldini needed cadavers with heads, so he had to go to London to find specimens for his work in 1803. In Europe, they preferred execution by beheading. He found the perfect specimen, a man sentenced to hang for killing his wife and daughter. After he acquired the body, he set up his experiment in public, attaching electrodes to various parts of the body. When the current was turned on, he was able to make the cadaver lift its arms and legs, open its mouth and eyes, and move its chest as if it were taking a deep breath. The audience was convinced he had succeeded in bringing the body back to life, albeit briefly and temporarily.

So Shelley came up with the story of Victor Frankenstein, who created a monster using a secret technique for giving life to dead matter. He created an eight-foot monster whose one desire was that Frankenstein make a female companion for him so he wouldn't be alone in the world.

NICHOLAS KINSEY

Mamma loves the Frankenstein story so much. She reads it to children in our street. There are a lot of stories in the penny bloods about people who have died and come back to life.

Eleven

Gerty carried a pail of hydrated lime into Lucille's bedroom. The two maids were already at work, stripping the bed. They dumped the sheets in a pile near the bed.

"What are we to do with the sheets and bedclothes?" Gerty asked.

"Miss Millie says we gotta put 'em in boiling water," she said, "then we gotta wash 'em."

Gerty started to mop the floor with the lime solution as the maids gathered the sheets and bedclothes and left the room. She got down on her hands and knees to scrub the wooden planks with a brush and looked out the window at the back pasture. Near the far wall, she spotted Smiley under the oak tree where they had buried the dead child. He was busy hammering a wooden cross into the grave.

Curious, she dropped the scrubbing brush into the pail and opened the window. She was about to call out to him when she saw him put down the hammer. Even from a distance, she could see his lips moving. He was standing immobile over the cross and saying a prayer for the dead child.

The night was chilly, and a damp mist covered the ground. With a dirty white bandana pulled up over his nose and mouth, Paolo walked around the cholera pit with a spade and a bucket of quicklime which he spread over the new bodies. The calcium oxide was used to reduce the smell of putrefaction and to accelerate decomposition. Paolo finished the task and returned the spade and bucket to the shed nearby.

There was another task ahead for Paolo. Tonight was to be his first time on the job as a remembrance man while his uncle and Joey got a good night's rest. The Italian migrant workers were in charge of grave digging and maintenance at the cemetery. They were paid a pittance by Maloney, who ran the funeral business and managed the cemetery for the good citizens of St. Francis. The Grenville's had paid a bonus to have someone stand watch over their burial plot at night.

Paolo sat down under a tree near the Grenville plot and pulled out a briar pipe from his pocket. He stuffed the pipe with tobacco and lit a match. The sweet fragrance of tobacco swirled around his head and helped reduce the odour of putrefaction blowing in from the cholera pit.

He lit an oil lamp and put it on the ground near his notebook and lunch basket. He pulled a steel dip pen and ink from a canvas bag and started writing a letter in the light of the lantern. After a time he fell asleep, dropping the pen and notebook in the grass, as the lantern flickered and went out.

An hour later Paolo was awakened by loud, drunken voices as a wagon pulled up near the cholera pit. One man held a lantern while the other two hauled several bodies from the back of the wagon and dumped them in the pit. Paolo stayed put and watched from the darkness until the men climbed back on their wagon and hightailed it out of the cemetery.

Paolo was wide awake now and got up to have a look. In the shed, he refilled the bucket of quicklime and picked up the spade, then started toward the cholera pit. On the way, he stopped at several graves and listened carefully, hoping to hear voices. A lot of the new graves didn't have headstones yet, but the burial reeds were easily visible, sticking out of the ground. He heard nothing at any of them, not that he had expected to. Finally, he arrived at the cholera pit and looked down at the new arrivals.

He could see clearly in the moonlight and noticed right away that one of the bodies looked out of place. Usually, the bodies of cholera victims were wrapped in bedsheets or heavy cloth, but this man was not wrapped at all. Instead, he was wearing an expensive frock coat and pants. His white shirt had a large ragged tear, and a bloodstain had spread across its front.

It was, unmistakably, a knife wound. Paolo speculated that the man had been in a fight and had not died from the blue death. He puzzled over its presence in the pit as he shovelled lime over the bodies. The stink of rotting flesh was atrocious. He quickly finished the job and left, returning to the tree and his canvas bag. He sat down, contemplating the situation.

I wonder who the dead man is. His family must be looking for him, but, of course, they'll never find him. The cholera pit is the perfect place to hide a body. No one will ever bother looking for a body in a cholera pit.

The job of the remembrance man is crazy, watching over the graves of people he doesn't even know. Dead people don't resurrect from the grave. They remain dead and can't come back to life. I don't know whether I can do this for long. I don't like cemeteries, and the smell of decomposition here is overwhelming. It's everywhere: in the earth, in the trees, in the flowers. It's the stink of the devil. I want to go home, but I promised to work for my uncle for three months. They say that the cholera will be over when winter comes.

Twelve

Paolo had put away his pen and notebook and was finally drifting off to sleep when a loud wail pierced the night air. He nearly jumped out of his skin. He looked around nervously but saw no one. He struggled to get up, ready to make a run for it, but the cemetery was silent as a tomb.

His first thought was that the man with the knife wound had somehow come back to life and needed his help. He knew this was absurd, but he also knew he had to make sure. He hurried back to the pit. It took him only a moment to check on the new arrivals. Not a sound was coming from them.

He had just turned away from the pit when he heard the wailing sound again. He was frightened, but his curiosity was stronger than his desire to run. Besides, whether he liked it or not, he had a job to do. He went to one of the new graves and put his ear over the burial reed. He heard nothing, so he moved on to the next in line and listened again. Still nothing. He straightened up and started for the Grenville plot when someone or something raced past him in the dark.

When his heart stopped thumping in his chest, he realized that someone had been playing a joke on him. The wailing sound and the dark figure in the night had all been part of an elaborate hoax. This was confirmed when he heard the sound of a horse and wagon on the road. He pulled himself together enough to return to the tree and his canvas bag, whose contents were scattered over the ground. His lunch basket was nowhere to be seen. He picked up his notebook, pen, and things and sat down. It was going to be a long night.

Sleepless, Paolo's mind wandered. He went for a walk, hoping to calm his lively imagination. He walked down to the entrance in the moonlight. There was a chill on the wind as he took off into the cornfield and walked the entire perimeter before returning to the Grenville plot. There was no one around to bother him.

He sat down again and listened to the night sounds. There were the sounds of crickets, the rustling of leaves in the wind, the scratching noises of field mice and other small animals, a bird pecking on a branch in the distance, followed by the hoot of a screech owl out in the cornfield.

It was going to be a nice quiet night and Paolo was starting to relax when a new creepy sound came to his attention among the songs of nightingales. Or were they mockingbirds? He realized that he would have to listen carefully if he wanted to hear anyone calling for help from a burial reed.

There seemed to be a persistent wail in the background sound, but he couldn't be sure. It could be a human sound or maybe an animal sound. Was it the scream of a red fox or perhaps a barred owl? Paolo wasn't sure. He stood up again and made his round of the burial reeds.

When he returned to the Grenville plot, he put his ear to the burial reed belonging to Lucille Grenville. It was silent, but there seemed to be an almost imperceptible keening coming from the daughter's reed. He jumped back, shocked at the realization. Could the woman still be alive? No, it was not possible. He must be imagining things.

He put his ear close and listened again. Then he got up and ran over to the grey mare tied to a tree near the entrance. He jumped on its back and galloped away in the dark.

Thirteen

"You better be sure, Paolo," Vito complained. "You wake me up, maybe for nothing."

"I'm sure," Paolo insisted. "I heard it. There can be no doubt."

"Hope it's not your imagination, young man," Vito told him sternly, "or there will be hell to pay."

"I swear I heard it."

Vito shook his head as he put on his shoes in the dark. Only moments before, he had been sound asleep, his only escape from the backbreaking work of digging graves. Then Paolo had come crashing into the cabin and shouting for him to wake up. He knew it wasn't in the boy's nature to play tricks. He must have heard something or he wouldn't have ridden hard through the night to tell his uncle the news. Vito stared at his nephew for a moment longer on the front steps and then made up his mind. He stood up and went to harness the wagon.

Getting back to the cemetery took longer in the wagon, but if Paolo was right, they would need it. Paolo's mare had been lathered up and exhausted from her early morning gallop, but they had tied her to the back of the wagon and brought her along. Paolo fidgeted with excitement the entire way and jumped down from the wagon, running ahead to the Grenville plot.

"This one," he called impatiently to Vito as he stood over the burial reed.

Vito collected the shovel from the back of the wagon and hurried over. He put his ear close to the reed. He listened for a long time. Nothing. Finally, he stood up and glared at Paolo.

"Stupid kid."

Shaking his head, Vito picked up his shovel and started back towards the wagon. Desperate, Paolo put his ear again to the reed as he watched his uncle prepare to leave, throwing the shovel into the wagon and grabbing the reins.

"Wait, Uncle, please."

Paolo listened as Vito returned, treading quietly.

"Put your ear to the reed," Paolo said. "It's hard to hear, but it's there."

Vito sighed as he kneeled next to his nephew. Together they heard a distinctive wailing sound coming from the burial reed. Paolo jumped up and ran back to the wagon to get the shovel while Vito remained immobile, frozen in fear. He had spent countless nights in the cemetery alternating with Joey, and neither man had ever heard a voice from a grave. A dead woman was calling to them.

Lit by an oil lamp on the edge of the grave, Vito and Paolo worked fast, removing the dirt from around the coffin. Vito grabbed a crowbar and hooked it under the cover, popping the lid. Paolo brought the lantern in close and the two perspiring men watched for some sign of life from the pale, sunken cheeks of an attractive young woman. Nothing. There was not a sound or movement from the corpse. She looked dead.

Paolo got up and took a shiny steel pocket comb from his pocket. He slipped it near the lips of the woman for a short moment before pulling it clear. He noticed the damp breath marks on the metal.

"Uncle, she's alive," Paolo whispered, his eyes wide.

Vito grabbed his nephew and embraced him, dancing a jig in the moonlight.

"You did it, Paolo! *Questo è meraviglioso.* We'll get a bonus for this."

Fourteen

It was a lovely day as Gerty exited the manor house, wiping her hands on an apron. No one was around, so she walked over to the back pasture. She stopped at the child's grave and admired the wooden cross that Smiley had whittled from a piece of cedar board and stuck in the ground. On the cross, he had carved the following words:

> One blue-eyed boy
> with no name,
> who was too young to die,
> August 1832

As she stood under the oak tree admiring the cross, she noticed a young man on a chestnut horse fast approaching along the road.

Paolo was eager to bring the good news to the Grenville family. He was feeling the adrenaline rush of recent events and hardly felt tired after a sleepless night. He rode up to the Grenville manor and dismounted at the front door, tying the horse to the railing. He climbed the steps and knocked.

After a few minutes, Baxter opened the door and looked down with a surly air at the unkempt and filthy young man in a threadbare waistcoat and top hat on the doorstep.

"I need to see the lord of the house, please," Paolo asked, smiling from ear to ear.

"What's your business, young man?" Baxter demanded, looking annoyed.

"It's about the young woman, sir. I must speak with the master of the house."

"Wait here."

Paolo waited impatiently on the front steps after Baxter left the door half-open. From inside, young Jimmy approached Paolo, followed by his younger brother, Tommy.

"You looking for work, mister?" asked Jimmy.

"No, I'm not, but thank you."

Paolo smiled at the two boys, who were curious to know who he was.

Lionel looked up from the Grenville accounts as Baxter entered the drawing room.

"There's a man here to see you, sir. He says it's about the woman."

"What woman?"

"I really couldn't tell you, sir. He didn't mention a name."

"Send him in, Baxter," said Lionel.

Lionel poured himself a cup of tea and continued his work in the big ledger. Moments later Paolo entered in his dirty clothes, looking quite out of place in the Victorian finery of the room. Baxter waited on the threshold.

"You can go, Baxter," said Lionel. "Who are you?"

"Morelli, sir... Paolo Morelli."

Cap in hand, Paolo looked around the room in admiration.

"Out with it, man."

"Yes, sir. I work in the cemetery with my uncle. I dig graves for Mr Maloney. I'm a remembrance man, sir."

"You don't say."

"Yes, sir. I was in the cemetery last night..."

"Oh, God!"

Lionel recoiled, looking fearful.

"Don't come any closer, Morelli. Stay where you are, don't touch anything."

"Of course not, sir. I have some good news for you. The woman is alive. She's come back."

"You're joking?"

"No, sir."

"The young woman is alive?"

Lionel seized a bottle of whisky from the cabinet and poured himself a large drink as he tried to maintain his composure. He looked out the window for a long moment.

"It happened last night, sir."

Lionel took a long draught of whisky and then turned to Paolo.

"You've done very well, mister...?"

"Morelli, sir."

"Where is she?"

"She's at our house, sir. We brought her from the cemetery last night."

"Has she said anything?"

"She's still asleep, sir. I mean unconscious, but breathing normally."

"Good work, Morelli. You've done well. You see this?"

Lionel held up a Spanish silver dollar and flipped the coin in the air, catching it.

"Yes, sir."

"I want you to keep her for a day or two while I make arrangements. Can you do that, Morelli?"

"I don't know."

"It's very important. You must not breathe a word of this to anyone. Do you understand?"

The man's reaction was not what Paolo had expected. He had hoped this would be a joyful moment for the lord of the house and had not expected to be bound by silence.

"We have had so much of the blue death," Lionel said. "It would be a terrible shock for the family to think the poor girl suffered. You'll keep this quiet, Morelli. Do I have your word?"

Paolo nodded quietly, and Lionel dropped the silver dollar into his outstretched hand.

"I will come for her in a few days. Cheer up, Morelli. This is wonderful news."

Paolo grinned at Lionel, admiring the 'piece of eight'.

"What's her name, sir? We don't know her name."

Lionel gave Paolo the shrewd look of a man who trusted no one. The girl must remain anonymous.

"Go now, young man. I'll contact you soon."

"Thank you, sir. We'll take good care of her."

Paolo turned and left the room. As he descended the steps, he ran into two boys playing with a ball and bat.

"Sir, do you know how to play baseball?" Jimmy asked.

"No, sorry," said Paolo as he climbed on the old mare. "I'm from Genoa, so I never learned to play. Why don't you show me how you hit the ball?"

Jimmy threw the ball in the air and swung hard with the bat, but missed it completely.

"You ain't no good, Jimmy," said Tommy.

"I am too. I always beat you."

REMEMBRANCE MAN

These kids are learning to play baseball. They are lucky. I never had time for games when I was younger. I always wanted to be an artist. There's a man in Detroit who does 'sun drawings'. He makes them with a camera obscura. He is doing what a man named Niepce did five years ago in France. He was able to make an image from an engraving of the famous Cardinal D'Amboise. It took hours, but he did it.

I would work for such a man for free, just to learn his trade, but no, I'm off in the wilds of Upper Canada, digging graves instead. Well, I was happy to see Uncle Vito and Nelly, who I didn't know very well. I don't want to appear ungrateful. I will do my share of the work and happily return in the autumn.

Fifteen

In the barn, the emaciated blonde girl with sunken cheeks and blue lips lay asleep on a straw mattress. Nelly, in a faded white dress, approached and held a wet face cloth to her forehead. Nearby, horses were making feeding sounds among the harnesses and saddles hanging from the beams. Paolo came in with a triumphant look on his face.

"Nelly, how is she?"

"She woke up about an hour ago, then she drifted off."

Paolo pulled the Spanish dollar from his pocket and held it up to the light, grinning at Nelly.

"See this, Nelly. Mr Grenville gave it to me."

"Well, I'll be damn'd. That's eight pieces of silver, Paolo. It's worth about five shillings. Yer gonna be rich one day!"

"Five shillings!"

"That's about one dollar in Detroit, Paolo. You did good."

Paolo approached the bed and looked down at the girl.

"She looks better."

"I gave her some water and a wee bit of soup."

"We gotta keep her a bit longer, Nelly."

Nelly stared at Paolo, looking alarmed.

"We can't, Paolo. We gotta get her out of here."

"Mr Grenville wants us to keep her for a few days."

"But Paolo, anyone could walk in here and see her. They catch a blue death in the barn, they gonna kick us out of here for good."

"We have no choice, Nelly," Paolo pleaded. "I promised Mr Grenville that we would keep her for a day or two."

Nelly looked at Paolo with rising anger and frustration.

"Vito ain't gonna like this one bit. They kick us out, we lose our jobs, Paolo. Then, what we gonna do, go back to Detroit to work at the mill?"

"You think you're good, Paolo, but I'm better," said Vito as he arm-wrestled his nephew.

They were drinking cheap whisky with Joey at the picnic table behind their dogtrot, one of two log dwellings with a breezeway under the same tarpaper roof. An oil lamp hung from the branch of a tree, and a few scrawny pigs grunted near a mangy dog on the porch.

Paolo started to feel a formidable pressure on his arm.
"Juss, cause you got yourself a Spanish dollar for the girl, doesn't mean you can beat your old Uncle Vito."

Joey laughed at this, watching his two friends intently. Paolo's arm was no match for his uncle's short but muscular forearm. The pressure was soon close to unbearable and Vito snapped Paolo's arm down.

"A few more weeks and the boy gonna catch you good, Vito," said Joey.

"How many you dig, Paolo?" asked Vito.

"I done fifteen graves already, Uncle."

"That's good. You do another thirty, and you beat me, no question. When are they comin' for the girl, Paolo?"

"I don't know, Uncle. They didn't say."

Paolo glanced at Nelly.

"Well, we can't keep her here, can we? We gonna be in big trouble if anyone finds her."

"The man asked me to keep her for a few days, Uncle. I couldn't say no."

Vito looked at Nelly and then at Joey.

"Did you know about this arrangement, Nelly?

"Yeah, Paolo told me. What can we do with her? We can't move her or throw her out, 'cause she's still too sick to travel. Anybody sees her and they come looking for us."

"You're sayin' our best bet is to keep her in the barn until the man comes?"

"Yes, dear."

Vito was not happy as he drank his whisky, but like the others, he didn't see any other options.

Sixteen

The sick girl was propped up on a mattress as Paolo spoon fed her a beef broth. She had a generous mouth, full lips, and perfect teeth. Her blue eyes were rimmed in red and fixed on the ceiling. Paolo was enchanted by the young woman, who seemed oblivious to his presence.

Nelly arrived with more broth and took over the job of feeding the girl.

"She's getting stronger, Paolo. She's sure got an appetite."

"That's good news, Nelly. I wonder what her name is?"

"They didn't tell you?"

"I asked Mr Grenville, but he wouldn't give me a name."

"Marge was talkin' down at the creek 'bout these twin sisters out at the estate. She used to work there. She says they were a sight to see growing up. They're identical twins."

"So you think she might be one of the Grenville twins?"

"Yeah, she could be."

"I better go, Nelly. See you later."

Paolo got up and left.

Wilbur was sixteen years old and strong for his age, but he was still only a boy. He struggled with the weight of the man in the wheelbarrow. The man was Wilbur's dad, Darius Barnes, a local farmer. He was on his back, folded up inside the wheelbarrow, his arms and legs spilling over the sides. Wilbur couldn't bear to look at his vacant eyes and the deathly blue tinge of his face. Barefoot and ragged, he pushed doggedly on in a desperate attempt to save his dad's life.

He stumbled past the houses of his neighbours and family friends, calling tearfully for help, but no one came. The good people of St. Francis wanted nothing to do with this kid and his sick father. The man was just another victim of the blue death. It was a common sight in the village. People standing on their front porch watched the boy and, one after the other, closed their doors to him.

What could they do? They had suffered enough, having abandoned their own sisters and brothers, mothers and fathers, on the same road. No one had offered to help them, and now young Wilbur was carrying his dad to the doctor's office.

Gerty and her younger brother, Alfred, were the only people who dared approach Wilbur, and even they kept a careful distance.

"Where you goin', Will?" asked Gerty, running alongside.

"Gonna see the doctor. Dad ain't dead yet."

"But Will, there ain't no doctor in town no more," said Alfred. "He up and left weeks ago."

"Where's he at?" Wilbur asked, desperation in his voice.

"He's long gone," Gerty said. "Go on home. Let your dad die in peace."

"He ain't gonna die on me," said Wilbur obstinately.

Gerty knew Wilbur well enough to know that he wouldn't change his mind. She took Alfred's hand, and they walked away. There was nothing else to do.

They watched Wilbur for a while, struggling with the load as he continued down the road. The boy stopped to catch his breath from time to time, and then carried on.

Seventeen

"Paolo, there's a letter for you," said Vito.

He was just pulling into the cemetery in the wagon as Paolo and Joey lowered a coffin into the ground using straps. The men removed the straps and Joey stepped into the grave to drill a hole for a burial reed.

Vito gave the letter to Paolo, who broke the wax seal. He read the brief note, running his dirty fingers over the rich vellum.

"What's it say, Paolo?" asked Vito.

"They're comin' for the girl tonight."

"That's good. The sooner the better," Joey said from the hole in the ground.

Paolo examined the letter again and then showed it to Vito. His uncle couldn't read, but his brow furrowed when he saw the signature.

"Why's it signed by this fella B-u-r-k-e?" asked Vito. "He ain't no Grenville."

"He must work for the Grenvilles, Uncle. He's the man in charge."

Vito nodded, returned the letter to Paolo, and started to unload the wagon.

Paolo helped lift the blonde girl from her bed and held her upright in her nightgown. She was awake and very docile as Nelly took a washcloth from a pail of soapy water and washed the girl's back and bum as Paolo looked away.

"Sorry to put you through this, Paolo," Nelly said, "but we can't send her back smelling like she does."

Paolo had noticed the rank smell about her as Nelly ran the washcloth around under the nightgown, dipping it frequently in the water.

"We'll put her in clean clothes and burn what she has."

"How we gonna get her out of here without no one seeing her?" asked Paolo.

"Vito says we can back up the wagon to the door. No one will see her."

The sick girl was coming around and supporting herself on her own two legs. Paolo held her loosely, and she seemed surprised to see him standing so close to her.

"Time to go home, dear," Nelly said.

"What's your name?" the girl asked.

"I'm Paolo and she's Nelly, miss."

"She's talking, that's good," said Nelly.

The girl closed her eyes and whispered their names before losing consciousness again.

Wilbur had finally given up. He wasn't sure if his father had been dead or alive when the weight of the wheelbarrow and his father's body had become too much for him. The front wheel had caught on something and the wheelbarrow had pitched over on its side, spilling his father into the ditch. Wilbur had fallen back, exhausted, on the side of the road. He stayed that way for hours. A neighbour had approached to a safe distance and tossed him a gourd of whisky. The whisky helped, but it changed nothing.

The hours passed slowly. Night was falling, and Wilbur was still guarding his father's body. He didn't even look up when two men in a cholera wagon pulled up alongside. One of them, a young man named Reuben, who was only a few years older than he was, climbed down from the wagon. He had a shaved head and straggly side whiskers.

"He's gone, Will. You cain't do nothin' more for him."

Wilbur said nothing as Reuben took the gourd from him and had a drink. He looked back at the bearded driver named Thaddeus. The man nodded at Reuben, who turned back to the boy.

"Tell you what, Will, my boy. We gonna help you carry your daddy over to the cemetery. Whadda you say to that?"

Wilbur remained silent. Thaddeus climbed down from the wagon and took the gourd from Reuben. He had a drink and returned the gourd to the boy. Wilbur didn't move or try to stop the men when they pulled bandanas over their noses, gathered up his old dad by his arms and legs, and swung the body over the side into the wagon.

Reuben climbed back on the wagon, followed by Thaddeus. They waited to see what Wilbur would do, but he just kept staring dully at the road from his position on the grass.

"What you gonna do, kid?" Thaddeus asked impatiently. "You can't stay here."

Thaddeus exchanged a look with Reuben. They were about to leave when Wilbur suddenly got to his feet and stumbled over to the wagon. Reuben waved to him to climb aboard.

It was almost midnight when Paolo and Vito laid the girl down on the straw in the back of the Grenville wagon. Nelly had provided her with a clean nightdress and given her a blanket to ward against the cold.

"She'll be a lot better at home, sir," Nelly said.

"Yes," Lionel Burke nodded. "I can see you have done well by her. In a few days, she'll be back on her feet."

The girl muttered something from the wagon as Paolo and Nelly looked in at her. There was a pained expression on her face and she seemed to be crying, but then she drifted off again into sleep.

"A splendid job, Mr Morelli. Thank you."

Lionel climbed into the driver's seat and whipped the horse into action. The wagon rolled out of the barnyard as Paolo looked on with a growing sense of unease.

Who is this girl? Why is Mr Burke so secretive? It makes little sense. She can't be a maid at the manor, not with those hands and fingernails. She didn't get them from scrubbing floors. She was buried in the Grenville plot, so she must be a member of the family.

Nelly says she's must be a Grenville, otherwise, Mr Burke wouldn't have paid a Spanish dollar for her. She thinks the girl may be one of the Grenville twins. But if she is family, then they should be celebrating her return, not sneaking her out of our barn in the middle of the night.

Eighteen

Two men waited near a wagon in the back alley. It was the middle of the night and the men were nearly invisible in the dark. The larger man, Biggs, was a colossus with an unkempt beard and a chiselled face, while his comrade was a skinny, raw-boned picket fence in comparison. They heard the creak of a door and looked up as Maloney appeared on the threshold of the cottage under an oil lamp. Biggs worked for Maloney as a supervisor at the quarry. He had done jobs like this for his boss before and knew it required the utmost discretion. He motioned his partner to silence as he led him to the back of the wagon. Together, they slid the pine box out of the wagon and carried it up the steps towards the cottage.

Inside, an old man in long red underwear lay immobile on the floor with a head wound. Nearby, Maloney was talking to a man in a frock coat with a large beard and spectacles. A young woman in a dressing gown and sleep cap hunched over the old man and examined the wound, which was still bleeding.

"He's good and dead, Pa," said the girl. "I'll clean up."

"Good girl," said the father, handing Maloney a wad of bills.

Biggs and his helper moved in and picked up the man by his arms and legs. They threw the body in the box and placed the arms over the chest.

"Gently does it, you eejits," growled Maloney.

"Sorry," said Biggs as he helped the other man slide the lid into place. "We're done."

"Good night, sir," Maloney said to the father.

Maloney followed Biggs and his helper out into the night with the heavy coffin. Behind him, the girl was already down on her knees, washing away the bloodstains from the floor.

Maloney drove the wagon out of the alley and turned left onto the road. Biggs and his helper worked hard during the day, and the night jobs for Maloney were particularly exhausting. They were soon fast asleep, slumped one against the other on the front seat. The road was deserted, but Maloney didn't like to be seen at this hour of the night. He whipped the horses to go faster.

The silence of the night was soon broken when the dead man woke up. It took Maloney a moment to realize what was happening. It started with a pounding on the lid of the coffin, which grew louder and louder until it was joined by the sound of splintering wood. The dead man had managed to smash his fist through the lid of the cheap coffin and was climbing out of the box as Biggs woke up. It took him a moment to scramble down from the wagon and to find a weapon. He came around the back of the wagon carrying a hammer and looked up at the dead man, his face bloodied and his eyes wild, crouching near the coffin. Biggs climbed up onto the wagon and took a roundhouse swing at the dead man connecting with his temple. The man collapsed and was thrown out of the wagon into the roadway.

"Is he dead?" asked Maloney, who hadn't moved from the front seat, but looked shaken.

"He is now," Biggs growled. "There ain't no money in live ones."

Biggs jumped down and joined his helper to haul the dead man back to the wagon, throwing his body carelessly into the coffin. They slammed the lid back on and went on their way.

Nineteen

Paolo had just finished shaving at the water pump in the backyard when Nelly brought him a towel and a clean shirt. She waited for him to wipe his face as they stood near a load of washing on the clothesline.

"There you go, young man," she traded him the shirt for the towel, then went back to the house. Paolo put on the shirt and was buttoning it up when Nelly reappeared with Paolo's worn frock coat.

"Here's your coat," she handed it to him. "I gave it a good brushing."

"Thanks, Nelly," he said gratefully.

"You'll look very handsome. Remember to take off your hat at the door."

"You think it's too early?"

"No, it's been about a week. She must be up and around by now."

Paolo looked reassured.

The door to the Grenville manor's summer kitchen was wide open, and a child was sitting on the grass, playing quietly with a toy horse. Paolo, in his best clothes, dismounted from the grey mare and tied the reins to the railing near the front door. He then walked back to the kitchen and looked inside.

In the kitchen, young Gerty was pouring water into a pail and singing to herself. She turned instantly as Paolo's shadow flitted across the wall.

"Good day, miss."

"Good day, sir."

"I've come to see Mr Burke."

"He's at church. He won't be back for a while."

"How's the girl, the one with the cholera?"

Gerty looked about uneasily.

"Ain't no more cholera here, sir."

"What 'bout the young woman? Is she any better?"

Gerty dumped quicklime into a pail. It bubbled noticeably as she stirred it up with the mop.

"I wouldn't know nothing 'about a woman, sir. Ain't no more cholera in the house after Madame Lucille and the cook passed away. We still scrubbin' the floors three times a week."

Paolo looked puzzled.

"Didn't they bring a sick woman here a few days ago?"

"I wouldn't know 'bout that, sir."

"They brought her here in the night."

"I don't think so. I ain't seen no sick woman."

Gerty turned away and started to mop the kitchen floor while Paolo watched her impatiently. With a heavy heart, he climbed back on the mare, and after taking a long look at the silent manor house, rode away at a fast trot.

It was a dark, rainy night and Paolo was huddled under a tree in the cemetery, wrapped in a rain slicker. He was back working as a remembrance man, listening to the sounds of the night. He tried to remain awake and attentive, but the patter of the rain made it impossible to hear any other sounds. He soon succumbed to sleep and dozed with his head against the tree. He was awakened by the sound of horses stamping the ground near the gates to the cemetery. He got up to have a look and walked down to the road in the rain.

At the gates, he noticed several bodies in white sheets abandoned on the road. The deceased were probably abandoned by family members, too frightened to bring them into the cemetery and give them a decent burial.

Paolo returned to the cemetery and got the mare and a long piece of rope. One at a time, he tied the rope under the arms of each cadaver and ran it back to the mare. The horse moved forward, pulling the head and shoulders of the victim up off the road with the torso and legs dragging in the dirt. He was exhausted and wet through after hauling the dead over to the cholera pit and pushing them in.

It took me several hours to clear the dead from the road. Uncle Vito says we cannot leave the bodies at the gate. Our job is to keep the site clean and everything as orderly as possible. Maloney has complained several times about the abandoned cadavers left on the road.

I didn't hear any wailing sounds coming from the graves, what with the rain coming down and the wind in the trees. I was so tired after the long night that I didn't wake up until well after sunrise when Vito and Joey arrived for work.

Twenty

The town folk were gathered in the tiny guildhall near the hotel on Main Street to hear Dr Walker talk about the cholera epidemic. The good doctor was a short bald man in his late sixties with side whiskers, dressed in a dark frock coat and monocle which he used to read from his notes. He had fled St. Francis in early July when the outbreak began in earnest, with an overwhelming number of cholera victims knocking on his door. He had gone to the city to rest up and confer with his medical colleagues. He had decided it was now time to provide advice to the people of the town and regain their trust.

Next to the doctor sat Constable Riley, who used the gavel to quiet the anxious crowd that filled the seats and spilled out into the entrance.

"Quiet, please, quiet! Ladies and gentlemen, Dr Walker is back in town and has some words for you about the cholera epidemic," said the constable. At a nod from Riley, the doctor stood up to address the crowd.

"Ladies and gentlemen," Walker began, "I do not need to tell you how we are ravaged by this disease in St. Francis and the region. We have lost many good people and we will lose more until this terrible epidemic is over. I have just returned from York after consulting with my medical colleagues there who claim to know the causes of cholera. They say that cholera is conveyed in the air and is prevalent in impure and damp air. I repeat impure and damp air."

There was a loud, derisive snort from somewhere in the audience. People turned to see who had the temerity to interrupt the good doctor. There were whispers and clucking noises when they saw that it was Colonel Butler, a man who had distinguished himself in the military many years ago but had entered into a sad and sometimes public struggle with gin and whisky. The last vestige of his former status as an officer and a gentleman was a scarlet mess dress jacket. He was tall, with bushy white hair and unkempt side whiskers. He would have looked imposing without the obvious food stains down the front of his jacket and the telltale red nose of a heavy drinker. The colonel glared back at the disapproving faces and was about to say something when a young man from the row in front of him stood up.

"Doctor, how do we treat it? My daughter came down with it this morning and is in very bad shape. What can I do to save her?"

"I'm so sorry to hear that, young man," said Dr Walker. "I'll get to that. First, you must understand that when you inhale the poison of cholera, it slows the function of the ganglionic nerves which line the surface of the lungs, so the lungs are no longer functioning properly. This explains the coldness of the body, which is typical of cholera. The blood thickens and turns black, so the patient is asphyxiated and dies. Other symptoms of the disease are the purging and the vomiting."

"Balderdash," roared the colonel, struggling to his feet. He ignored Walker and addressed the crowd.

"Ladies and gentlemen, do not believe this man for an instant. It is not the air, but the water. I say: do not drink the water and you will not suffer the illness."

"Come, come," interrupted the doctor. "The most eminent physicians in the country say it is carried on the air."

"Rubbish," said the colonel, his face red with anger. "I was with the 80th Regiment of Foot in India during the outbreak in Hyderabad fifteen years ago. I saw dozens of cases of cholera, sir. A regiment might be stationed in a small town near the market and would come down with the disease along with the natives, but those stationed further away would often avoid the disease entirely. We were breathing the same air, but we were not drinking the same water. In India, it was the water, not the impure air."

The colonel sat down as people around the room demanded to be heard.

"Nonsense," barked Dr Walker, who had expected to find a room full of quiet locals, not this room of rowdy troublemakers. "For heaven's sake, man, I have just consulted the best people in this country and the consensus is that it is the impure air that is contaminating our bodies, not the water."

"Your so-called 'best people' are wrong, doctor!" said the colonel, who shook his head sadly, the anger replaced by bitter memories. "In India, we tried everything. The disease would crop up in one town and then move to another. Everywhere we went, we brought the disease with us. Our people noticed that the only way to reduce the propagation of the disease was to discard the soiled blankets and bedclothes of the victims. I am not a medical practitioner, but anyone could tell that we were responsible for spreading the illness. The native people were infected soon after we left a place, not before we arrived."

Colonel Butler had the room's full attention.

"So how would you treat the disease, Colonel?" asked the young man who had questioned the doctor.

"We couldn't do much for the victims," Butler admitted. "All we could do was to try to prevent other soldiers from getting sick. We noticed that not all the men were affected. None of the men who were drinking their daily ration of gin or whisky were affected, nor were most of our tea drinkers. Only the men who were drinking the local water were getting sick."

"Colonel," said Dr Walker in a calm and collected voice. "Your theory has been discredited by our best medical specialists. Let me be perfectly clear, you cannot catch cholera by drinking water."

"But cholera attacks the alimentary canal," the colonel insisted, "causing diarrhea which passes out of the intestines through the so-called "rice-water" discharges. So the poison is ingested through the mouth, not the lungs. It has to be the water."

Dr Walker had heard enough. He was used to having his pronouncements accepted without question. He turned his attention back to the crowd.

"Please do not believe this man, ladies and gentlemen," said Walker, raising his hands for quiet. "His theory has been discredited by the best physicians of this country. As for medicine, the recommended treatment is to take two drops of laudanum, two grains of calomel, and brandy to stimulate the victim, to apply hot flannels to the body, poultices of mustard, cayenne pepper and hot vinegar, tobacco enemas."

The colonel again interrupted the harassed doctor in his parade-ground voice and the room hushed.

"Boil your water before you drink it!" bellowed the colonel. "That is the only way to reduce your chances of infection from cholera. Boil the water."

Unable to tolerate the colonel's interruptions any longer, Doctor Walker gave up and headed for the exit. He had been summoned by several local families with pressing needs and was frustrated by his public confrontation with that old fool Butler. *What a ridiculous hypothesis! Water had nothing to do with the blue death. It was the air. Everyone knew that.*

Twenty-one

Paolo was dozing in a new part of the cemetery during his lunch break when he was awakened by voices. He got up, shaking the dust from his clothes, and headed over to a grave where Vito and Joey were talking to a shrimpy little guy in a top hat and expensive coat.

When Paolo arrived, Vito and Joey were digging up the grave at the request of the stranger. Vito's spade soon struck the coffin and Joey removed the surrounding dirt with his shovel. The smell of rotting flesh was self-evident. Vito looked up at the bereaved client for further instructions.

"Sir?"

"Get the top of the box off. You're paid to do that," the man insisted, perspiring in the heat.

"Your son is dead, sir. There can be no doubt."

"I must see him with my own eyes," insisted the man. He removed his hat, his hands shaking with nervous energy.

"It serves no good to see the boy," said Vito, still hoping to spare this man the sight of his dead son.

Vito nodded at Joey, who was busy wrapping his bandana tightly around his nose and mouth. With their faces covered, the men stepped into the grave and leaned down to pop the lid with a crowbar and a shovel.

The bereaved man watched silently as he ran his hand over his eyes and wiped the sweat from his face. Paolo was worried that he might be feeling faint, so he brought over a folding chair for the man to sit in.

"Please, sit down," said Paolo. "You don't look so good."

"He was my only son," said the man, ignoring the chair.

"How old was your son?" asked Vito.

"He was 18 years old," said the man sitting down.

"What was his name?"

"James Albert. He was named after my father. He was the nicest person you could ever meet, respectful of his elders and the joy of our family. We miss him so."

"Give him a minute or two," whispered Vito to Joey, who stood ready to pop the lid off the coffin.

The man nodded to Vito when he was ready, and Joey slowly removed the lid on the coffin. Looking out at them from the grave was the blackened death mask of a man struck down in the prime of life.

The father's mood changed as abruptly as if he had been slapped across the face. He was back in control and his sentimental longing for the boy was gone. He stood up decisively and turned away.

"Thank you, gentlemen. Thank you."

He tossed a shilling to Vito and walked with great dignity back to his buggy while the men looked on.

A lot of people don't believe their child is dead, so they'll go to extraordinary lengths to test the body for signs of life. Tobacco smoke enemas are common in Detroit and we laugh at it, making jokes when we talk about "blowing smoke up your arse". It is supposed to warm the body and stimulate respiration. Another thing they try is to manipulate the tongue by force or by taste. They pull and pinch the tongue, or pour bitter liquids on it, hoping to revive the dead person. But the worst are those who shock the body with pain, burning a finger, pouring scalding water or shoving a needle into the heart. The methods used are too gruesome for words.

Twenty-two

Paolo was desperate for information about the sick girl. She occupied his thoughts day and night. What had happened to her? He tied his horse to a tree some distance from the Grenville Manor in the moonlight and came the rest of the way on foot. There was light spilling from a window at the front of the house. Paolo stayed in the shadows and pressed himself against the wall next to the window. It was a hot, muggy night, and the window was partly open. He could hear voices from within and cautiously raised his head to have a look.

Four people sat at a table in the centre of the parlour. Lionel Burke, in evening dress, was dealing cards to an older gentleman, a society lady of a certain age, and a young elegantly dressed blonde woman with her back to the window. The young woman played a card, followed by the gentleman on her left.

"So Lionel, what are your plans for the estate?" the older man asked.

"Well, I'm not sure. We're going to be short of men during the harvest. Lucille ran a tight ship, but she could have done more with the land. The price of wheat is up, but we've only got a few hundred acres planted this year."

"You could rent it out to settlers."

"George, you know as well as I do," Burke said with exaggerated patience, "that settlers don't have any money, they're buying everything on credit. Then when the harvest fails..."

"George has told me," said the society lady, turning to the young woman, "that you sing very well. Why don't you sing us something?"

The woman's diversion seemed like an effort to forestall some latent bad feeling between Lionel and George. She laid a comforting hand on George's and Lionel seemed grateful for the distraction.

"Go ahead, girl," said Lionel. "Sing us a song."

Paolo instinctively ducked as the young woman stood up, fearful that he would be seen. When he looked again, she had disappeared from view, but he could hear the notes of a piano and the sound of her voice as she sang a soft, melancholic tune. *Long, Long Ago* by Thomas Haynes Bayly was a popular song at the time.

"Sing me the songs that to me were so dear
Long, long ago, long ago
Tell me the tales I delighted to hear
Long, long ago, long ago

Out of the past on the winds of the years
Sung by a voice that could still all my fears
Softened by laughter and gentled by tears
Long, long ago, long ago

Sing me the songs that were mine at the start
Long, long ago, long ago

Tell me the tales that were dear to my heart
Long, long ago, long ago

Now I shall share with a child at my breast
All of those songs that once put me to rest
Safe in the arms of the one I loved best
Long, long ago, long ago
Long, long ago, long ago."

Paolo risked another look through the window when the song came to an end with applause.

"That was lovely," said the older woman.

"Yes, it was. You have a wonderful voice," said George.

"She's very talented," added Lionel.

They were returning to the card table when Paolo finally got a glimpse of the young woman. He gasped in shock and backed away from the window. A branch knocked against the windowpane as he scrambled away from the house on his hands and knees. He had seen her face, and she was even more beautiful than he remembered. She was none other than the girl in the coffin.

She's alive and well, she's a Madonna. She sings like an angel. I have never heard such a sweet voice. Maybe Mr Burke wanted to hide her from the Grenville household, and that's why no one had heard of the cholera victim. She certainly looks much better. I can't wait to tell Nelly and Vito. They'll be so happy.

Twenty-three

At the quarry, Paolo waited with the wagon as two bearded men, whose hair and clothing were covered in a thin layer of white dust, emerged from a shed carrying a headstone. The wagon shook with the weight as they loaded the headstone flat on the floor. The quarrymen returned for the last headstone and Paolo watched them load it near the others. Something about the inscription caught his eye.

Here lyes buried
the Body of Daphne Grenville,
Born 1812, Dyed 1832

The inscription had to be wrong. Paolo jumped down from the wagon and went back to get a better look. He looked perplexed as he read the words. This must be the daughter of Lucille Grenville, who was now alive and well after having escaped being buried alive in the cemetery.

Biggs, the man in charge of the quarry, was coming out of the shed with some papers for Paolo to sign.

"Sir, there is a mistake on this headstone," said Paolo, pointing to the Grenville headstone in the back of the wagon.

"We don't make mistakes," Biggs said as he handed Paolo a bill of lading. "Sign this."

"This woman is not dead."

"Wouldn't know 'bout that, ain't none of my bizness. Juss scratch yer name over here on the line."

"But the woman is not dead!" Paolo insisted.

"And I'm telling you," Biggs snarled, "it's none of my bizness. Now sign the paper and be on yer way."

Biggs looked suspiciously at Paolo as he took the pencil and scratched his name on the paper.

"It don't mean nothin'," Joey insisted.

"Then why is Mr Burke putting a headstone on an empty grave?" Paolo asked as they sat at the table in the yard.

It was the end of a long day, and Paolo was still upset about his encounter with Biggs. He had told Vito and Joey all about it over a supper of pork and beans washed down with homemade beer.

"Burke took the girl, killed her, and put her back in the grave. That's what I think," said Joey.

Nelly exited the cabin and collected the plates, kicking the neighbour's pig out of the way.

"Go on with you, Joey," Nelly said. "This ain't Detroit."

"He must have ordered the headstone earlier," Vito said.

"Sure," Paolo admitted, "but why pay Mr Maloney to put that headstone in place? The grave is empty."

"It is strange, my boy," Vito said, drinking his beer. "But it ain't none of yer bizness. Best you keep your nose out of it, Paolo."

"We filled the dirt into that grave a week ago," Joey said. "There ain't nobody in that grave."

REMEMBRANCE MAN

Uncle Vito told me to drop it, but I cannot understand why someone would put a headstone on an empty grave. Maybe they ordered the headstone before we found her, and they are just going through the motions. I don't like that man Biggs. Something is going on over at the quarry. They are making money hand over fist these days with the transport of the dead and the burials. Mr Maloney doesn't seem to be the most honest person in these parts.

Twenty-four

Paolo rode up to the post office near the coach station on the grey mare. He dismounted as a man was unloading boxes and hauling them into the post office. He followed the man inside and stepped up to the wicket where the station master, wearing a green visor and round spectacles, was counting figures off a sheet of foolscap. He looked up at Paolo and removed his spectacles.

"What can I do for you, young man?"

"Good day. I hear you have a letter for me."

"Name?"

"Morelli."

"Ah, yes." The man's eyes lit up. "I know an Italian man, Morelli, over at the cemetery. He watched over my sister Agnes."

"That's my uncle, sir. I work with him at the cemetery."

The station master looked at the dirty young man and his demeanour changed in an instant.

"Damn it," he snapped. "Keep your distance. Stand back."

"Sorry, sir," Paolo said meekly as he stepped back.

"I see his missus from the time to time," said the man in a more conversational tone. "Nelly, I think her name is."

He turned around and began searching the mailboxes.

"So you are the nephew who writes the letters?"

"Yes, sir."

The station master found what he was looking for and turned around, slipping a letter under the wicket.

"Thank you, sir."

Paolo picked up the letter and looked at his name inscribed in capital letters in a feminine hand. It wasn't his mother's handwriting, and she was the only woman who had ever written to him. He pulled the wax seal from the paper and read the short message.

> I HAVE BEEN BETRAYED.
> YOU ARE MY SAVIOUR. PLEASE COME.
> YOURS TRULY, DAPHNE

Under the name, there was the address of the Provincial Lunatic Asylum in the town of York. Paolo looked perplexed.

"Bad news, Mr Morelli?" the station master asked.

"No, sir," Paolo stammered. "It's fine. Thank you."

Paolo walked out of the building, his heart pounding, and quickly climbed on his horse.

"You're not looking so good, Paolo," said Vito. "All those nights. I think you been workin' too hard."

"I'm fine, Uncle."

"Your mamma will never forgive me if anything happened to you, son."

It was a hot day in the cemetery. They were digging new graves side by side. The boy looked distracted and tired. His body was filling out with the hard labour and he was getting stronger by the day, thought Vito, but it would not be a good idea to overwork him.

Vito took a breather and wiped his brow as he watched his nephew digging the hole next to him.

Paolo had been working every night in the cemetery for a week and trying to catch up on his sleep during meal breaks and rest periods. It had been several days since he had received the letter from Daphne. He had abandoned any idea of going to see her. There was no way that he could get off work and York was a long way away.

"Maloney wants me to run into Hamilton for burial reeds, but I hardly have time, what with the new arrivals. I was thinkin' you might go."

"I can go, Uncle."

"You don't mind?"

"Course not."

"Okay, how about tomorrow? You could get some rest tonight. Joey will look after things in the cemetery."

"Thank you, Uncle."

"It'll do you good to get away for a bit, Paolo."

Paolo nodded at his uncle and rested for a moment as he thought about the trip.

"Before you go, you better talk to Nelly and find out what provisions she needs in town."

The mystery girl is called Daphne, and she's at the Provincial Lunatic Asylum. What is she doing there? Can this be the same girl? She looked like an angel when she was in Nelly's care. I don't know what to do. Should I go and see her? Maybe it is better if I leave her alone. Mister Burke might not be too happy if I were to visit her in the city. Then again, I could go to Hamilton for Vito's supplies and then go on to York from there.

Twenty-five

On a leafy street in the city, Paolo trotted up and down on the grey mare looking for the Provincial Lunatic Asylum. He had never been to York before, so it took some time to find the place. He eventually located a large, imposing building some distance from the road behind a gate. He tied his horse to the railing near the gatehouse. He was painfully conscious that his threadbare frock coat and top hat made him look like a down-on-his-luck businessman in this rich and fashionable town.

A wagon drove through the gate, followed by several young men carrying shovels. Paolo joined the men and was waved in by a fat guard wearing a peaked cap. He climbed the steps and went to the front desk, where a man was drinking tea and cleaning his pipe with a knife.

"Sir, I'm here to see Miss Grenville."

"Grenville? Sorry, I don't have that name," said the clerk.

"She arrived a week ago. A young woman, Daphne?"

"A new arrival, you say. Daphne? We have a Daphne on the third floor, but she's been with us for a long time, sir."

Paolo nodded at the man.

"Visits are 10 minutes, sir. Sign here."

The clerk pushed the visitors' book across to Paolo, who scribbled his name in the book.

"Up the stairs to the third floor, then down the hall to your right. She's in 305. Don't forget. Keep it quiet up there and no baiting the inmates."

"Yes, sir. Thank you."

Paolo started up the stairs. When he got to the third floor, he noticed several white-clad guards in the lounge near the door. They were having a laugh about something, and Paolo kept his eyes straight ahead and continued into the women's section. He had only gone a short distance when he found number 305. It wasn't a room; it was a locked cell with a sliding metal food tray slot in the door. Paolo didn't know what to do. He hesitated and then tentatively knocked on the door.

"Go away!"

The voice from inside was faint, but the woman's anger was unmistakable. Paolo slid the cover aside and caught a glimpse of a thin blonde woman sitting on a hardwood chair in the far corner. As his eyes adjusted to the darkness of the isolation cell, he realized she was wearing ankle bands and wrist muffs to prevent scratching and self-abuse. He hardly dared to look at her face, but when he did, there was no doubt. It was Daphne; it was the same girl.

"I can see you out there. I got ears, you know. Go away."

Through the slot in the door, Paolo observed her watching him. She could hobble around, but she couldn't move her hands and legs much.

"Want to see my tits? Want to see me pee in the pot?"

Paolo blinked and tried to speak, but Daphne cut him off.

"How much you got?"

She stood up and collected her petticoat over her hips, then turned around to show him her naked backside. Paolo was shocked into silence. He was about to go away when Daphne awkwardly made her way closer to the door.

"OK, mister, that's a penny," she told him in a saucy tone.

Paolo realized she had no idea who he was. She hadn't heard him speak, and all she could see of him were his eyes through the narrow slot.

"It's me, Miss Daphne," Paolo whispered. "Paolo from St. Francis."

Daphne suddenly realized her mistake and started to cry.

"You've come for me?" she whispered.

After what he'd just witnessed, Paolo wasn't so sure anymore.

"I'm not mad, Paolo," she insisted. "Did my sister send you?"

"Why have they put you in here?"

"Lionel put me in here. You've come to set me free?"

Paolo watched Daphne wiping her tears away. The resemblance to her twin, the elegant young woman at the manor house who sang so beautifully, was striking.

"I saw your sister at the house."

"That's my sister Emily, Paolo. Lionel wants her to inherit the Grenville estate. He's gonna marry Emily and then kill her so he can have the estate, the money, everything."

"He would do that?"

"Paolo, he had me buried alive," she said, furious at his naivete. "What do you think?"

"You're looking better now, Miss Daphne, much better."

Daphne moved closer, locking her pretty blue eyes on Paolo. She didn't appear to be mad. She had been treated badly. She was vulgar, but perhaps it was the hostile environment of the Asylum that had made her so. He sincerely wished to avenge her honour.

"You must help me, please, I beg of you."

"I don't know what I can do for you here, Miss Daphne."

"I know where the key is."

Paolo stared at her and was moved by her predicament.

"Will you help me? You are my only hope. I must have my revenge on Lionel. I hate him, hate him, hate him. I will pull out his eyes and ears. He's a snake, he's a devil."

"I must go now, Miss Daphne."

"You could come here disguised with a mask and a cape. We could go away together arm in arm like a handsome young couple, no one the wiser."

Paolo knew that she was flirting shamelessly with him, but deep down, he wanted desperately to be the object of her desire.

"Please say you will come back. You will not abandon me."

"No, of course not."

"Will you help me escape?" said Daphne, grinning at Paolo through the slot in the door.

Twenty-six

The following day Paolo returned to the front gate of the Asylum. He tied his horse to the railing and went to the gatehouse, where he was immediately waved through. He headed to the side of the building where there was a wagon parked near the bakery. He slipped into the building through a large basement kitchen where dozens of loaves of bread lay on racks near the ovens. It was very quiet, and the staff were off on their lunch break. He found several white tops and cowls thrown over a chair, so he grabbed one of each as he headed for the stairs.

Paolo arrived at Daphne's cell and peeked in through the food tray slot. He whistled to Daphne, who was sitting on her bed of straw talking to herself.

"Is that you, Paolo? You came."

"How do we get you out of here?"

"That's easy. Give me a few minutes. Hide yourself."

Paolo looked around and then disappeared from view as Daphne started to bang on her cell door.

A male guard was smoking a cigarette in the stairwell when he heard the banging. He dropped the butt on the ground, stamped it out and then hurried along the corridor towards Daphne's cell. It was strictly forbidden for inmates to make any kind of noise on the floor during visiting hours.

The guard stopped at Daphne's cell and peered inside. Daphne was hidden from view from the door as she banged on the wall with her chamber pot. The guard slipped his key into the lock and opened the door. Just as he opened it, Daphne came out from behind the door and swung the metal chamber pot down on the man's skull. He crumpled onto the floor. Daphne poked her head out the door.

"Come on then," she hissed.

Paolo came out of his hiding place and joined Daphne in the cell. He was taken aback when he saw the unconscious guard.

"Don't you worry 'bout him," Daphne said. "He'll be coming 'round soon enough. He thinks he can get it for free."

Paolo snapped out of it.

"Help me get rid of the ankle band."

Paolo used his knife to cut the leather strap, and Daphne removed the band holding her ankles together. She stood up as Paolo pulled a white top and cowl from under his jacket.

"Put this on," he told her. She looked like she was going to laugh, but Paolo gave her a warning look.

"We're going out through the bakery."

Daphne pulled the white top over her clothes and slipped on the cowl to cover her hair and shoulders.

"Lovely. Let's go."

It happened so fast that no one had time to raise the alarm. Paolo reminded himself not to hurry, but to move slowly, as if he was just following his daily routine. He took his time driving the baker's wagon through the front gate and out on to the street. Daphne, in her white uniform and cowl, looked like a baker off to make deliveries in the neighbourhood with her sacks of flour, tools and a water barrel in the back. Paolo stopped the wagon briefly across the street from the front gate and went to fetch his grey mare attached to the railing. No one came after them, but Paolo felt much better after they had turned off the main road and headed out into the country.

After an hour, Paolo pulled off the dirt road into the woods and stepped down. He drank from the water barrel as Daphne ran off to pee in the woods. He looked away as Daphne pulled up her petticoat and squatted in the long grass. She finished her business and returned with a smirk.

"You were watching me, Paolo. I can tell. Never seen a woman pee, have you?"

Paolo looked perplexed.

"You saved me from that horrible place," Daphne said as she touched her throat and shivered. "I guess I owe you, young man. Give me your hand."

Daphne took Paolo's hand and put it on her breast.

"How does that feel?"

The softness of Daphne's breast aroused Paolo, who was embarrassed by this intimacy. Daphne frowned suddenly and slapped his hand away.

"Please, sir, remove your hand from my tit."

Paolo stepped back as Daphne laughed.

"We better go, Miss Daphne. It's a long way."

Paolo checked the saddlebags on the mare before climbing back on the wagon.

"Whatcha got in those bags, young man?"

"Nothing much, just some supplies for my uncle."

Paolo whipped the horse, and the wagon rolled forward. Daphne took his arm, sitting in close, but Paolo was tired of her tricks and shook her off.

Twenty-seven

It was getting late when Paolo noticed a small creek near a stand of trees and pulled the wagon off the road into the long grass. Daphne had fallen asleep, and Paolo was careful not to wake her as he stepped down. He walked down to the creek and noticed small animal tracks and telltale rabbit droppings leading near the water's edge. There was a clump of scrub trees crowding the trail, the lower branches close to the ground. Paolo shrugged - it was as likely a spot as any, and it would be dark soon.

He picked up a heavy branch and took out his penknife, cutting off several bits to set a trap. He installed a dead branch over the trail and pulled out a piece of thin wire from his pocket. He looped it around, making a noose, which he hung from the branch in the middle of the trail, inches off the ground. Then, using bits and pieces of branches, he blocked off the trail so the rabbit would be forced to jump through the wire noose if it ventured along the path.

Paolo stood up and returned to the wagon where Daphne was waking up.

"Want to make us a fire?" Paolo asked.

"A fire?"

"Sure, we might need it to cook up the food."

"You brought food? I'm starving. Aren't you an enterprising young man?"

"Maybe, maybe not. Let's get that fire going."

Paolo stepped away from the wagon and started looking for combustibles to make the fire.

It was a dark night on the prairie as Paolo cooked a rabbit on a spit over the fire. It had taken no time to snare the rabbit. The field was full of them. The meat was well done, so Paolo speared a haunch and handed it to Daphne who was sitting nearby. He then took some meat for himself.

"So when did your cousin Lionel have you put away?"

"Three years ago."

Daphne frowned, looking increasingly agitated as she tore into the rabbit meat.

"I hate the bastard. I hate him."

"So you think Lionel wants to inherit the manor?"

"Not just the manor, the land. It's a vast estate. It runs all the way down to the river."

Paolo sat silently chewing on his meat, watching Daphne across from him.

"My father sent me away to live with my aunt. She was a horrible woman."

Daphne shivered at the memory. "My sister got to stay at home and even had her own tutor."

"Why? What had you done?" asked Paolo.

"Nothing. I didn't do a thing. Father always preferred Emily to me. He said I was the bad one, and I needed a stern hand."

"What happened after you lived with your aunt?"

"Let's not talk about that."

The look on her face told Paolo he had asked enough questions. He was going to the wagon to get a drink from the water barrel when he thought he heard something. He froze and then pulled a flintlock revolver from his leather satchel. It belonged to his uncle and was a Collier five-shot with a rotating barrel.

"Be quiet now," he whispered. "There's a wagon on the road."

He pulled Daphne to the ground, and they crawled away from the fire into a nearby gully. When they looked up again, they could see the dim outline of a wagon pulling to a stop on the road. Paolo's first thought was that someone from the Asylum had succeeded in tracking them down. As the four men got closer to the fire, Paolo knew they weren't from the city.

"There goes our supper," whispered Paolo, lying on his belly in the gully.

The men stumbled forward, looking around, and soon were fighting over the remains of the rabbit on the spit. They didn't seem to care who they had disturbed as they feasted on the rabbit meat.

"Who are they?" asked Daphne.

"Riffraff. You can smell them from here. They're cholera men, see their wagon. Stay down."

Paolo gave the fire a wide berth and made his way over to the cholera wagon with his gun drawn. The cholera men sounded like they had been drinking. They didn't look like much, but there were four of them. Paolo was glad he had the revolver. He didn't know much about guns and wasn't sure how many barrels were primed and held balls.

He got to their wagon, recoiling from the smell coming from the back. He looked in and saw two bodies wrapped in bedclothes in an advanced state of putrefaction.

As the men argued over the rabbit meat, Paolo approached the tired horse, caressing its mane gently. He gave the horse a hard slap on the rump and the startled animal reared up and took off, the cholera wagon clattering along behind it. Paolo dropped to his knees in the high grass as the four men ran past him, trying to catch up with the wagon.

Daphne was sitting near the fire when Paolo returned.

"You should have shot them," she said.

"I think I only have three barrels loaded. There were four men."

"You could have shot three of them."

"I prefer not to fight, Daphne."

"We could have killed them all."

Paolo looked at Daphne with consternation.

"I met an axe killer in the Asylum. A tiny woman, shorter than me. She killed a man, smacked him in the head with an axe."

Paolo remained silent.

"You aren't very brave for a cholera man."

"I'm not a cholera man, Miss Daphne. I don't collect dead bodies on the road. I'm a remembrance man. I watched over your grave and pulled you out just in time. Remember?"

"Oh, my. Aren't we sensitive all of a sudden? The cholera man is getting all uppity. I do believe I've offended him."

"I saved your life, Daphne."

"As you keep reminding me. Well, I would have shot those dirty scum. They ate our supper and now we have nothing."

"We have our lives, Miss Daphne. That is good, isn't it?"

"No, it's not good. I hate them. Let's go after them. Come on Paolo, we can catch them and make them pay."

Paolo looked genuinely surprised at her desire for vengeance.

"You can go," he said finally. "I need my sleep. We'll be up at dawn."

"You're gonna go to sleep now?"

"Yes, I am. I'm tired. Good night."

Paolo put his gun back into his leather satchel and lay the satchel down as a headrest. He then pulled a wool blanket around himself and lay down near the fire. Daphne steamed in silent frustration.

In Detroit, they treat cholera with cupping and bloodletting. My mamma swore by it. She said it can cure any disease, but I've seen several neighbours who've died from the blue death after such treatments. In my street, there was a man who used cauterization to treat cholera victims. He applied a red-hot iron along the spinal column and said it worked very well. There were rumours that plugging the anus with a cork and giving acid baths helped revive the victims, but I don't believe it.

Out here in the country, there aren't any doctors around to treat cholera victims, so all we have is the bloodletting and the calomel treatment which I hear is made from a mercury compound and very expensive. Mamma sent me some medicine to ward off the cholera, but it tastes bad. Nelly says it won't help much. She thinks the best way to protect oneself is by getting a lot of rest and fresh air.

Twenty-eight

It was a sweltering summer day in the vast sea of empty grassland as far as the eye could see. Paolo had been driving the wagon for hours. Daphne had fallen asleep on the seat beside him, and Paolo was having trouble keeping his eyes open.

In the middle of the afternoon, Paolo had an apparition. Two small, stick-like figures stood immobile in the distance. At first Paolo thought his eyes were playing tricks on him. When he got closer, he saw they were just children, a little boy and a girl, holding hands and standing barefoot in the muddy road. The boy looked to be about six years old, while the girl appeared to be older by a year or two. Paolo looked around and saw no sign of a house or any sign of human habitation. The children seemed to be waiting for them or for anyone to come along. He pulled up next to the children.

"Hello, where do you live?"

The barefoot boy pointed to a sharecropper's mud-walled hut hidden in a copse of trees behind him.

"Where's your mama, your papa?"

"Dey catch de cholera, mister," said the boy.

"Somebody looking after you?" asked Paolo as Daphne woke up beside him.

"We lookin' after ourselves."

"Do you have any food?"

"Not much, juss a bit of grain."

"Got any eggs, maybe a chicken?"

"We got a hen, not layin' no good," said the girl.

"Got any family in the area?"

"An uncle, he lives west of here," said the boy.

"Well, you can't stay out here alone. I can take you up the road aways," Paolo offered, "but first we need to eat. Let's go find that hen."

Near the sharecropper's hut, Daphne and the two children watched hungrily as Daphne slowly turned the hen on a spit over the fire.

"What's your name?" she asked.

"Neil," said the boy.

"Neil Francis," said the girl. "Dat's his name, miss."

"No, it ain't. It's juss Neil."

"And your sister?"

"My name's Fran 'lisabeth, miss."

"No, it ain't. It's juss Fran. Nobody call you no 'lisabeth.'"

"Mama, she called me dat."

"Yeah, she'd be callin' you dat when she got her dander up," insisted Neil.

As the children watched Daphne preparing the food, Paolo silently dragged a man's body out of the hut and then returned for the wife. With a shovel he found in the house, Paolo started to dig a shallow grave for the couple in the loamy soil. The bluish tinge on their faces confirmed what the little boy had told him. Somehow, the children had escaped the same fate.

The next day, the two children were up at the crack of dawn. They sat together on a blanket, watching Daphne snoring near the remains of the fire. Paolo had gone to fetch some water from the wagon. When he returned with a wooden bucket, Daphne was just waking up. Paolo sat the bucket on the ground near Neil and Fran.

"Go ahead," he told them, gesturing at the bucket. "That's what it's there for."

They both cupped their hands and scooped water out of the bucket.

"Time to have a pee before we go, ladies," Paolo announced.

"Fran ain't no lady, mister," Neil said. "She's my sister."

"I am too a lady," Fran protested.

Daphne got up and stepped behind a tree to do her business while Fran just squatted in the dust near the remains of the fire and let it fly.

"See, mister," said Neil. "That ain't no lady."

Paolo laughed and drank from the bucket. He then took some water to wash his face and neck.

"We best be on our way, but before we go, let's say a prayer for your parents."

Paolo and the children walked over to the gravesite behind the sharecropper's hut. They kneeled and Paolo led them in the Lord's prayer.

"Our Father in heaven, hallowed be your name. Your kingdom come, your will be done, on earth as it is in heaven. Give us this day our daily bread, and forgive us our debts, as we also have forgiven our debtors. And lead us not into temptation, but deliver us from evil... *Nel nome del Padre, e del Figlio, e dello Spirito Santo*. Amen."

"What was that, mister?" asked Fran.

"In the name of the Father, the Son and the Holy Spirit in my language, in Italian."

After the prayer, Daphne joined them as Paolo and the children were putting together a makeshift cross from two pieces of wood and a bit of twine.

"Let me tie them together," said Paolo as Neil held up the pieces of wood.

After he tied the knot, making the cross, Paolo took a rock and hammered the wooden support into the dirt. Neil and Fran looked down solemnly at the grave. Their parents were buried in a proper grave with a cross, just like normal people.

I met these two children, Neil and Fran, on the road returning to St. Francis. Their parents had just died, and they were alone and abandoned. What will become of them? I'll take them as far as I can. Such is the state of this country. One day you have a mother and a father, and the next they are gone. Pray for them.

Twenty-nine

While Daphne slept in the back of the wagon on a pile of gunny sacks, Paolo and the children sat up front with Paolo as they approached St. Francis. Neil and Fran's eyes were wide with fascination as they drove down Main Street. Paolo had to smile. It was obvious they had never been to a town before and were amazed to see so many people walking about. Paolo stopped in front of the coach station and took the children inside.

Daphne woke up and looked around. It took her a moment to realize where she was and that she was alone. No one came out or went into the coach station. She sat up straight and searched Paolo's leather satchel, pulling out his revolver and a journal. The pages were written in elegant Italian script and were incomprehensible to her. She sighed in frustration and put it back in the satchel, then hid the gun behind a sack of flour. She lay back and watched a dark cloud, heavy with rain, coming in from the west.

The lights of the migrant dogtrots appeared through the woods. Paolo pulled up near his cabin and jumped down from the wagon. He untied the grey mare and threw the saddlebags with Nelly's supplies over his shoulder.

"You remember the road now, Miss Daphne? Just follow the trail through the woods and you'll be home within the hour."

"Thank you, noble sir," added Daphne with a laugh as she climbed clumsily into the driver's seat.

Paolo looked up at the darkening sky.

"It might be better that you stay here for a while, Miss Daphne. There's a big storm coming in."

Daphne looked at the sky and grinned at Paolo.

"I'm not worried about a bit of rain, Paolo. I want my old life back. I will have it. No one can stop me."

Daphne touched Paolo's arm affectionately as he removed his leather satchel from the wagon. She leaned over and kissed him hard on the mouth. Paolo stepped back uneasily, never having been kissed that way before.

Daphne laughed and whipped the horse into action. The first raindrops fell as the wagon raced off through the woods.

Thirty

After a night of heavy rain, the Grenville calash appeared on the road in the morning haze. Miss Emily always enjoyed driving the calash herself. She was at the reins of her favourite horse, a frisky young mare, and she reminded herself not to go too fast. Mrs. Henderson, her sixty-year-old housekeeper, was sitting beside her, and Emily knew the older woman was easily frightened when she went too fast.

Emily had spent a few days out at the lake cottage with the housekeeper who was cleaning it in preparation for the arrival of the two Grenville boys who would spend their days, fishing with Smiley off the dock and running wild in the natural splendour of the lake.

As the calash pulled off the road and went through the gate, Emily noticed how quiet it was. There was none of the usual activity around the stables and the kitchen, and while the front door was open, no one came out to greet them. Mrs Henderson, sensing Emily's unease, stepped down from the calash with her basket and went up the front steps as soon as Emily pulled the mare to a stop.

"Baxter," she called, stepping through the open door. "We've arrived."

Emily was tired and took her time collecting her things from the calash when she heard Mrs Henderson scream.

It was late morning by the time Constable Riley arrived at the Grenville manor. A servant woman ushered him through the hall to the garden, where Miss Emily and Mrs Henderson sat at a table under a shade tree drinking tea. Both were visibly upset, and Miss Emily had tears in her eyes. Riley exchanged a few awkward words with them and then followed the servant back to the house.

The staff, who lived nearby, had left the manor house as soon as they could get away. Miss Millie has assembled the rest in the kitchen to wait for the constable to arrive. The whole room was deathly quiet as they waited. After what seemed like an interminable time, the constable appeared in the doorway.

"Well, ladies," he began, "you've all had a bad fright, so I will be quick. What time did you hear the gunshots?"

"Oh, I couldn't say, sir," said Miss Millie.

"It was after three o'clock in the morning, sir," said a scullery maid. "I had gone up for a glass of milk around half past two. It was after I was back in bed."

"What did you do when you heard the first gunshots?"

"I got up and locked my door," Miss Millie told him. "That's when I heard the second shot on the floor above."

"We were wakened by the gunshots," said Gerty. "I stepped out into the hall with the other girls, but we were too frightened to go up, sir."

"So you didn't hear a voice or see something through a window?"

"No, sir," Miss Millie and Gerty said in unison.

Riley tried not to show his frustration. The servants weren't being much help, but they had had a terrible shock. He would just have to be patient.

Thirty-one

Paolo was back at work in the cemetery. It was hot as he toiled in a hole in a new area of the ever-expanding cemetery. Working with a pick, he softened up a rocky layering of shale before shovelling it out. Looking up, he spotted Constable Riley looking down at him from his horse.

Paolo stepped back and had to crane his neck to look up at the man. Riley dismounted as Deputy Fuller, a thin man with a moustache and side whiskers, arrived on horseback. Riley looked at Paolo and then spat a wad of chewing tobacco on the ground.

"That's a hard job you're doin' there, young man," said Riley. "I'd appreciate it if you'd step out for a moment."

Paolo nodded and climbed out of the grave, dropping his shovel just as Vito and Joey came over. The constable turned his attention towards Vito.

"Nice to see you again, Mr Morelli. I hear that you and your nephew here are 'remembrance men'. Fine upstanding work, I might say."

"Yes, sir. We do what we can," Vito replied.

"It must get mighty lonely out here, watching over the dead."

"It does, but we're used to the work. No complaints."

"You fellas got any firearms?"

"No, sir. Don't need none out here."

The constable laughed and said, "No, I don't suppose you do." He smiled briefly, then his manner changed.

"Gentlemen, I want you to follow us," said Riley. "That your wagon over there?"

"Yes, sir."

"You follow me and Deputy Fuller here will bring up the rear."

"Where we goin', sir?" Vito asked nervously.

"I have something to show you. It won't take long, Morelli. Just follow us."

The arrival of the lawmen at the dogtrot had frightened Nelly, who looked with alarm at Vito. Riley was busy searching their cabin while Fuller kept an eye on Paolo, Vito, and Joey. Neither Fuller nor Riley had explained why they were there, but Riley had looked under the bunk beds, gone through the pantry, and searched their clothes and valises.

Finally, he straightened up and exchanged a look with his deputy before taking Paolo out through the back door and sitting him down at a table in the yard. Fuller kept everyone in the house, but he let them watch from just inside the doorway.

"I've been talking with the servants at the Grenville estate," Riley said, his eyes on Paolo. "They tell me they've seen you lurking around the manor."

"Me, sir? No. I only went out there to talk to Mr Lionel."

"So you had business with Lionel?"

"Yes, sir."

"What kind of business?"

"I'm a remembrance man, sir, so one night I was in the cemetery and heard Miss Daphne calling from the grave. She had been buried alive. We dug out her grave and nursed her back to health. I went out to the estate to tell the family the good news that she was alive."

"You're pulling my leg?" Riley said, incredulous.

"No, sir. It's the truth. You can ask Lionel."

"What were you doing yesterday?"

"I went to York for supplies for my uncle, sir. I got back last night, just before the rainstorm."

"Where did you go after you got home?"

"I didn't go anywhere, sir. I ate my supper and went to bed."

The constable waved to Fuller, who went to his horse and brought back a package wrapped in cloth. He gave it to the constable, who removed the oilcloth and held it aloft so everyone could see it.

It was a Collier five-shot flintlock revolver.

"Do any of you men recognize this gun?" Riley raised his voice so that Vito and Joey could hear. "This is a fancy weapon with a capacity to fire five shots."

There was a long silence.

"It's mine, sir." Vito stepped out of the doorway. "I bought it in Detroit this last year. It ain't been used in a long while."

"I see." Riley turned to his deputy. "Mr Fuller, was this gun recently fired?"

"Yes, sir," Fuller replied. "You can smell the gunpowder."

The constable brought the gun to his nose and sniffed the musty charcoal and sulphur smell coming from the barrel.

"That's impossible. I never used the gun," blurted Paolo, while Vito lifted his eyebrows in dismay.

Paolo realized that the cat was out of the bag. Riley gave the Collier back to Fuller and stepped closer to Paolo.

"So where've you been with this gun, young man?" he asked.

"I went to York with it, sir."

"You took this gun with you?"

"Yes, sir. It was for protection."

"You ever fire it?" Riley asked.

"No, sir."

"I see." Riley stared down at Paolo, then glanced at his deputy. "Mr Fuller?"

"Sir?"

"Arrest this man."

Thirty-two

The front door of the manor house was wide open, and there was a sound of flies buzzing in the heat. Fuller and Paolo waited on the front steps as Constable Riley stepped out.

"We're ready," he told Fuller. "Bring him in."

Paolo followed the constable into the drawing room. He could see Lionel Burke, sitting at a desk in the far corner of the room. There was something terribly wrong with his head. It was thrown back and his face was covered with dried blood from a head wound. His hand rested near a pen on the desk, as if he had been writing something right up until the moment he had been brutally assassinated. The constable turned to Paolo and held up the Collier flintlock revolver.

"We found your gun on the premises, young man. This is the gun that was used to kill Mr Burke here. It had blood all over it."

"Sir, that is not possible. I never came here."

"That's not what the servants tell us."

"I had nothing to do with this."

"Why'd you kill Lionel Burke, son? Money, was it?"

"No, sir."

"Miss Emily and the housekeeper discovered the bodies when they arrived early this morning."

Paolo remained silent, too stunned to speak.

"Come along now. Let me show you the rest."

Riley left the room, followed by Paolo and Fuller. They headed to the kitchen. On the floor, a man was lying flat on his belly with a bullet wound in his back.

"I think you two have met," Riley said quietly. "This is Baxter, the butler."

"Oh, God!" cried Paolo.

"We think your gun was used to kill him, too."

The constable turned and headed up the stairs to the bedrooms on the second floor. At the top of the stairs, there was the body of young James in his nightgown with a gunshot wound to the chest as if he had run straight into the bullet.

"I think you were going up the stairs as the boy was coming down towards you, so you shot him because he could identify you, you heartless bastard."

Paolo looked on, speechless at the horror of it all.

"Now, you have no more bullets left, so you ran after the other kid."

Riley angrily grabbed Paolo's arm and dragged him up to the top of the stairs and into the bedroom. The younger brother lay dead on the floor with a hideously, smashed skull.

"I think you struck him a fatal blow with a hammer, or maybe an axe."

Riley backhanded Paolo across the face and sent him flying. The constable struggled to recover his composure as he stared at the young man for a long moment.

"Son, this is a horrible crime," Riley said, shaking his head. "What did these people ever do to you that you had to come out here and kill them in cold blood?"

Paolo wiped the blood from his nose and slowly picked himself up off the floor.

"Son, I think it is time to own up for your crimes."

Thirty-three

Constable Riley had to get out, if only for a few moments. He looked tired and dispirited, as he reflected on the horrible crime. In his career as a constable, he had never witnessed such a slaughter. He stepped off the veranda and went to his horse tied to the railing. He collected a notebook from a saddlebag and then put his arms over the saddle, resting his head against the worn leather. He stood that way for a long moment as he watched his horse slapping flies with its tail.

St. Francis was a small country town and nothing much ever happened in the region. Now all that had changed. He would have to deal with a sensational murder that happened on his patch. The inevitable enquiries of newspaper reporters and the meddling of the political class poking their noses into his business, made him cringe. He never came to St. Francis looking for fame and fortune.

He was about to go back into the house when he noticed deep wheel ruts in the muddy ground tracking west. He stared at them for a moment, then dismissed the thought.

Paolo was still in the drawing room, sitting on a straight-backed chair with his wrists cuffed behind him. He watched the constable arrive and pull up a chair.

"I tell you Daphne Grenville is alive and well," Paolo said. "Dig up the grave and you'll find it empty."

"Sir, I believe he's lying," said Fuller. "I've seen Daphne's headstone in the cemetery."

"Miss Emily told us that Daphne never left the Provincial Lunatic Asylum," said Riley. "As far as she knows, she's still there."

"I told you that Daphne caught the blue death and was sent home to be buried next to her mother in the Grenville plot," said Paolo. "I'm not making this up. Talk to my uncle and Nelly, who nursed her back to health."

"So you're saying Lionel sent her back to the Asylum after you found her?" asked Riley.

"Yes, sir. She sent me a message asking for my help, so I visited her at the Asylum in York and helped her escape."

"You helped her escape?"

"Yes, sir. We arrived yesterday evening. She stole my gun and took the wagon."

"But no one has seen her since she returned to St. Francis," Riley said. "What do you think, Mr Fuller?"

"His story is a lie, sir."

"She must be hiding out somewhere," insisted Paolo.

The constable sat silently reflecting on Paolo's culpability, then spat a wad of tobacco into the spittoon near the desk.

Thirty-four

It was late in the afternoon. The bodies of the dead were laid out on tables covered in white shrouds in the parlour of the Grenville manor. Several women, including kitchen staff and servant girls, were sitting near the tables.

There was a stir in the room and a great wail of grief as Emily appeared in the doorway. She showed no sign of being aware of it, going instead to an open window and staring out at the back pasture with tears in her eyes. The loss of her mother and her two brothers was just too much for her. She felt totally alone in the world.

When she turned around, Emily saw Smiley standing near her in the window light.

"My condolences, miss."

"Smiley."

"I came as fast as I could."

"Please, Smiley, sit with me."

They took chairs near the kitchen staff, who fell into a respectful hush as they sat down. After a few moments, the general murmur of conversation resumed, although Smiley remained silent for a long time.

"I'm sorry for the young'uns," he said, "and your mum."

Emily burst into tears. Smiley waited, with infinite patience, for her to get hold of herself.

"The constable has arrested a man," he said in a whisper.

"Yes, I've heard."

"He'll hang for this crime."

"Yes."

"You must go and see him."

It was Paolo's second day in the town jail. Sometimes he managed to doze fitfully on the filthy straw mattress, but most of the time, he paced within the tiny confines of the cell. There were bars on a high window offering some illumination. A miserable candle burned in a wall holder and stank of animal fat, barely penetrating the obscurity where rats scurried back and forth in the corners. The meals were delivered on a tray by the deputy, who never said a word.

No one had come to see him, but he had gotten a note from Vito and Nelly. He knew Nelly had done the writing, but most of the words came from Vito. The note blamed Paolo's arrest on the fact he was a foreigner and a convenient scapegoat. That's how these things happened in Detroit, and it was the same in St. Francis. The rest of the note must have come from Nelly, because it said that Constable Riley would soon realize his mistake and then Paolo would be set free.

What have I done? Daphne stole my gun. She killed these people. Now they blame me for the crime? I have no motivation to hurt anyone. I don't even know these people, except for the two boys who I met briefly on my visit to see Lionel. None of that matters, according to Deputy Fuller, who says they're going to hang me as soon as they can find a judge.

Thirty-five

The crowd at the funeral service overflowed the local church. In spite of their fear of cholera, they made an exception for the murder victims - now known as the Grenville Four in the newspaper reports. The entire town seemed to be present at the ceremony. At the end of the service, they gathered respectfully outside and waited for the signal to depart.

The funeral director Maloney, in a top hat and black frock coat, sat up front next to the driver. The team of horses started off slowly and the hearse advanced, followed by the Grenville family calash and the citizens of the town. The silence was oppressive as they made their way over the flat grassland to the cemetery.

Emily alone represented what was left of the Grenville family. She was accompanied in her calash by Gerty and two maids, with Smiley driving. Nelly had bravely attended the funeral wearing her best hat and now she walked along with the rest of the townspeople, ignoring the stares and whispers. Constable Riley and Deputy Fuller followed the anonymous crowd of sympathizers on horseback.

The errand boy from the post office crossed the street and entered the jail. He knocked on the door to the office.

"Come in," Riley growled.

"Constable, I have a letter for you," the boy said, opening the door and nearly bumping into Fuller in his haste. "It's marked urgent, sir."

The kid handed the letter to Riley, who tore it open.

"Thanks, Billy. How's your dad?"

"He's doin' fine, sir."

Billy took a moment to look around the room and was impressed by the large collection of old flintlock muskets and pistols in the gun case on the knotted pine wall behind the constable.

"Tell him I said hello," said Riley as he reached into his pocket and flipped the boy a coin. Billy nodded happily and ran out of the office.

"Well, Fuller," Riley said. "You were right. It's from the Provincial Asylum. They don't have anybody there with that name. They never heard of her."

"Just what I thought, sir. Morelli was lying through his teeth."

"Well, it's possible that she was there under another name. Families do that, you know, to avoid the shame of having a lunatic in the family."

Riley was about to say something when they were interrupted by the sound of women's voices in the hall. Fuller got up to investigate. A moment later, he returned.

"Miss Emily is outside, sir. She wants to see the prisoner."

"Does she now? This could be interesting."

The constable stood up and went out into the hall. Emily and Mrs Henderson were sitting together on a bench in the waiting room.

"Miss Emily, Mrs Henderson. I'm sorry for your loss."

"Thank you, Constable," said Emily, wearing a hat and veil.

"My deputy says you have come to see the prisoner."

"Yes, sir. I have some questions for him."

"I'll wait here, dear," said Mrs Henderson. "If you need me, just call."

"Well, you better come in then," said Riley. "Mr Fuller will see that you are comfortable and safe. The prisoner will be cuffed to a chair."

"Thank you, sir."

Emily rose, leaving the housekeeper on the bench, and followed Riley into his office.

Paolo was shackled and cuffed, and sat on a wooden chair in the corner of the room as Fuller brought in the visitor. Emily sat down opposite the prisoner, examining him closely.

"I'll be outside, miss," said Fuller. "Juss holler if you need me."

"Thank you."

Fuller left the room.

"Mr Morelli, I am Emily Grenville. They say you are responsible for killing my cousin and brothers. I have come to ask you why."

"I'm innocent, miss. I told the constable, but he doesn't believe me."

"The constable says you met my sister Daphne."

"Show me your face."

Emily lifted the veil momentarily and looked away. She was the spitting image of Daphne.

"You're very beautiful, miss."

Emily blushed and dropped the veil to cover her face.

"My sister is dead, Mr Morelli. She died of the blue death a fortnight ago. I don't know how you can..."

"She's alive, miss. I was with her only a few days ago."

"You say you have met my dead sister. I don't understand, Mr Morelli. How can this be so?"

"I'm a remembrance man, miss. I saved your sister from the grave."

"I know nothing about you, Mr Morelli. Where are you from?"

"I'm Italian from Genoa, miss. I arrived last year and live in Detroit with my family."

"I don't know Detroit. Is it a big place?"

"Yes, it is. It's a big town with over two thousand people. It's a port on the Detroit River, a lot of ships go through there, coming from Buffalo. My mother is a seamstress and makes dresses for wealthy patrons. She has a small shop on Farmer Street. My dad works as a carpenter when he can find work."

"Is there a lot of cholera in Detroit, Mr Morelli?"

"Yes, it's worse than it is here. It started with the Black Hawk War."

"What war is that, Mr Morelli?"

"The Indian war in Wisconsin, miss."

"I never heard of this war. We don't get the news much in St. Francis."

"The troopships passed through Detroit on their way west, miss. Some of the ships carried soldiers infected with cholera. There was a big panic in the town and the mayor ordered all the ships to keep a distance of 100 yards offshore. The passengers weren't allowed to land until they had been seen by a health inspector, but it was already too late. People were fleeing the city. That's why my parents sent me here to work with my uncle."

"How are your parents, Mr Morelli?"

"They're fine, miss. They closed down the shop in June and don't go out much."

"You're lucky to have your parents. My father died of typhus and my dear mother recently of cholera."

"Yes, I know, Miss Grenville. I'm very sorry for your loss."

I've met the twin sister. Her name is Emily, and she is just as beautiful as her sister in a quiet understated way. She came to see me and I told her about Detroit and how the cholera arrived there. She asked a lot of questions. I can see that she is deeply troubled by the murders. She is lucky to be alive with that crazy sister of hers running amok.

Thirty-six

It was a scorching day as Vito and Joey proceeded to dig out Daphne's grave. Fuller directed operations standing near the grave while Constable Riley sat in the shade on a folding chair, smoking a cigar. Maloney, formally attired as always, stood perspiring in the heat.

"So, Mr Maloney," Riley looked up at the funeral director, "you say you had this one buried good?"

"There is no doubt in my mind, sir."

"And Lionel Burke paid you for the headstone?"

"Absolutely, sir. He wanted the best for his niece."

Vito and Joey's shovels struck the wooden surface of a coffin. Vito looked at Fuller, confused.

"What is this, Mr Fuller?"

"It's a pine box, Morelli," Fuller said with a grin. "You handle them every day."

"Open it up," ordered Riley from the shade.

Vito and Joey hauled the coffin out of the grave with their straps and put it on the grass nearby. The smell of putrefaction was all too evident. Riley, Fuller, and Maloney gathered around as Vito popped the lid. They peeked inside at the deceased woman and then quickly pulled back and away from the coffin. Vito and Joey were astonished.

"Well, gentlemen, I think we have our answer," said Riley. "Thank you, Mr Maloney."

"Any time, sir."

"All right, gentlemen, you can nail it down again."

Vito and Joey grabbed the cover and quickly nailed the coffin shut as Riley and Fuller climbed onto their mounts and left Maloney with the two gravediggers.

"I don't get it, sir," Vito said. "We pulled a body from this grave in the middle of the night."

"Maybe you are mistaken, Morelli. There are so many graves here and at night?"

"No, it was here in the Grenville plot."

"A strange business, if you ask me. I hear your nephew Paolo is being held at the jail."

"He ain't guilty, sir."

"Rumour has it he is a murderer. I hope, for your sake, it's not true, Morelli. You won't last long in this town if he's found guilty. Don't forget to dig the new one I asked for."

"Yes, sir."

Vito watched as Maloney climbed on his wagon and drove away.

Emily sat alone in the garden, observing the ducks on the pond. The silence was broken by the arrival of Mrs Henderson and Constable Riley with hat in hand.

"I'm sorry for the interruption, Miss Grenville."

"It's no trouble, sir."

"Please sit down, Constable."

Riley nodded and sat down, wiping sweat from his brow, as Mrs Henderson returned to the house. They waited in an awkward silence as Gerty arrived with an elegant tea service. Emily smiled her thanks and Gerty withdrew to the house.

"There can be no mistake, your sister Daphne is buried in the cemetery. We did the exhumation this morning. Morelli was lying, miss."

Emily tried to remain calm and composed, but her heart was all aflutter.

"Would you like a cup of tea, constable?"

"Thank you, miss."

Riley noticed a tremor in her hand as she poured the tea.

"Milk?"

"Yes, please."

Riley took the cup and put in three teaspoons of white sugar. He hadn't seen a sugarloaf and a bag of coffee beans in over two months because certain foodstuffs were being hoarded in the Eastern cities during the epidemic. He made a satisfying grunt as he sipped the sweet tea and then turned his attention back to Emily.

"I know I asked you this before right after the murders," he said, "but now that some time has passed, have you noticed anything missing, any valuables, from the house?"

"No, nothing. Everything is in its place."

"Did Morelli ever come into the house?"

"He may have met with Lionel, but I have no knowledge of that."

"After your mother died of cholera, your cousin Lionel arrived here from York to help with the estate?"

"Yes, sir. My mother said I should call on him to help me manage the estate after her death."

"And how did you get along with Lionel?"

"He was a good man, I suppose," said Emily, "but he lied to me about Daphne. I never knew that he had buried her body here in St. Francis."

"Daphne was sent away in '29, I believe. Did she ever come back for a stay?"

"No, mother refused to have her back. Daphne suffered from delusions and frequent hallucinations, according to her doctor. She was not dangerous."

"What was her treatment?"

"According to Lionel, she was placed on a restricted diet and had to be physically restrained when she had her fits. The doctor said that her insanity was in her blood, so she had some cupping and bleeding to reduce excessive animal spirits."

"I have been in contact with the Asylum, but they have no record of Daphne. Could she have entered the Asylum under an assumed name?"

"I wouldn't know, sir. Lionel handled everything when my mother was alive."

"Were you angry with Lionel for having sent your sister away?"

Emily sipped her tea, looking at the ducks.

"No," Emily said, shaking her head. "Daphne had become impossible to live with. Lionel was only following my parents' desire to keep her away from the family."

"You know that Morelli will hang for this."

Emily listened in shocked silence.

"How can you be so sure it is him, sir? Why would he do such a thing?"

"The murder weapon, miss. It belongs to Morelli. With time, we will find out why."

Thirty-seven

The Smythe Manor was a beautiful house with French windows overlooking the river and well-tended lawns and trees, now left in abandon. The lawn was overgrown and brown, and rubbish of all kinds littered the grounds. Constable Riley rode up to the house, passing wagons carrying pieces of furniture and driven by a motley assortment of looters.

His thoughts went out to the Smythe family who had abandoned the house and returned to Hamilton after the death of old man Smythe in July. Since then, looters had taken over the building and were stripping it clean. Some of them were borderline thieves, but others were ordinary citizens, who before the blue death would never have done what they were doing now. One wagon groaned under the weight of an upright piano.

Riley remembered old man Smythe as a bible-thumping firebrand, the scourge of his family. After their mother had died, the children wanted nothing to do with their old man and had fled the manor one after the other over the years. The blue death had caused this ignominy and so many others in St. Francis.

Riley made no effort to stop the looters. The Smythe family would not be returning to the abandoned manor. Looters were one thing, but squatters were another. Sooner or later, Riley feared that somebody would start a fire, either accidentally or on purpose, and with the hot weather and dry grassland, it could become a serious threat to the surrounding farms.

The last of the wagons clattered by him. Riley noticed the broken glass from the windows on the first-floor patio. There was no sign of life from inside the house. The constable dismounted at the front door and removed his Nock repeating musket from its scabbard. He pointed it at the sky and fired a shot into the air. He could hear running footsteps from inside the house as he rotated the second of the Nock's six barrels into position and waited. A moment later, a couple of teenage boys came tumbling out the front door, stopping up short when they saw the musket and the man behind it.

"Git," Riley said with a mean look.

The boys took off down the front steps and kept on going. Riley kept his attention on the house and the front door and counted off a full minute before he swung down off his horse. He kept the Nock in the crook of his arm as he tied his mount to the railing and climbed the stairs to the front door.

The hall had a beautiful curved wooden staircase, surrounded by pieces of wrecked furniture and torn paintings. He went into the parlour to have a look. It had been stripped by the looters and was now littered with torn furnishings. He returned to the hall and climbed the stairs to the second floor. He noticed a little boy kicking a wooden ball in the corridor.

Riley kneeled down to play with the child, who kicked the ball over to him. He recognized the boy as soon as he saw his smiling face. It was the Ross child, but what was he doing in the abandoned house? Riley kicked the ball back, and as he stood up to complete his search, he saw the boy's mother holding a musket.

Nelly and several migrant women were washing clothes in the river. The laundry was left to dry on boulders in the sun. The women looked up as a farmer in overalls and a straw hat pulled up in a wagon. Next to him sat two children, Neil and Fran.

"My name's Peters," said the man. "Any of you ladies know a young gentleman by the name of Morelli?"

Nelly stepped forward, holding a basket of wet clothing.

"Yes, sir. He's my nephew."

"Hello, ma'am. I have a farm west of here. I want to say a few words of thanks to Mr Morelli for saving my niece and nephew. Where can I find him?"

Constable Riley watched Eleanor Ross as she worked at the stove in the downstairs kitchen of the Smythe Manor house. She looked less emaciated and drawn than she had when he'd last seen her. She put a plate of eggs and grits in front of her son and looked over at Riley.

"You sure you don't want any, Constable?" she asked. "We got more than we need. We got the eggs from the henhouse out back and the grits from a bag of cornmeal in the basement. The Smythe family won't be needin' them no more."

"No, I'm fine, ma'am. I tried to contact your sister Rebecca, but she'd left town."

"She's always takin' off with bad men, but it never lasts long before they start beatin' on her."

Eleanor served herself and sat down to eat with her son. She took a mouthful and looked up at Riley.

"I want to say how sorry I am about shooting at you and your men the other day."

"Don't worry yourself, ma'am. I don't hold a grudge," Riley said as he turned to the boy. "How old are you, Virgil?"

The boy looked at his mum and held up a hand to show off five fingers.

"One, two, three,..." said the child as he counted each finger and smiled triumphantly when he got to the last one. "I'm five."

"He's learnin' to count, constable. I'm teaching him."

"Well, that's a good thing."

The boy finished his plate and ran off to play with the ball.

"We buried your husband in a marked grave, ma'am."

"A marked grave? I hear most everybody without a penny to their name gets thrown in the pit."

"I had a talk with the funeral director. He's in a numbered grave, so you can find him any time you want to."

"Abe Ross was a good man when I married him. We were sweethearts from our school days, but out there on the prairie, he became a different man. I can't say I regret losing him."

"Sorry to hear that, ma'am."

"Ain't nothin' to feel sorry about, Constable. That's life."

"You know you can't stay here for long with looters coming and going."

"They don't bother us much. We lock the doors upstairs at night and keep to ourselves. I got my musket with me and I can shoot."

"Yeah, I know you can," Riley smiled. "That's what worries me."

Thirty-eight

A dandy in a frock coat and bow tie sporting a goatee examined the collection of old muskets and pistols on the wall in the Sheriff's office. Deputy Fuller sat quietly in Constable Riley's chair as the newspaper reporter from the big city expounded on the crime of the century.

"This is going to be very big," said the man, pulling a notebook from his pocket. "Let me get your name. It's Fuller, isn't it?"

"Yes, it is. E. A. Fuller, Edward A. Fuller," said the deputy who had come back after lunch and found the man waiting for him in front of the jail. Now they were in Riley's office and Fuller wasn't sure he should be talking to him.

"When will they transfer him?" asked the reporter as he scribbled the name in his notebook.

"We must finish the inquiry first."

"Deputy Fuller, I would very much appreciate your help in doing a portrait of the killer."

"A portrait?"

"Yes, a drawing of this man. His likeness will attract readers. You could be in the picture too, as the arresting officer. What do you think?"

"Better to talk to the constable first."

Nelly poked her head into the constable's office and saw the reporter talking to the deputy.

"Can we have a word with the prisoner, Mr Fuller?"

The reporter stood up and shook hands with the deputy.

"I'll be over at the hotel. Call me when you have talked to the constable. This is going to be big, Mr Fuller. Very big."

Fuller nodded at the reporter as Nelly entered the office.

"I need to have a word with Paolo, sir."

"Mrs Morelli, I don't think it is a good idea for you to be seen coming in here."

"I've brought the children and Mr Peters, sir."

"The children?"

Neil and Fran appeared in the doorway, followed by Mr Peters.

"Mr Peters wants to thank Paolo for saving Neil and Fran."

Fuller looked genuinely surprised.

"See, their parents died of the blue death," Nelly said. "They were abandoned and starving when Paolo found them. He buried the parents and then brought the wee ones all the way to St. Francis."

Deputy Fuller had refused to allow the children to see Paolo. Now he sat, shackled and cuffed in the interview room, as the deputy went to get Nelly and Mr Peters. Nelly rushed over to embrace Paolo and then stepped back.

"Paolo," she said, "this is Mr Peters. You gotta listen to what he has to say."

"Mr Morelli, I just want to express my thanks to you for saving the kids. We had no idea that my sister and her husband had died."

"They were standing in the road, sir. We couldn't leave the children alone out there."

"Well, I wanted to thank you personally. It was remarkably generous of you."

"Mr Peters is willing to put in a word with the constable," said Nelly.

"I'm not sure it will help, Nelly," said Paolo, scratching at his new growth of beard. He looked downright sorry for himself.

"Paolo, you mustn't lose hope."

Mr Peters is a nice man. My only hope is that the children will be able to identify Daphne and, God willing, the constable will spare my life. I wish I had never come to this place.

I should never have trusted Daphne. She was so beautiful, I wanted to save her. I should have known she was crazy from the moment I met her. Back home we have a saying: bella in vista, dentro è trista (a fair face and a foul heart).

Thirty-nine

Constable Riley couldn't stop thinking about Eleanor Ross and her child living as squatters in the abandoned manor house. He knew it wasn't his responsibility to look out for them and they were free to come and go, but he had continued to have misgivings about them after he left them the day before.

So when he rode up to the house late in the day, it looked like he had been worrying about nothing. The house was quiet, and the looters appeared to have gone home. He dismounted and removed a package from one of his saddlebags, tucking it under one arm. He went up the front steps and through the front door.

As soon as he stepped inside, Riley could hear men's voices and the scrape of furniture upstairs. He backed slowly out of the front door and went to get his Nock musket, returning the package to the saddlebag. He went back inside with the musket and silently crept up the stairs. The noise was coming from the upstairs bedroom that Eleanor had shared with young Virgil.

Riley passed the first bedroom on the floor, which was empty. The bed and most of the furniture had been removed. In the second bedroom, two men were struggling with a large cabinet.

"What are you doing?" exclaimed the constable.

The two men dropped the cabinet, seeing the armed constable in the doorway pointing his musket at them.

"We were told to collect these things, sir."

"You were, were you? Who hired you?"

"Mr Maloney, sir. He told us to collect what was left."

It took a moment, but Riley recalled seeing one of the men around St. Francis. He had a familiar face and was a working man, not the kind to take something that didn't belong to him. Riley lowered the musket.

"There was a woman with a child living here. Have you seen them?"

"No, sir," replied the man from St. Francis. "We ain't seen no woman."

Riley left them to their work and headed downstairs. He entered the dining room and then went through to the kitchen, but there was no sign of Eleanor and Virgil. He tried to imagine what could have happened to them. Where could they have gone?

He walked out the front door and around to the back of the house. There was a wagon full of furniture parked near the door, but no one was around.

He returned to the front of the house and climbed back on his horse. It would be getting dark by the time he got back to town. The woman and child were off in the wind. He had done his best to help them.

As Riley rode away from the manor house, he noticed a faint light coming from the window of a shack at the end of the vegetable patch. He decided to go over and have a look. The patch was overrun with weeds and looked abandoned. As he approached, he saw young Virgil run out of the shack and heard the voice of his mother.

"Virgil, get back in here. You ain't hardly eaten."

"Mama, a man is coming."

With these words, Eleanor appeared in the doorway with the big musket pointed at Riley.

"Constable!" she lowered the musket and leaned it against the wall. "How are you? We weren't expectin' no visit."

"You moved out of the manor?"

"Yeah, we had no choice," said Eleanor. "The looters are stripping the place clean. This shack ain't so bad."

"I brought you something."

The constable dismounted and gave Virgil the package wrapped in newspaper.

"The butcher in town had it prepared," Riley said. "The meat will tide you over for a while."

"Thank you, constable," said Eleanor, taking the package from the boy.

"It's a pleasure, ma'am. Remember, you gotta feed that boy if you want him to grow up strong. You get enough to eat from the garden?"

"Yeah, it's got everything: carrots, beets, beans, onions. We can't complain. It must have been paradise here when the Smythe family had it."

Eleanor turned and gestured toward the shack's interior.

"This is the summer kitchen. It has a stove and a couple of bunk beds in the back. It's comfortable enough."

Riley supposed it was. The Smythes had been a big family with a lot of servants, at least until the old man had driven most of them away. The kitchen would have had to feed a lot of people.

"You got time for a glass of elderberry wine, Constable?" Eleanor asked.

"Please," Riley said, a little bewildered by her hospitality. "I would like that."

Eleanor pulled a chair from inside the door and parked it in the sun next to a wooden crate and a battered table. She then went back inside to fetch the wine. Riley was just sitting down when Virgil came over to him.

"You see this," Virgil said, holding out an angular piece of flint. "It's a real arrowhead!"

"Well, it sure looks like one," Riley smiled. "See the way it's tapered at the end so it can be fixed to the shaft of an arrow."

Virgil examined the arrow head's tapered end with awe.

"Where'd you find it, son?"

"It's mine," said Virgil as he closed his hand over the arrowhead, afraid that Riley was going to take it away.

"He found it in the house," said Eleanor, arriving with two jars and a bottle of homemade wine. She poured a measure into Riley's jar and handed it to him.

"You can keep it, son. I'm sure the Smythe family won't be needing it no more."

Virgil smiled at the constable and ran off into the garden. Eleanor poured herself a glass of wine and took a seat on the crate.

"What's your name, Constable?"

"John Riley, ma'am."

"You married, John?"

"No, ma'am. Not anymore. My wife died of typhus a few years ago."

"You gettin' long in the tooth, John?"

"Not that old, ma'am," said Riley. "Still gotta bit of fire in me."

Eleanor laughed as Riley tried the wine, which was dry with a fruity taste and a dark red colour.

"That's a nice brew. It's got a lovely taste to it," said Riley. "Where'd you find it?"

"The Smythes left several bottles in the basement. Did you know the family?"

"Yeah, I knew old man Smythe back in the day. He was a hard man, always off on a crusade about some tomfool thing. I think his family suffered."

"What happened to them?"

"Most of the young ones left the estate, anything to get away from their old man. I think his wife died of consumption a few years back. Smythe lived here alone for quite some time until he died of the blue death, along with a couple of his servants."

Virgil came back to the porch and settled himself in his mother's lap, contentedly examining several smooth stones that he had found in the garden. The boy must have had a terrible shock when his dad died out on the prairie, and now he was living hand to mouth in abandoned buildings with his fearless mother.

The light started to fail, but the evening was still warm. Riley leaned back in the chair and fought the urge to close his eyes for a moment. After all the human drama he had witnessed this week, it was relaxing to simply observe Eleanor interacting with her child.

Forty

Paolo in cuffs and shackles was led out behind the jail by Fuller, holding a musket and a Collier flintlock five-shot revolver. The yard led down to a dry stone wall in the trees where the reporter was waiting for them with a sketch easel.

"Can we stand him up against the wall, Deputy?" asked the reporter.

Fuller led Paolo over to the wall and stood next to him.

"Can you put yourself just behind him on the right?"

Fuller moved over and pointed the Collier revolver at Paolo's head.

"Very good. A bit higher for the revolver. Lovely."

The reporter was a talented artist and sketched the men in fast and furious strokes.

"Mr Morelli, can you lift your head a little?"

Paolo raised his chin and smiled.

"Thank you," said the reporter, who stopped sketching and came over. "Look, Morelli, we can't have you smiling. You don't look like a killer. Remember that you hate the law. Gimme a scowl or a sneer. That's much better. Mr Fuller, gimme a mean look like a real lawman."

The reporter quickly returned to his easel and sketched Morelli's scowling face and then the stern expression of Fuller, making both men look their part in his portrayal of good versus evil in the old West.

Eleanor had put Virgil to bed in one of the bunk beds at the back of the summer kitchen. She sat quietly with the constable on the porch, drinking the elderberry wine and listening to the noise of crickets in the warm summer evening. She stood up and came around the table, putting her hand on the constable's shoulder. Her eyes sparkled with pleasure in the presence of this rough-hewn lawman with his weather-beaten face, his mutton chops and his straggly beard. He was a lot older than her late husband, but that didn't seem to bother her.

Eleanor had lived a hard life out on the windswept plains with a man who was not always kind to her. She had suffered through childbirth and long winters, living rough with little or nothing to feed her family. There was no way that she was going to let an eligible male slip away without making a play for him.

Eleanor sat in his lap, kissing him lightly on the lips as he held her. The constable had been attracted to Eleanor the very first time he saw her aiming her musket at him. She pushed Riley's glass away and took his hand in hers, which she pressed gently to her breast. They kissed for a long time, his hands moving over her body until finally Eleanor pulled herself away and stood up. He looked at her, confused. He started to say something, but she put her finger to her lips for silence. She went into the summer kitchen for a moment to check on Virgil and then reappeared with a blanket. She took Riley's hand and led him off the porch into the tall grass.

"So what's this Morelli fella done?" asked Eleanor in the moonlight, pouring the rest of the elderberry wine.

"He's murdered four people, two were children."

John held Eleanor in his arms as they drank their wine on the porch.

"Why did he do it, John?"

"We don't know."

"Sounds like a crime of passion. My dad was a constable over in St. Marys for a couple of years," said Eleanor, noticing the surprise on Riley's face. "What? You didn't think a woman like me could have a lawman as a father."

"I reckon I am surprised, a little."

"My dad used to say it was a hard job, 'cause you never knew what people were going to do."

"That's true, you never do know."

Riley fell into a thoughtful silence. *He was thinking about his years as a bounty hunter and how some of the worst criminals he'd bagged looked positively harmless. No, you could never tell what someone might do.*

Eleanor glanced at Riley and wondered if she'd said something wrong.

"You know something, John?" she said, taking his hand in hers. "You've got nice hands."

Riley looked embarrassed.

"Eleanor," he said finally. "I'd like to find you lodging in town. I could put you and Virgil up at the hotel for a couple of weeks while things are quiet. Maybe get you a job in the kitchen."

It was her turn to go quiet.

"John, I'd prefer to stay here," she said. "This is a nice place. The creek is just down the hill and we have the garden to ourselves."

"It's not safe for you being alone out here with a child and looters coming and going."

"I can take care of myself."

"I know you can."

"But, John, in town, I'll be that poor Ross woman who lost her man. I don't want people to pity me."

"Don't worry, Eleanor, there's not much pity left in town. Everyone has lost a family member or a friend. Everyone has suffered."

"But they'll say..."

"It doesn't matter what they say."

"They'll say who's that woman with the constable? It will only make for a lot of gossip."

Riley pulled Eleanor into his lap and kissed her.

Today, a newspaper reporter did a sketch of me with Deputy Fuller. I'm the dangerous outlaw, and Fuller is the brave lawman. What a joke that is. Fuller, with his ridiculous moustache and insolent face, looks more like a killer than I do. The reporter had me scowling and giving off menacing looks. He said that all self-respecting bandits look like that. The sketch will go on the front page of some newspaper in York. Maybe I'll join a circus if they release me one day.

Forty-one

Deputy Fuller hadn't seen Riley all morning. That was unusual, but Riley was the boss and if he wanted to come in late, that was his prerogative. It was getting on to noon as Fuller left the jail and made his way across the street to the hotel. As he entered the hotel dining room, he saw his boss sitting in a club chair, having a cup of tea. He tried to hide his surprise and went over to see him.

"Hello, sir."

"Mr Fuller, how are things at the jail?"

"Fine, sir. We had that reporter around yesterday."

Fuller had decided not to say anything about the Morelli sketch. He secretly hoped the newspaper would not publish it.

"Vito Morelli's wife came by with two kids and their uncle."

"What did they want?"

"The man had this story about Morelli and some girl finding the two kids on the road and taking care of them."

"Who is the uncle?"

"The fella's name is Peters, sir. He's a farmer. The kid's parents died from the blue death. He says he didn't know nothing 'bout it until they showed up on his doorstep."

"Is Peters still around?"

"Don't know, sir. He came by to thank Morelli for saving the kids. You ask me, I think it's just a trick to help get Morelli off."

"Sounds like it." Riley nodded. "You have your lunch, Fuller. I have some errands to do. When I get back, I want you to tell me all about the reporter."

In the midday heat, a white gelding trotted along the rutted track, pulling the Grenville calash. Constable Riley drove the calash in the company of young Emily, wearing a fashionable summer hat and dress.

"I don't know why you want me here," complained Emily.

"I'm sorry for the inconvenience, miss, but this is a murder inquiry," said Riley with a grim look on his face.

They arrived at the Morelli dogtrot just as Nelly was preparing food for lunch. She put down her spoon and removed her apron before she stepped outside to greet the constable and the lady.

"Good morning, Constable Riley," she said, but then looked embarrassed in front of the well-dressed young woman.

"Good morning to you, ma'am."

The constable climbed down and helped Emily step out of the calash.

"This is Miss Grenville, ma'am. Has Mr Peters arrived?"

"Yes, but he's out helping Vito and Joey," Nelly said, glancing from Riley to Miss Emily and back again. "He'll be back soon."

"Do you mind if we come in for a moment?"

"No, sir."

"It won't take a minute," Riley assured her, ushering Emily ahead of him as they followed Nelly into the one-room cabin.

Neil and Fran were sitting on a bench near the window. They hardly noticed Riley but stared at Emily, who felt only distaste as she looked around the miserable lodging with its bunk beds and brown newsprint-covered walls.

"Miss Emily, we've searched this room, but you might want to look around a bit."

"I see nothing here that belongs to me or any of my family, Constable. I really don't think we need to see anymore."

Riley nodded and smiled at the children.

"Hello, children. I'd like you to meet Miss Grenville. Her name is Emily."

"No, it ain't," said Neil sharply.

Emily looked speechless.

"What's her name, then?" asked Riley.

"She's that nice lady that cooked our old hen," said Fran. "Didn't she, Neil?"

"Yep, but her name ain't Emily. She goes by Daphne, sir. Dat's what I heard."

"But Daphne's dead," shrieked Emily, alarming the children. "Why are you doing this to me, Constable?"

Riley silently took Emily's arm and led her outside to the calash.

"The night of the murder, Miss Emily," he said quietly. "You travelled with Paolo Morelli and those two children, arriving late in St. Francis. Morelli left the children with the station master, and then you left Morelli here before returning to the manor with the wagon."

Emily was mesmerized by Riley's story.

"Sometime later that night, Morelli joined you at the manor, and you began your killing spree. Is that exact, miss? Did Morelli do the killing? Tell me, miss."

Emily was about to say something, but remained silent. Riley sensed movement out of the corner of his eye and turned long enough to see Nelly watching them from the porch.

"Did he force you to help him, miss? Or were you the one

behind this horrific crime?"

"Constable, you can't believe I would participate in killing my own brothers. This is insane."

Forty-two

The front page of the York Colonial Advocate was dominated by a drawing of the depraved criminal Paolo Morelli in the custody of Deputy Constable Edward A. Fuller of St. Francis. The reporter had taken some liberties with his illustration and unless the reader had read the story beneath the picture, he or she would have thought it was a picture of a Mexican desperado apprehended by a fierce Texas Ranger. Underneath the picture was the headline:

GRENVILLE KILLER
MORELLI CAPTURED

Constable Riley put down the newspaper and looked up at Fuller, standing in front of his desk.

"Mighty fine picture, Fuller. I only hope we got the right man."

"You have the weapon, sir. You have Morelli and the woman arriving in St. Francis with those children. You got the motivatin' factor, sir. Revenge. You always tellin' me how we gotta have a motivatin' factor."

"Yes, but I would give it all up for a nice, clean confession."

"When are they arriving for the transfer?"

"A couple of days."

"Good, we'll be clear of them," said Fuller confidently.

"I wish it were as simple as that, Fuller," said Riley. "There are a lot of holes in this case. It may come back to bite us in the ass."

Paolo listened to the rain patter against the window in his jail cell. It had been a long day. Nothing was happening in his case. He had hoped that the constable would find evidence to clear him, but it hadn't happened. Deputy Fuller had brought in his lunch tray and told Paolo that he would soon be transferred to York for trial. This did little to raise his spirits until Peters paid him a visit in the afternoon.

"Morelli, you got a visitor," Fuller yelled from the door.

Peters came in, holding his hat in his hands.

"Mr Morelli, I thought you might need a bit of company," Peters said from the doorway.

"Good day, Mr Peters. There's not much new, I'm afraid."

"I saw your picture in the newspaper, young man. It was not a good likeness."

"Yes, that damned reporter made a drawing."

"Well, sir. It wasn't a complete loss. There was this very interesting article about the new developments in rail travel under the picture."

"Rail travel?"

"Yes, sir. Railways are the thing of the future, Mr Morelli. Ever hear about the Tom Thumb?"

"No, sir."

"Tom Thumb is a steam-driven locomotive in Maryland," said Peters. "There was a race between the Tom Thumb and a horse-driven cart a year or two ago. Imagine that, a race between a locomotive and a horse."

"That's amazing."

"The Tom Thumb wanted to prove that it could go faster than any horse-drawn cart, so they had a race side by side along a rail track near Baltimore."

"A race like this can only happen in America, Mr Peters," said Paolo, fascinated by the idea. "Who won?"

"Well, the Tom Thumb is this huge four-wheel locomotive with a vertical boiler, so it took some time for it to catch up to the horse and overtake it. It was going great guns until the belt came off the blower pulley and it lost power. The horse then caught up with the locomotive and won the race."

"The horse won?"

"Yes, it did. It made a lot of money for the betting crowd."

"I would have put my money on the locomotive, Mr Peters."

"Me too, Mr Morelli."

"In England, there are a lot of new developments," Peters said, pulling up a chair and sitting down. "The home country is way ahead of us in the colonies."

"How so?"

"They've had steam locomotives hauling coal and minerals for several years now in England. Back in '29, they had a competition at Rainhill in Lancashire to test which steam locomotive would best perform for the Liverpool and Manchester Railway. Five locomotives were entered into the competition on a one-mile track. The 'Rocket' built by George Stephenson was the only locomotive to complete all the trials. It averaged 12 miles per hour with a thirteen-ton load and reached a top speed of 30 miles per hour."

"That's very fast."

"Yes, it is. Locomotives and railways are coming to America, Mr Morelli, mark my words."

"I hope I get to see it one day, Mr Peters."

Forty-three

Miss Emily was arrested in the morning and Fuller put her in the cell next to Paolo. She was in an angry mood and paced up and down, refusing to speak to Paolo. It was the ultimate indignity for a woman in her position to be locked up without any privacy, like a common criminal. She took her time to hang a blanket over the bars separating her cell from Paolo's so that she could use the chamber pot in the corner. When she finished, she stood up and continued her pacing. After a time, Paolo tried to make conversation.

"I'm sorry, miss, to mix you up in all this," said Paolo.

"I've done nothing," said Emily, "and now they arrest me as your accomplice."

"Well, those kids took you for your sister. You look so much alike. It's not their fault. Until the constable finds Daphne, we'll both remain in jail."

"But I've done nothing wrong," Emily said, sitting down.

"Tell me about Daphne."

"I was so stupid. That sister of mine is completely insane, and it was me who sent you to York to help her."

"You sent the message?"

"Of course I did," Emily exploded. "I wrote that damn message!"

She recalled seeing Paolo for the first time. *He was on his horse and riding away from the manor when Emily entered the summer kitchen.*

"Who is that man, Gerty?" asked Emily as Gerty mopped the floor.

"I don't know, miss. He was askin' about a sick woman with the cholera. He wanted to see Mr Lionel."

"What woman?"

"I tole 'im we ain't had no cholera in this house for a good while. He said a sick woman was brought here in the night."

Emily looked perplexed as she gazed at the lone rider disappearing in the distance.

Emily stood near the bars, reflecting on her conversation with Gerty. She turned to look at Paolo.

"Lionel told me how you nursed Daphne back to health. We thought Daphne was still at the Asylum. None of us knew she had nearly died, and you had saved her. That was very generous of you and your family."

"We were paid for the work, miss. It was what anybody would have done."

"Still, it was very kind. After you saved her, I couldn't believe Lionel had sent her back. He wanted her out of the picture so he could steal the estate away from me and my brothers without us raising a finger to stop him."

Paolo remained silent.

"I went to the cemetery that day to see who you were," Emily said. "I was curious about the man who had saved Daphne and nursed her back to health."

On her white gelding, Emily rode up to the perimeter fence near the cemetery. From a distance, she could see the Italian migrant workers digging graves and the funeral director Maloney arriving with a casket. The men emerged from the graves and stood to attention as they watched Maloney's wagon arrive, accompanied by five or six solemn-looking men and women.

"Paolo, get out of there," Vito yelled. "Mr Maloney has arrived."

Paolo grabbed his shirt and climbed out of the grave, where he stood to attention in the heat. The men watched Maloney come through the gate with the casket while the family stopped near the entrance. They slipped bandanas over their mouths and noses as they watched the casket rolling on towards the family plot.

Emily turned her horse and rode away from the cemetery.

"I wanted to see Daphne's knight in shining armour," said Emily to Paolo in the jail cell. "That's when I wrote you the note. I had it mailed from York."

"Where is she now?"

"I don't know. I haven't seen her."

"Why are you protecting her?"

"I'm not protecting her. She's my sister, but we were never close."

"Well, she's mad as a snake."

Paolo looked at Emily's sad, but beautiful face.

"We will hang for this," Emily said. "They can build their case with me as your accomplice."

"No, you will not hang. They do not hang women like you, Miss Emily. You're a Grenville."

Paolo didn't know what more to say.

"Well, who is she?" Emily asked. "The woman in Daphne's grave?"

"Probably some poor local girl who died from the blue death and was abandoned by her family. We usually put them in the cholera pit with the unclaimed bodies, but Maloney had her put in Daphne's grave."

"Why would he do that?"

"I think he wanted Daphne to disappear, miss."

Forty-four

Clara had nearly missed the house altogether. It was nigh on midnight as she drove the wagon along the road. The Smythe Manor house was dark, set back from the road and screened by a tall hedge. Clara was dead tired after the long day and it was a miracle she'd noticed the house at all. She glanced back over her shoulder. Ten women were sleeping in various positions in the back of the wagon.

"What do you think?" she asked her colleague on the seat beside her.

"It must be the right place," Juba said.

That was enough for Clara. She turned off the road and drove the wagon toward the front door of the large manor house. In appearance, the two women couldn't have been more different. They had met a year ago in Kingston at a Methodist camp meeting. Clara was a short, 40-year-old white woman with dark hair and a lined face while Juba was a slim, free-born African American woman in her twenties from Western New York where she had established a reputation for herself as a 'pretty shouter'. This referred to her religious fervour and enthusiasm during prayers, singing, and exhortations at camp meetings. Clara had earned respect among her fellow Methodists through her wisdom and commitment to the cause over many years.

Clara pulled the wagon to a stop near the front door, and she and Juba stepped down to wake up the other women. They were a sorry lot, dressed in old hand-me-downs and half asleep as they stumbled sleepily off the wagon. Clara led the way up the front steps. She was surprised by the broken windows and the poor state of the building. She looked through a window and screamed, then whirled around and started herding Juba and the others back down the steps.

"What's wrong?" Juba demanded.

"Two men in there. They scared the bejesus out of me," Clara said. "They're looting the place."

Juba didn't ask any more questions, just helped the other women scramble back into the wagon. They had been attacked on the road before and weren't going to take any chances.

Suddenly, a fat bearded man with red hair appeared on the porch, holding a flintlock pistol.

"Get down from that wagon!" he bellowed, slurring his speech.

A skinny, long-haired man followed him out the door and stopped short as soon as he saw the women.

"Red, what the fuck are they doin' out here?" he asked. "In the middle of the night?"

"I don't know, Eugene," Red grinned, starting down the steps. "I say we run 'em off or maybe we could take a prisoner or two. Whadda you say, boy?"

The women stood in a line near the wagon, unsure as to their fate.

"Sure, we could have some fun," said Eugene, laughing. "Cut 'em up a bit."

"No need to get nasty," Red told him. "We'll just pick a couple we like and run the rest of 'em off."

The terrified women shrank away from the big man as he came closer. Clara stepped in front of him.

"We're sisters of the Methodist church. You ain't got no right to hold us, mister."

"I ain't gonna hold you, sister," said Red, seizing Clara by the neck and sticking the pistol in her ear.

"Eugene, go get that young blonde bitch in the back and maybe that little dark-haired one next to her."

Eugene pushed his way through the women and grabbed the pretty blonde, who looked to be barely sixteen years old, and her dark-haired neighbour. He tried to pull the girls away from the other women, but they refused to let them go.

"Stay where you are," said Clara bravely. "He can't force you."

"I'm warning you," Red yelled at the women. "I'll shoot the sister if I have to. Let them go!"

The women reluctantly released their hold on the two girls. Eugene grinned and dragged the girls away from the others. A voice was heard from the front porch.

"Drop the pistol, you fat pig!" yelled Eleanor, pointing her musket at Red. "I said drop the pistol."

Forty-five

In the summer kitchen at the end of the garden, young Virgil climbed out of his bunk bed and came over to whisper in the constable's ear.

"Constable, I hear voices coming from the house. Mama's not here."

Riley woke up in a hurry and looked over at Eleanor's empty bed. He slipped on his boots and stood up. He put on his belt and grabbed his pistol, making for the door.

"Stay here, son. I'll go check on your mother."

Virgil returned to his bed and pulled the covers over his head as Riley ran out into the night.

Red turned in astonishment, waving the gun at Eleanor, who stood firm on the porch.

"I said get rid of the gun, arsehole."

"Who is this bitch?" demanded Red, aiming the pistol at Clara's head.

"She ain't gonna shoot you, Red," said Eugene. "She's just bluffin'. That musket probably ain't even loaded."

"Is that right, lady?" Red asked. "You bluffin'?"

"I said drop the gun."

"Okay, okay," said Red, lowering the gun.

For a big man, Red moved very fast. He swung the pistol back towards Eleanor, but she had seen it coming and didn't hesitate. The boom of the musket reverberated against the building and Red fell to the ground like a rag doll. Eleanor calmly reloaded as Eugene quickly lost interest in the sisters and ran off.

Riley heard the shot as he ran towards the house. As he got closer, he saw the dim outline of someone coming his way. He slowed and crouched low in the cabbage patch, then came up suddenly from the ground and flattened the man with an uppercut. He paused only long enough to make sure the man was unconscious, then kept going. He soon caught sight of a group of women gathered around the front steps. They seemed to be attending to someone on the ground.

"Eleanor!" he shouted.

"I'm here, John," she called back.

Riley breathed a sigh of relief as she stood up. The rest of the women parted to let him through, and he saw a man lying on his back with a bloody wound to the shoulder.

"What happened?"

"He was going to shoot her," said Eleanor, waving a hand in Clara's direction.

Clara stepped forward, looking very pale.

"I'm Clara Torrey, sir. We're Methodists. The late Mr Smythe lent us the house."

"You've come to live here?"

"Well, just temporarily. We're organizing camp meetings in these parts for Reverend James Wigan."

Riley turned towards Eleanor.

"He was going to shoot Clara," said Eleanor. "I was on the porch."

"You shot him from the porch?"

"Yes, John. I aimed for his shoulder. I'm a good shot."

"Don't I know it?"

A sister picked up Red's pistol and handed it to Riley just as young Virgil ran up to his mother. She bent down to give him a hug.

"This is my son Virgil," Eleanor said, smiling. "John Riley here is the constable in town."

"It's a pleasure to meet you ladies," John told them. "Sorry about the reception."

"Don't worry, sir. We sometimes get worse from our Catholic brothers and sisters," said Juba, laughing. "I'm Juba, this is Abigail, Lucy, Amelia, Louise, Martha, and... I'll let them introduce themselves."

"We'd better get installed. It's very late," said Clara.

Riley kneeled near the wounded man and examined the damage.

"He's going to lose a bit of blood, but I think he'll survive," said Riley.

"There was a second man, John. He ran that way," said Eleanor.

"I got him. He's sleeping it off in the field. Don't worry about him."

The sisters started moving boxes of foodstuffs, kitchen utensils, and printed pamphlets out of the wagon into the house.

"What do we do with the wounded man?" asked Clara.

"There's not much I can do for him in town, sister," said Riley. "Our doctor is away for a bit."

"Abigail was a nurse. Maybe she can extract the ball," said Clara.

"Good, let's get him inside," said Riley.

As Riley and the women helped lift the wounded man up the steps and into the house, Eleanor turned to Virgil.

"Let's get some tea going for the sisters, shall we, Virgil?"

"Sure, Mama."

"Can you start the stove in the kitchen, young man?"

Virgil nodded and ran into the house as the women lit candles to light the passageways.

Forty-six

In St. Francis, a mob of migrant workers and farmers approached the Morelli dogtrot in the dark. They yelled threats and carryied torches, the flames visible for miles.

"Murderin' eye-talian riffraff! Papists! Go home. Murderers."

The angry voices could be heard across the migrant camp. Neighbours watched silently as the Morellis hastened their departure. The grey mare was already harnessed to the wagon. Nelly ran out of the cabin with an armload of clothes and threw them into the back of the wagon on top of the valises, the bedding, and the kitchen supplies. Joey climbed up onto the driver's seat and prepared to leave just as Vito arrived with a box of tools. He dumped the box in the wagon and jumped onto the seat next to Joey. They pulled out in the nick of time. The vigilantes, surprised by their sudden appearance on the road, managed a few angry shouts as Joey whipped the horse into a fast trot.

In the light of a candle, Abigail worked on the wounded man's shoulder. He was lying on a bench in the hall of the Smythe Manor house and cried out as the sister probed the wound with a sharp paring knife. She succeeded in removing the ball and cleansed the wound with boiled water.

"Bloody hell," Red Buckley whined. "You fuckin' witches almost killed me."

"We'll pray for you, sir," Abigail said primly. "You are very lucky to be alive."

"He doesn't deserve to be," Eleanor said, glaring at the man.

"You shot me, you bitch."

"I should have shot you through the heart. That would have shut you up, you worthless old fart."

As Red growled at the women, Eleanor went looking for Virgil. She passed by the large parlour where the sisters had laid down blankets on the bare floor. Some were already asleep, while others sipped tea and chatted quietly. She headed for the stairs, where she found Eugene cuffed to the bannister in the hall. The constable planned to take the two looters to town first thing in the morning.

Eleanor found Riley in the kitchen drinking tea and put her arm around him. She kissed him and then collected young Virgil asleep in a chair near the stove. She tried in vain to wake the boy, and then gave up, lifting him into her arms. They left the house together, with Riley holding her musket and walked down to the summer kitchen at the bottom of the garden.

Paolo was scared. He had heard about lynchings in the American South, and it seemed to always happen at night. Only minutes before, Deputy Fuller and his youthful assistant, Johnny, had burst into his cell and dragged him out of the jail through the back door. They threw him into a wagon and shackled him to the floor. Moments later, they returned with Emily. Her hands were tied behind her back, and they'd put a gunny sack over her head. They helped her into the back of the wagon and put her next to Paolo.

Fuller tied his horse to the back of the wagon and then climbed up on the driver's seat next to Johnny. Fuller cracked the whip, and the horse leaped forward. They took off along the riverbank, heading for the road out of town. Paolo didn't want to think about where they were going.

Forty-seven

"We gonna hang him, deputy?" Johnny asked, sounding excited by the idea.

"That's up to him," Fuller said, loud enough for Paolo and Emily to hear.

The wagon was parked on a stone bridge over the river in the moonlight. Fuller had removed Paolo's shackles and pushed him with his arms tied behind his back over to a small wall overlooking the river. Paolo thought of running, but didn't think he would get far in the dark before he got a bullet in the back. He was terrified as he watched Fuller fashion a loop at one end of a long coil of rope. When Fuller slipped the loop over his head, Paolo tried to duck, but the deputy pulled it tight under his chin. He gave Johnny the other end of the rope.

"OK, Morelli," said Fuller. "One last chance to tell the whole story before you go in the water."

"I didn't do it!" protested Paolo.

"They all say that," said Fuller, shaking his head. "Are you going to pin it on your lady friend?"

"She had nothing to do with it. It was her sister."

"Okay, Morelli, you've had your chance," said Fuller.

Together, Fuller and Johnny grabbed Paolo and pushed him off the bridge into the water. Paolo made a huge splash as he hit the water and dropped like a stone beneath the surface. As

Johnny started to pull up on the rope, Emily cried out in terror from the wagon, blinded by the gunny sack. Paolo's head popped up at the surface as he struggled for air.

"What kind of justice is this?" he screamed, trying to keep his head above the slow-moving water.

"Pull him out, you're going to drown him," screamed Emily.

"Don't you worry, Miss Emily. It won't be long now before he confesses," said Fuller. "Anything you want to say before we dump you back?"

Paolo said nothing and Johnny let him sink out of sight.

"Leave him be," shrieked Emily.

"Won't be long 'fore he'll be givin' up his secrets," Fuller said with a laugh as Johnny pulled gently on the rope.

Paolo's head again appeared at the surface. "Do I get a last request?" he sputtered.

"Now, you talkin', Morelli," said Fuller, still hoping for a full confession. "We ain't got no time to waste on murderers."

"I want you to free Miss Emily because she had nothing to do with the murders."

In the wagon, Emily stopped moving, hearing Paolo's confession.

"And my family had nothing to do with them, either."

"Anything else?" asked Fuller.

"I want to be buried in a nice pine coffin with a brass burial reed, just like Daphne's."

"You won't be needing no remembrance man to check up on you," said Fuller, grinning at Paolo from the bridge. "You're gonna be deader than a doornail."

Johnny let Paolo slip underwater again as Emily managed to slip her head out of the gunny sack. She struggled to her feet with her wrists tied behind her and jumped off the wagon.

Fuller and Johnny were looking down at the water and watching for Paolo. Fuller lit a cigar, cracking a match as Johnny played with the rope, hauling it in slowly. Paolo's head appeared at the surface again as he struggled to free his hands.

"OK, Morelli. One last chance. Let's hear it," said Fuller, anticipating the nice, clean confession he would take back to Constable Riley.

"I am going to put a curse on you, Fuller."

The deputy smiled as he flicked ash down on Paolo.

"You are going to regret this, you swine. I'm gonna yell my indignation from the grave."

At the same moment, Emily barrelled into the two men, who tumbled over the small wall into the river. Two enormous splashes were heard from the water below. Paolo managed to free one arm and swim for the riverbank as Fuller and Johnny struggled to gain the surface.

"Help, help. I can't swim," Johnny yelled as he sank below the surface again.

"Damn it, Johnny," complained Fuller. "He's getting away."

Johnny's head appeared at the surface a second time, and he managed to keep his head out of the water by doing a furious dog paddle.

Paolo got into shallow water and quickly climbed out of the river. He removed the noose from his rope-burned neck and scrambled up onto the bridge. He put his arms around Emily and untied her hands.

"Let's take the horse and get out of here," said Paolo.

He grabbed the reins to Fuller's horse tied to the back of the wagon and climbed into the saddle. He hauled Emily up, sitting side-saddle in front of him, before trotting off into the night.

Forty-eight

Paolo and Emily rode up to the dogtrot in the dark. Paolo jumped off the horse and ran inside. He came out, stripping off his wet shirt.

"My folks are gone. They left in a hurry," said Paolo. "Do you need anything?"

"No, I'm fine. Let's get going."

Paolo ran back to the cabin to change his clothes. He grabbed a few things before rejoining Emily. He hooked a leather water flask over the saddle horn and handed Emily a bag of clothes and some household items, including an iron cooking pot. He laid some blankets over the saddle and swung his leather satchel over a shoulder before climbing back on the horse behind Emily. It was going to be a long run to Detroit, and he had no intention of ever returning. He kicked the horse, and they took off in a westerly direction, avoiding the main road.

Deputy Fuller and young Johnny returned to town in their wagon, looking wet and disconsolate. They pulled up behind the jail and saw a light in the window. There was a wagon parked there with a fat, red-haired man tied up in the back.

There was no sign of Riley, but the back door of the jail was open.

"Damn it!" Fuller swore, looking at Johnny.

As they climbed down, Riley stormed angrily out of the jail.

"Where the hell are the prisoners?" he demanded.

"They escaped, sir. I'm gonna get after them."

"What happened to you? You're wet through, you fall in the river?"

"Yes, sir. We were crossin' the bridge and they jumped us."

"Jumped you?" Riley roared, incredulous. "That scrawny Italian kid and the girl? How'd they get out of jail?"

"It's a long story, sir. I'll tell you later if you don't mind."

"Bloody hell, Fuller! I've got the York police coming at noon today to pick them up."

"Don't worry, we'll find them, sir," Fuller said, hoping to appease his boss. "We're just gonna get some dry clothes and horses, sir. Then we'll be off."

"Before you go, give me a hand getting that man into a cell," said Riley. "His partner's already in there."

Fuller looked down at the wounded man in the wagon.

"What happened to him?"

"He got himself shot," Riley growled. "They were looting out at the Smythe Manor. Now stop asking questions and get him inside. Then go find Morelli and the girl."

The sun was coming up as Paolo and Emily rode west over the prairie.

"You tried to frame me," said Paolo bitterly.

"Pardon me?"

"You are as bad as your sister. Daphne stole my gun and disappeared. Then you had her body exhumed. You must have known there was a body in the grave."

"That was the constable. He requested it."

"Yes, but you went along with it. Quite convenient, putting the blame on me."

"I couldn't very well refuse, Paolo. It was the constable's idea." Emily touched Paolo's face with her free hand. "Do you know you are quite handsome when you're mad?"

"You think I'm stupid," Paolo blushed, embarrassed and angry, "just 'cause I'm not from a rich family like yours. I can read and write in English and Italian. I can do sums. I'm gonna study law when I get back to Detroit."

"My, my," Emily said, removing her hand. "You're very sensitive."

"You wanted to prove that my story was a lie. That's why you went to see the constable, to have him dig up the body."

"That's not true. At first, I didn't know she had died from cholera and had been buried in the cemetery. It was only later that Lionel told me you had nursed Daphne back to health. Then the constable came to see me and asked to exhume the body. I couldn't refuse. How was I to know there was a body in the grave?"

Emily looked at Paolo's intense face and laid her hand over his on the saddle horn to console him.

Forty-nine

Constable Riley sat on a bench on Main Street as he waited for the mail coach from York to arrive. The coach and horses soon swept into view and came to a stop in front of the station at precisely five minutes past noon. While the horses stamped their hooves and wheezed from exhaustion in the heat, two police inspectors in bowler hats and suits disembarked. Riley stood up and approached the big lawmen. One man carried a rifle under his arm and the other, a handgun in a holster.

"Hello, gentlemen," said Riley.

"You must be Constable Riley?" said one of the lawmen, shaking hands with the constable.

"Yes, I am. How was your trip?"

"There were a lot of bodies on the road, sir. The blue death is bad out your way?"

"It's been terrible in these parts. Just terrible."

"We had to shoot over the heads of some cholera men on the road to keep them away from the coach."

"Let's have a drink first," said Riley, leading the men over to the hotel bar.

Riley wondered where Fuller had gotten to. *If only his deputy could find Morelli and bring him in, Riley would be rid of the problem. His investigation was going nowhere, and although he didn't want to admit it, he believed Morelli was innocent. The only connection between Morelli and the Grenvilles was the firearm.*

Riley pulled out his watch chain to check the time as the barman served whisky to the lawmen.

"So where you from?" asked the older cop.

"Texas," replied Riley.

"You're a long way from home, constable. You a rancher?"

"Nope."

"A farmer maybe?"

"Nope."

"Ain't that Mexican territory down there, sir?"

"Yep, sure is. The Mexicans run the place. You ever seen a cattle drive, Inspector?"

"No, I don't think I have."

"Well, you'll never forget it if you see it: a herd of longhorns spread across the prairie and the thunder of hooves. It's quite a spectacle. As a kid, I delivered beef to New Orleans."

"So how'd you get into police work, sir?"

"A rancher sent me to Chicago to find a man who had killed one of his friends. I found him in a bar, playing poker."

Riley drank from his whisky as the lawmen waited with bated breath for the rest of his story.

"Go on, sir. What happened?"

"The man had just pulled a jack of diamonds and had himself a straight flush with all his money on the table. That was when I shot him dead."

The older cop grinned.

"He pulled a gun?"

"Nope. I stuck my gun in his ear and pulled the trigger."

"You shot him in cold blood."

"Yep, I didn't give him the chance to draw his gun. I ain't no hero."

The lawmen looked shocked by the constable's story.

"Earned me a nice tidy sum from that rancher, I did. The only problem was that I had to get outta town fast. The police down there don't take too kindly to a killing in their town."

The younger inspector looked very uncomfortable.

"Well, well. That's quite a story, sir. You ain't bullshitting us?"

"Nope. I shot him in the ear once and then shot him again to be sure," said Riley with a smile. "His hearing wasn't too great after I left."

The older cop laughed at this, convinced the constable was pulling his leg.

"So how'd a man like you get a job as a police constable?" asked the younger inspector.

"Gentlemen, ten years ago this place was the Wild West. The constable at the time had been shot dead by two feuding brothers. There was no law west of Hamilton. You had revenge killings, burning barns, and shootouts right here on Main Street. Nobody wanted the job. I put my name in and the Grenville family supported me. The town council doubled the pay 'cause they figured I might not survive for long."

The lawmen reflected on their own careers, how they struggled from patrol to desk jobs to qualify later as detectives in the city. Riley was the exception, a fugitive killer who took a job in a piss-poor town that no one wanted.

"Is your man going to be on time?" asked the younger cop.

"I hope so, gentlemen. Another drink, perhaps?"

"No thanks," said the older cop.

"Let's go over to the jail," said Riley.

The two lawmen stood up and walked out of the bar as Riley threw down some coins for the drinks.

170

The constable thought about how these fellas were typical cops from the city, the kind of yahoos who worshipped Western heroes and couldn't get enough of the life. He'd learned over time that his colleagues weren't interested in where you came from or how you got there, but only wanted to hear a good tale. Tell them a good story and they'd become friends for life.

He hadn't shot that gambler in public; he wasn't that stupid. He'd simply waited for the man in the livery stable and shot him in the back from the shadows as he'd climbed on his horse. Then he'd put one in the head for good measure.

Hunting men was like hunting game. Once you'd killed the animal, then the real work began. You had to dress an animal and haul it out of the forest. He'd stolen a wagon in Chicago to carry the body back to St. Louis and had to pack it in ice to keep down the smell. That was his first job as a bounty hunter. He'd liked the pay but didn't like the job or the people.

When a wanted poster said 'dead or alive', Riley had always preferred 'dead'. He didn't like to take chances with outlaws. He would never draw down on a target in public. He preferred to bushwhack a man in a quiet place. He'd tried 'alive' a couple of times but didn't like the risks. He was always in danger of getting shot or knifed by some ornery bastard. And the conversation with these arseholes was never worth putting your life in danger.

He'd often chased down men hiding in Upper Canada. That's how he ended up in St. Francis. He'd shot a man dead, who was wanted for murder in Detroit, and was busy hauling the body home when the locals found him and figured a gunman from Texas might make a decent constable. He wasn't proud of his past and he'd been happy to turn the page. Older folk in town still remembered the gunslinger with the dark past and disapproved of him. The gossip provided him with an aura of authority, but kept people at a distance.

Fifty

Joey threw the dregs of his morning tea into the campfire.

"Someone's coming!" he said, standing up.

Nelly looked to where Joey was pointing. A rider was advancing rapidly across the prairie.

"It's a woman," Joey yelled, squinting. "She's got someone with her."

Vito looked up, surprised.

"He's right," Nelly told him. "I think it's one of the Grenville twins, with Paolo behind her."

After a moment, Paolo and Emily arrived. They rode up to the campfire and Paolo jumped down to embrace Nelly and Vito. He shook hands with Joey and then helped Emily down off the horse.

"Paolo, my boy, you're a free man," said Vito. "Your mama will be so happy."

"Uncle, this is Miss Emily Grenville."

"Good day, miss," said Vito.

Emily nodded, but stayed back.

"How'd you get free?" asked Nelly. "No, I don't want to know."

"They were going to hang us," Paolo said, "but we managed to escape."

The others were stunned by this revelation.

"Both of you?" Nelly blurted.

"Both of us," Paolo nodded. "They think Emily was my accomplice and arrested her."

"You can't stay here, Paolo," Vito said, shaking his head. "They're gonna be right behind you."

"I know," Paolo said. "We just need to rest up for a few minutes."

"You're gonna have bounty hunters runnin' all over this patch within the hour," Joey added.

"Sit down and have some tea," ordered Nelly. "You need to eat something."

They sat down on a blanket near the campfire as Nelly poured them the remains of the black tea and brought them some bread and cheese from the wagon.

"You gotta get to the States as fast as that horse can carry you," Vito said.

"If I go to the States, I'll never clear my name," insisted Paolo.

"There's nothin' you can do now, my boy," said Vito. "By escaping, you've proved yerself guilty. Nothin' gonna stop 'em now."

"I don't want to be runnin' from the law, Uncle. If I can just find Emily's sister, Daphne. That should be enough."

"Paolo, use your head," Vito said, exasperated with his nephew's logic. "They've got your gun. You're a fugitive from justice. You'll hang if you stay here."

"The police will be in Detroit by tonight," Joey said. "You better head west, as your uncle says. You can slip across the border into St. Clair tomorrow. Nobody will be the wiser."

Deputy Fuller was sweating profusely with his cowlick plastered to his face as he sat in a chair in the outer office. He had two angry lawmen from York peering down at him, and Constable Riley watching him from the door.

"After we dumped him in the river, I asked him if he had anything to confess," said Fuller.

"You were hoping for the big confession?" asked Riley.

"Yeah, you're always sayin' how we gotta get them confessions."

"Yeah, but we don't drown our prisoners or pistol whip them for a confession, son. We always try to work within the law."

"Damn right, Constable," scoffed the older inspector, remembering a certain poker game in Chicago.

"So what did Morelli have to say for himself?" asked Riley.

"Nothin' much, sir. He said that Miss Emily was innocent, same as his family."

"Anything else?"

"Well, sir, he wanted to be buried in a nice pine box, that's what he said and he wanted a brass burial reed."

"A brass burial reed?"

"Yep, that's what he said. Wants one just like Miss Daphne so he can holler his indignation at the world."

Riley laughed, as did the lawmen.

"Holler his indignation at the world," said Riley. "The kid's got a gift for words."

Billy from the post office came running in, as the constable exchanged a glance with the York lawmen.

"Constable Riley, I got a message for you from my dad," said the boy.

The constable tore open the note from the station master.

"Looks like they've been seen on the road west of here," Riley said. "The driver of the mail coach spotted them at first light. They must have ridden all night. I suggest, Mr Fuller, that you and our colleagues here find some fresh horses and get after them."

Fuller jumped up, happy to be working again, and followed the lawmen out of the jail and over to the stables. Riley sat down at his desk and thought about young Morelli. He was a smart kid, but Riley was glad to be rid of him.

Fifty-one

Paolo and Emily made their way west across a vast sea of grassland. The sun beat down mercilessly. Emily was napping on and off, propped up against Paolo in the saddle.

Paolo pulled up near a river and climbed down. He helped Emily off the horse and then went down to the river to fill the water flask. Stepping gingerly around the marshy land, he found a spot and got down on his knees to drink from the river. He heard a sudden splash just in front of him and looked up. Emily was in her petticoat and up to her knees in the water busily washing her face and arms.

"It's hot," said Emily, "and nobody's around. Go on, take off your shirt. I won't look."

Paolo hesitated, then took off his shirt and tossed it behind him. When he turned back, Emily splashed water in his face.

"I lied," she teased. "Get in there. It's not that cold."

Paolo waded in and grimaced from the cold as water splashed across his torso. He then splashed Emily in return and soon they were two kids, splashing about in the river and laughing without a care in the world.

Emily had retreated to the riverbank as the sun was setting in the west. Paolo remained in the river with the water up to his knees. He tried not to stare as Emily stripped off her sodden petticoat and sat innocently on the riverbank in her bloomers, drying in the sun. Paolo was standing in the shallow water and observing something on the bottom.

"What are you doing?" asked Emily.

Paolo looked up and made a sign to keep quiet as he used his shirt and a stick to drive some fish into a shallower part of the river. Emily watched him working the fish close to shore when he suddenly lunged underwater and came up seconds later with a good-sized spotted bass wriggling in the folds of his shirt. Emily squealed in delight as he tossed the fish onto the sand near her feet.

Paolo picked up the stick again and returned to herding fish close to shore. Moments later, he caught a smaller bass and threw it on the sand near the first one. He grappled with a third, but lost it and then caught a fourth before giving up.

"Well done, Paolo," said Emily as he waded ashore. She took the shirt from him as he went to look after the fish.

"I'll give it a wash," she said, wading into the river. "Then we can dry it on the sand."

He grabbed the fish flopping about on the sand and used his knife to cut gut them. He then went looking for dry kindling wood for a fire.

It was dark by the time Paolo had built a fire and finished cooking the bass. Emily speared a piece using Paolo's knife and gave it to Paolo, who bit into it hungrily. Emily took a piece and ate it. They were silent for a while as fireflies flashed around them in the dark.

"I'm going back," Emily blurted. "When we get to the border and I know you're safe, I'll return to St. Francis."

"They'll put you in jail."

"No, they won't." She smiled mischievously. "I'll tell them I escaped, and that it was you who did all the killing."

He stared at her, alarmed.

"Yes, they might go for that."

"I'm a Grenville. They wouldn't dare hang me."

Paolo looked dubious and started to protest, but she put a finger to his lips.

"I can't keep running, Paolo. I have the house and the servants to look after, and you'll have a new life back in the States."

Paolo threw the fish bones into the fire.

"I'll miss you, Emily."

"No, you won't!" Emily said playfully. "Not in Detroit you won't."

"Yes, I will. I'll miss you, *la mia bella ragazza*."

Emily blushed as she realized how attached she had become to this young man in such a short time.

Fifty-two

It was nearly dawn when Maloney's wagon pulled up near a little house with a white picket fence in St. Francis. Maloney climbed down and ordered his two assistants to wait at the wagon. The men were scruffy cholera men whom Maloney had recruited at the last moment. He opened the gate and walked up the path to the front door. He knocked, and a man appeared in bedclothes and a nightcap. He looked distraught and frightened.

"Mr Maloney, I'm sorry, but she's not ready yet."

"Mr Benton, we agreed that the pickup time was to be four o'clock," said Maloney, looking at his pocket watch. "What do you mean that she's not ready?"

"She's my wife, Mr Maloney. It's not so easy."

"Benton, look at me. I don't care. Just do it. I'll give you five minutes, that's all. Then we've got to be off."

"She's locked herself in the bedroom. I've been trying to talk her out, but she won't come."

"Five minutes and I don't care a whit who I have to put in the pine box. Got it?"

Maloney stepped outside and lit his pipe. The sweet smell of tobacco filled the cool night air. From inside the house, he could hear George Benton pounding on the bedroom door. Maloney let it go on for a while, and then checked his pocket watch before he went back inside. Benton was frantically assaulting his wife's bedroom door with a hammer. He had put a hole in the door large enough to put his arm through and open the lock. As he opened the door, Maloney heard the terrified woman whimpering inside the bedroom.

Benton looked exhausted and seemed at a loss as to what to do next with the hammer.

"Here, take this," said Maloney, handing Benton a pistol he carried in his coat pocket.

"Just go in there and do it. I don't have all night."

Benton stared at Maloney for a moment, then took the pistol and went inside.

Across the street, Gerty was sound asleep in her own bed after Miss Emily had sent all the house and kitchen staff home. She never wanted to hear a gunshot again, but that was what woke her. She was sure of it and the sound was coming from across the street. She crept to the bedroom window and looked out. Maloney's wagon was parked in the street, and two men were unloading a pine box from the wagon. They carried it up the front steps and into the Benton house.

She wondered what the undertaker was doing at her neighbour's house in the small hours of the morning. Maybe there had been a death in the family.

"What is it, Gerty?" asked Alfred from his bed along the wall.

"Quiet, Alfred," whispered Gerty. "Go back to sleep. You'll wake the twins."

From the window, Gerty saw Maloney on the doorstep stand aside to allow the men to enter with the coffin. Moments later, the men exited the house with the pine box nailed shut, followed by the undertaker.

Gerty was perplexed. She knew the Benton family well. They were an odd couple with no kids. George worked at the sawmill while his wife, Elizabeth, was a seamstress and took in sewing jobs. She repaired clothes for Gerty's brothers and sisters. She was a frail, gentle spirit and was well-liked in the community.

On the other hand, George was a bad apple, constantly complaining about his lazy wife who couldn't do anything right and flirting incessantly with other women. He frequently beat Elizabeth, who hid her bruises behind extravagant shawls and scarves. It was well known on the street that George had his eye on several young women half his age.

As the undertaker's wagon set off in the early dawn, Gerty returned to bed and wondered who had died. The rumours would spread soon enough.

It was a wet dawn and Paolo shivered in his blanket near the smoking embers of the campfire. He opened one eye and then the other. The light was just coming up in the east. He saw the horse munching grass nearby and then looked around for Emily, but there was no sign of her. Maybe she went for a walk, he thought, as he fell back and pulled the blanket close around his shoulders.

After a moment, he got up and did a proper search of the area, but there was still no sign of her. He thought she must have left during the early morning hours. Paolo quickly saddled up the horse and prepared to leave.

Fifty-three

A posse of lawmen rode across the wide plain. They ran their horses at the gallop in a westerly direction and then pulled up sharply at Deputy Fuller's command. Fuller took off his hat and wiped his brow as the lawmen gathered around him.

"We should split up," he said. "If we stay together, we could miss them entirely as we go west."

The two York policemen exchanged a look but didn't say anything. They came from the city and knew nothing about tracking a fugitive in open country.

"If anyone sees Morelli and the woman, fire your gun and we'll come running."

A young man holding a shotgun looked at Fuller.

"What's he got, sir? What kinda gun?"

"We don't know, but we figure that he met up with his folks and he may have a rifle. He won't be easy to take down. So you better shoot first and ask questions afterwards. That is, if you're still breathin'."

The men laughed loudly.

"Bob and I will take the left flank. You men take the middle and the others go on the right flank, keepin' yer distance."

The men separated into three groups and took off at a fast trot, heading west over the grassy plains.

Tracking Emily took time. Even though he was on horseback, Paolo had to go at a walking pace most of the time. It was the only way he could see the faint signs of her footsteps on the soft soil of the prairie. It was almost noon when he saw Emily's head pop up over a rise. He urged his horse into a gallop and went after her.

"Go away, Paolo," Emily said, running in front of the horse.

"Stop, Emily. I have to talk to you."

"I have nothing to say to you. Get away from me."

Paolo jumped down from the horse and tackled her to the ground near a copse of trees.

"I have to know about Daphne," he told her. "If I go back, she's the only one who can set me free."

"Are you crazy?" she hissed. "Don't go back, they'll hang you. You have no chance."

Suddenly, Paolo grabbed her arm and quickly forced her down in the grass.

"What are you doing?" Emily demanded angrily.

"Shut up," Paolo told her, crouching in the grass.

Off in the distance, there was the sound of horse's hooves fast approaching. Paolo grabbed the reins of the horse and led it under the dense foliage of the trees. In the distance, they could see three men on horseback riding straight towards them. Paolo held his breath as the riders veered off at the last minute, going west. He gave a sigh of relief as he looked at Emily.

"Let's go," Paolo said as he took Emily's arm and helped her mount up. He took the reins and jumped on behind her before setting off in an easterly direction.

Fifty-four

Paolo and Emily walked east all morning, often leading the horse and hiding behind the occasional tree or hill to avoid being seen. Late in the afternoon, they allowed themselves a rest and lay down on their bellies on a small hill overlooking the vast prairie. Paolo passed the water flask to Emily.

In the middle distance, they could see a line of trees blocking their view of the horizon, but on the left several miles away, they could just make out a man ploughing a field and, to the right of the trees, an isolated farm. The man stopped to wipe his brow and then whipped his horse forward, driving the iron plough into the soft loamy soil.

Paolo thought there could be a posse of lawmen hidden behind the line of trees. Nothing was visible to the naked eye. He recited a few lines of a poem in Italian.

> *"Sempre caro mi fu quest'ermo colle,*
> *E questa siepe che da tanta parte*
> *De'll ultimo orizzonte il guarde esclude."*

"What does it mean?" asked Emily.

"It's called '*Infinito*'. It's a famous poem by Giacomo Leopardi, Emily. I learned it at school. It's about our understanding of the infinite."

184

"The infinite?"

"It goes like this," Paolo said, reciting the poem in its English version.

> *"This solitary hill has always been dear to me*
> *And this hedge, which prevents me*
> *From seeing most of the endless horizon.*
> *But when I sit and gaze, I imagine, in my thoughts*
> *Endless spaces beyond the hedge,*
> *An all encompassing silence and a profound quiet,*
> *To the point that my heart is almost overwhelmed."*

"You see that line of trees?" Paolo asked, pointing into the distance.

"Yes, I see it."

"That is the hedge that prevents us from seeing the horizon."

Emily lay back and listened as Paolo recited the rest of Leopardi's verse:

> *"When I hear the murmur of the wind in the leaves,*
> *I compare its sound to the infinite silence*
> *And with my mind, I embrace eternity,*
> *and all the ages past and present with their sounds,*
> *And in this immensity, my own thoughts drown,*
> *plunging into the sweet, refreshing depths of the sea."*

"It's about the limits of human understanding. Leopardi is one of our greatest poets," said Paolo with pride. He turned to look at Emily, who had fallen asleep next to him.

Paolo hadn't had the heart to wake her. He had kept watch, nearly dozing off himself, and finally busied himself collecting wood for a fire. It was almost dark when Emily woke up, shivering from the evening chill. She got up and came over to the fire. They were both sunburnt and exhausted from their day on the prairie.

"Tell me about Daphne," Paolo asked. "You aren't telling me the whole story. I deserve to know."

"Do you?" asked Emily.

"Yes, I do," insisted Paolo. "I'm the one they're going to hang for Daphne's crimes."

Emily hesitated, not wanting to remember the details of that terrible night.

"Come on, Emily. I have to know."

"All right, Paolo. That night, I was staying at my aunt's house out by the lake. It happened in the middle of the night. Daphne arrived covered in blood."

Daphne jumped out of the baker's wagon and ran up to the porch. She banged on the door with one hand, a hatchet in the other.

"Wake up, someone! Wake up!"

She ran back down the steps and threw a handful of pebbles at the upstairs window.

"Emily, it's me. Your sister has come home."

The door opened slowly, and Smiley appeared on the threshold. Daphne hid the hatchet behind her back.

"Miss Daphne?" Smiley stared at her in shock as she ran up the steps towards him.

"Get out of my way, Smiley. I want to see my sister."

Smiley didn't see the weapon until it was too late. Daphne barged into the house and took a wild swing at him with the hatchet, hitting him with the blunt end and knocking him to the floor. She was standing over him when Emily appeared at the top of the stairs in her nightgown.

"Daphne?" Emily called as she hurried down the stairs and knelt beside the unconscious man. "What are you doing here? You've hurt Smiley!"

"Oh, shut up, sister. That's nothing. Lionel is dead. I shot him and that old fool, Baxter. They deserved it, locking me up like that and stealing my dowry."

"What about the boys?" Emily said, as she stood up, a look of dread creeping over her face.

"Those whining brats?" Daphne said, running into the kitchen. "I need some water. Get me water."

Emily followed Daphne into the kitchen as she picked up a pitcher of water and poured herself a glass.

"Where are the boys?" Emily demanded frantically. "Where are Jimmy and Tommy?"

"So what have you been up to, sister?" Daphne asked, her tone maddeningly casual. "You never bothered to visit me in York."

Emily grabbed her coat from a hook on the wall and started to pull on her shoes.

"Where are you going? I just arrived. Don't you want to talk about old times' sake?"

"I'm going to get the boys," Emily said as she finished putting on her shoes. "You left them in the house all alone. You are awful!"

"Go to them, sister," Daphne waved a dismissive hand. "I need to sleep."

Fifty-five

"I took the wagon and went to the house. I saw it all, Paolo," Emily shivered. "It was awful."

Paolo could think of nothing to say. He put his arms around her and pulled her close. He'd seen it himself and couldn't imagine how she felt.

"Those were my boys, Paolo. I helped raise them," Emily murmured, tormented by the memory. "They were just the sweetest kids you could ever imagine."

Emily turned to face Paolo.

"I sat there looking at their lifeless bodies. I could do nothing for them."

Paolo threw a branch on the fire.

"I wanted to kill Daphne when I returned. She'd murdered my boys and there she was, fast asleep at the kitchen table like nothing had happened. Smiley had fled the house when I got there. I wanted to kill her."

The Grenville Manor house was dark and silent as Paolo and Emily came in through the back door into the kitchen. After the murders, the household staff had been sent home. Emily lit an oil lamp.

"You can stay here tonight," said Emily, "but tomorrow at dawn you must leave."

Paolo nodded and looked around.

"Are you hungry?"

Paolo nodded.

"Why don't you go into the dining room? I'll fix us something."

As Emily put plates on the table, Paolo looked at an old engraving of a Hamilton street in a tiny frame on the wall.

"Is this Lionel's?"

Emily came over to look.

"No, that's my mother's. She always liked that picture."

"You know that they have the new heliographic drawings in Detroit. They are called 'sun drawings'. They are made with a camera obscura. There's a shop where they do them. It takes several hours to produce an image."

Emily looked intrigued.

"How marvellous! Have you had your picture taken?"

"Oh, no. It's far too expensive, and it takes hours for the picture to come out."

"I would love to have my picture taken. I would put on my best clothes. It would be wonderful."

"I've been studying the camera obscura. It's an old optical device. The light comes in through a small hole and is projected onto the opposite wall. The image is upside down and reversed back to front."

Paolo looked at their reflection in the sideboard mirror as Emily was still having girlish thoughts about getting dressed up for picture taking. Paolo saw Emily glance at the mirror.

"See?" Paolo put his hand on her shoulder and pointed at the mirror. "Just like a mirror, a picture of you is an exact reflection of your features, except for one thing."

He pointed to Emily's buttons on her dress.

"The buttons?" she asked. It had taken her a moment to realize what he was talking about. "They're on the wrong side!"

"That's right. The image is reversed, same as in the camera obscura."

Paolo made a show of peering at her reflection in the mirror and then gave her a mischievous grin.

"Who are you anyway? Are you Emily or Daphne?"

She turned and slapped him. He looked astonished and humiliated at the same time.

"That's not funny," she snapped, furious. "I'm not crazy like Daphne, Paolo. I'm not crazy!"

"I'm sorry, Emily," he stammered. "I didn't mean it."

Her anger vanished as quickly as it had arrived. She grabbed Paolo and kissed him hard on the mouth. It was exactly the way Daphne had kissed him on the night they'd returned from York. Emily let him go and left the room for the kitchen, leaving Paolo more confused than ever.

Fifty-six

"Have you seen the *Liberator* newspaper?" Emily asked, sitting at the dining room table eating cold cuts in the light of the oil lamp. "Lionel brought it from York. It favours the liberation of slaves in the Southern States."

Emily felt nervous entertaining Paolo in her home. She was so ignorant of the larger world and Paolo had lived in big towns like Detroit and Genoa. He had met with people of influence and knew how to talk. She wondered how much they had in common.

"Yes, I have. The abolitionists are distributing it in all the churches in Detroit."

"My mother said that William Garrison is in favour of sending the slaves back to Africa, but not all abolitionists are for it."

"I don't know much about slavery, Emily. We don't have any slaves in Genoa, just a few black people from Africa."

"Smiley was a slave before he escaped and came here. Mother helped him and gave him a job as a houseman. He lives in a shed out by the lake."

"I think your mother was a good Christian woman."

"Yes, she was. I miss her so very much."

Paolo nodded, and they ate in silence for a moment.

"What's it like in Genoa?" Emily asked.

"Genoa's a big port, Emily."

"Is it in the north or the south?" asked Emily. "I'm so ignorant of geography."

"It's in the north, in the *Regno di Sardegna*. The Sardinian Kingdom, it's called. It's a large state, including the Savoy and Piedmont. Genoa is the hometown of Giuseppe Mazzini, the famous Italian patriot. You may have heard of him. Last year, he founded *La Giovine Italia* for people who want political representation and unification. It means *Young Italy*. I'm a member now and there are many of us in Detroit."

"Italy is not united?"

"No, not at all. There are a lot of Italian states. In the north, there is the Sardinian Kingdom, the Lombardy-Venetia Kingdom controlled by Austria, Tuscany, the Papal States, Parma, Modena, Naples and so on."

"Why so many?"

"I don't know. Italy is an old country with a lot of powerful city-states. If America was like Italy, we would have states such as Detroit, Chicago, St. Louis and others. Each independent of the others with a king or duke."

"That would be difficult to manage, wouldn't it?" Emily asked.

"Yes, it would. Mazzini's idea is to build up small groups of nationalists around the country who will be ready for a revolution when the time comes. Mazzini says we need to be free of Austria and the popes to become one nation, a republic like you have in America. The new pope, Gregory XVI, is against Austria's occupation of the north, but he won't surrender his power. Mazzini says he must."

"You think there will be fighting?"

"Last year there was an uprising in Parma, Modena, and Bologna. The rebels formed a republic for a short time called the *Province Unite Italiane*. It had its own flag, the tricolour green, white and red, but it was crushed by the Austrians."

"Are you going to return to Italy to fight for freedom?"

"Mamma says my fight is in America now, but I don't know. Maybe I'll return one day."

There was a long silence as they ate.

"You didn't tell me what happened when you returned to the cottage on the night of the murders?"

"I arrived back at the cottage at dawn and found Daphne asleep at the kitchen table. I was a mess," Emily said, remembering the events.

Emily entered the kitchen and saw her sister quietly sleeping at the table. She grabbed the heavy clothes iron from the stove and slammed it down on Daphne's head. She collapsed unconscious on the floor. Emily was in shock seeing her sister sprawled out on the floor, bleeding from a nasty head wound.

Smiley entered the kitchen and looked horrified.

"Miss Emily, what have you done?"

Emily sobbed silently.

"She's dead, Smiley. I hit her with the clothes iron."

Smiley kneeled to have a look at Daphne.

"She killed Lionel, Baxter, and the boys, Smiley," Emily said. "I went to the manor last night. I saw it all."

Smiley stood up.

"Dear Lord, please pardon our sins," Smiley said, crossing himself. "Let me get a fire going and I'll help you clean up. We can't have anyone finding her body in here."

An hour later, Emily was sitting on the front porch in a clean dress, watching the road near the lake as the sun came up. She looked very pale, overwhelmed by her circumstances. Smiley in shirt sleeves arrived from the garden, perspiring heavily.

"I've found a site to bury your sister. It has a nice view of the lake. I'll need your help to carry the body."

"I don't think I can do it."

"Miss Emily, look at me, please," said Smiley, sitting down near her. "I pushed your baby carriage around the garden when you were just a little girl. You and Daphne were the joy of the Grenville house."

Emily looked puzzled.

"You are a grown woman now. You must be strong. Think of your ma and pa. They are with you this day. They'll make you strong."

"Mother and father?"

"Yes. Now buck up, girl, we have a body to bury. You must return to the manor as soon as possible. You do not want the servants to see the bodies before you get there. Take the calash and pick up Mrs Henderson on the way, as you do every Tuesday. She'll be waiting for you if you don't go."

Emily stood up and went into the kitchen to get her shoes. Suddenly, she screamed and ran out of the kitchen.

"She's gone. She was dead. I swear I killed her."

Smiley went into the kitchen to have a look and returned.

"God forbid you killed your sister, Miss Emily," Smiley said with a sigh of relief.

"But where is she? Where's she gone?"

"It doesn't matter where she's gone, miss. You need to get over to the manor house as soon as possible. All hell is about to break loose."

Fifty-seven

"So where'd she go?" Paolo asked as they were finishing their meal in the dining room.

"I don't know," Emily said.

"Well, how did she leave? She didn't leave on foot?"

"She left a wagon out front."

"So she must have stolen a horse?"

"I don't think so. Smiley would have told me if a horse was missing."

"We're lost without Daphne. The constable thinks you were impersonating your sister."

"I know, Paolo, but you must get away. I can get off, but you have no chance here in St. Francis. Go south to Lake Erie. You can catch a boat from there to Detroit."

Paolo remembered the crazy look on Daphne's face when she left him at his cabin on the night of the murders. He wondered where she was and what she was up to.

Daphne stumbled into the barn where she found three cholera men camped out on bales of straw with their few possessions. The men were drunk and passing around a bottle of whisky.

"Well, guess what we have here," said Reuben. "We found ourselves a real lady."

"Shut up, you moron," said Daphne, pulling out a small pocket pistol, a four-shot pepperbox, that she had stolen from the Grenville drawing room.

The young cholera man stopped grinning and stepped back, eyes wide with fear. Daphne observed the young men.

"Hey, are you boys twins?" asked Daphne.

"I'm Thaddeus, he's Reuben," said the other lookalike. "We got the same mother, but not the same dad."

"And what about you with the spectacles? What's your name?"

"I'm Wilbur," said the boy with long hair.

"Don't talk to him, miss," Reuben told her. "I'm the brains of this outfit."

"What happened to your head, miss? You're bleedin' somethin' awful," said Thaddeus.

"I'm bleeding, am I? Okay, don't just stand there. Go get me a bucket of water."

The three men looked at each other and then Wilbur collected the bucket in the corner and filled it with water from the rain barrel outside the door. He brought it over to Daphne.

"Miss, you want us to wash out the blood?" Reuben asked.

"Stay where you are. It won't take a moment."

Daphne put down her gun and dunked her head in the bucket, running her fingers over the bruise. She looked up at the three young men who hadn't moved and then dunked her head again in the cold water.

"You want me to have a look at that cut?" Reuben asked.

"You some kind of doctor?"

"No, but I've seen a lot of cuts and wounds, miss."

"OK, just you. Come over here and take a look."

Daphne picked up the gun and pointed it at Reuben as he approached. He stood behind her and ran his finger over the bruise.

"Ow, that hurts," said Daphne.

"You got a bad cut, miss. It's still bleeding. You might need some stitches," Reuben said.

"Any of you fellas good with a needle and thread?" asked Daphne.

The men shook their heads, one after the other.

"No, I didn't think so," Daphne said as she stood up. "Where's your wagon?"

Fifty-eight

Paolo went over to the piano in the drawing room. He ran his fingers over the keys as Emily approached.

"I heard you singing that night with Lionel. Why don't you play me something?" asked Paolo.

Emily nodded and sat down quietly at the piano. She ran her fingers over the keys and then started to play a traditional Scottish ballad, the *Barbara Allen* song, which was popular during the cholera epidemic.

> *"Twas in the merry month of May*
> *When green buds all were swelling,*
> *Sweet William on his death bed lay*
> *For love of Barbara Allen.*
>
> *He sent his servant to the town*
> *To the place where she was dwelling,*
> *Saying you must come, to my master dear*
> *If your name be Barbara Allen.*
>
> *So slowly, slowly she got up*
> *And slowly she drew nigh him,*
> *And the only words to him did say*
> *Young man, I think you're dying.*

He turned his face unto the wall
And death was in him welling,
Goodbye, goodbye, to my friends all
Be good to Barbara Allen."

Paolo was mesmerized by Emily's lovely voice as she sang for him. It was the first time he had heard the Barbara Allen song. He remembered evenings with his parents as a child singing songs and how his cousins could charm the entire family with just one song.

When he was dead and laid in grave
She heard the death bells knelling
And every stroke to her did say
Hard hearted Barbara Allen.

Oh mother, oh mother, go dig my grave
Make it both long and narrow,
Sweet William died of love for me
And I will die of sorrow.

And father, oh father, go dig my grave
Make it both long and narrow,
Sweet William died on yesterday
And I will die tomorrow.

Barbara Allen was buried in the old churchyard
Sweet William was buried beside her,
Out of sweet William's heart, there grew a rose
Out of Barbara Allen's a briar.

They grew and grew in the old churchyard
Till they could grow no higher
At the end, they formed a true lover's knot
And the rose grew round the briar."

As the song ended, Paolo applauded and put his arm around Emily.

"Emily, that was lovely," said Paolo, "*è magnifico, grazie.* I have a cousin back home who sings like you. She's got a lovely soprano voice."

Emily nodded and stood up.

"Will my rose grow round your briar?" asked Paolo playfully.

"You're no *Sweet William*, Paolo," Emily said with a laugh. "Besides, your rose is on its way to Detroit."

Emily collected the plates on the dining room table.

"Promise me you'll go, Paolo. If you stay here, they'll hang you."

Paolo nodded, looking exhausted.

"Are you tired?" asked Emily.

"Yes, I'm ready to drop," said Paolo. "We better sleep down here. If they come looking for us, we can be away in the nick of time."

"You can sleep down here, but I'm sleeping in my bedroom. I haven't slept in my own bed for three days. I need to wash. Look at this dress."

"It's a lovely dress."

"No, it's not. It's dirty."

"Just be ready to leave at a moment's notice. They might come looking for us."

Fifty-nine

It was dark in the drawing room, illuminated by beams of moonlight raking the floor. Paolo slept fitfully on the daybed and was awakened by the sound of footsteps on the front porch. He had just managed to slip down behind the bed when the front door opened. A man appeared in the doorway with a lantern, stamping his feet. He entered the room and sat down heavily at Lionel's desk. Paolo recognized the man immediately. It was the undertaker, Maloney. He found a glass and a bottle of whisky. He was pouring himself a drink when Biggs came into the house.

"All gone, boss, except for a horse out back."

"Take a look upstairs."

Biggs disappeared up the stairs as Maloney examined the paintings on the wall, hoping to find something of value. Moments later, Biggs came crashing down the stairs, dragging Emily along in her nightgown behind him.

"Look who I found, boss!" Biggs announced, proud of himself. "Miss Grenville was hiding upstairs."

"Tell this thug of yours to let go of me, Mr Maloney," Emily said, fuming. "I was asleep in my bed."

Maloney's eyes lit up, seeing Emily on the stairs. Behind the daybed Paolo was getting ready to jump out and seize Biggs when he heard Maloney's voice.

"Let her go, Biggs. Now scoot, out with you."

Biggs let Emily go and went outside as Maloney poured himself another whisky.

"I'm sorry for barging in on you like this in the middle of the night, Miss Emily. Where are your servants?"

"I sent them home, Mr Maloney, after..."

"I see. So you are all alone in the house."

There was a hint of menace in Maloney's voice. Emily looked at the glass of whisky in Maloney's hand.

"Lionel's whisky," Maloney smiled. "I have a weakness for a good whisky, miss. We were nearby and thought we saw a light in the window."

"Well, thank you for coming by," she said haughtily. "You can leave now. I think I'll go back to bed."

"Everybody in town is talking about your escape from jail with that criminal Morelli, miss."

"Don't worry about me, sir. I'm going to see the constable tomorrow to turn myself in."

"That's an excellent idea, Miss Emily. I have money. You will need money to hire a lawyer."

"Please go, sir. It's very late."

Maloney stood up and went to the door.

"Please let me help you. Lionel was a friend of mine. I owe it to your family."

"Thank you, but it won't be necessary. Good night."

"Good night, miss."

Sixty

It was a sunny morning as Gerty and Alfred crossed the street to the Benton house to offer their condolences and to pick up their mother's darning. An attractive young woman opened the door. Gerty had never seen her before.

"Hello, can I help you?"

"We've come for my mum's darning," said Gerty, trying to hide her surprise.

"Well, I wouldn't know about that. Mrs Benton died last week, came down with the blue death."

"We heard," said Gerty. "We're sorry for your loss. We liked Elizabeth. She was very kind."

"It was very sudden."

"How is the family coping? And Mr Benton?"

"He's doing fine, miss. Do you know him?"

"Not very well. Who are you?"

"I'm Ginny. I'm a friend of the family."

There was an awkward silence while Gerty tried to grapple with the idea of this pretty young woman living alone with old man Benton.

"I'm Gerty and this is my brother Alfred. So you still have our darning?"

"I'll check. Wait here, please."

As the woman went off to look, Gerty and Alfred stepped into the parlour and looked around. The room had been swept and scrubbed to Gerty's eye. There was a rocking chair near the fireplace and a ball of woollen thread with knitting needles on the daybed.

"Do you think he killed her?" Alfred whispered.

"Quiet, now," Gerty hissed, examining the bedroom door. Something had happened to the door because what looked like a hole had been patched up with a piece of cardboard and glue. They were still examining the door when Ginny arrived with a package of clothes wrapped in newsprint.

"What happened to the door?" asked Alfred nervously.

"I wouldn't know. That was before I arrived," Ginny replied with growing unease. "Are these yours?"

"Yes, they are. How much will that be?"

"I don't know. Just take it. I'm sure there won't be a charge now that she's gone."

"Thank you. Will you be staying for long, Ginny?"

"Yes, I hope so," Ginny said. It was obvious that she'd had enough of their questions.

Gerty and Alfred left the house and almost ran into a farmer's wagon coming their way.

"You saw the door?" asked Alfred.

"Yep, I seen it," said Gerty. "I think there must have been some kind of fight."

"You think he killed Mrs Benton?"

"I heard a gunshot that night, but it wouldn't account for that patch on the door."

"You think Benton shot her?"

"Anything is possible," Gerty said.

Alfred had a wild imagination, and she didn't want to encourage him. Their family had enough to worry about, without having a murderer living across the street.

Sixty-one

It had been a long night for Colonel Butler. It had started when Mrs Farley, his neighbour and occasional cleaning lady, had come over after lunch. She hadn't been feeling well to begin with and had taken sick after trying to put some order in his rundown house. She started vomiting repeatedly, and the colonel had taken her home to her little shotgun house across the way.

Butler quickly recognized the sickness. Mrs Farley was showing all the signs of coming down with cholera. He knew that after his public quarrel with Dr Walker at the guildhall, nobody in town took him seriously. People were still dying of cholera at an alarming rate, and Dr Walker's remedies didn't appear to be saving any lives. So he put Mrs Farley to bed and had a talk with her girls.

"Your mum's got the cholera, my dears," Butler said.

Both girls were stricken with fear and started to cry. Cholera was a death sentence in St. Francis. Everybody knew somebody who had died recently.

"But we're going to do our very best to try to save her, aren't we girls?"

"Yes, sir," said Grace, the older of the two, while Harriet remained silent.

"We're going to work very hard to save your mum," said Butler. "I'm going to need your help."

The girls nodded, drying their tears.

"We're going to get the stove going and boil water. Grace, I want you to fill a bucket at the pump. Harriet, you light the stove."

Grace was a tough little soldier at seven years old. She immediately ran off with a bucket to the water pump while her sister Harriet obediently lit the stove.

Mrs Farley was rapidly losing fluids, her bedclothes were soiled by watery diarrhea and vomit, and Butler feared for her life. He knew from his experience in India that rapid rehydration was the best recourse in cases of cholera.

"You listen to me," he told the girls when they were boiling the water. "I know it's going to be difficult for you, but you must not touch your mother or any of the sheets on the bed. If you do, you'll get sick too, and then your mother will be angry with you. We want her to get well, don't we?"

Grace and Harriet nodded solemnly.

"Very well," Butler said, observing the hope in the eyes of his young troops. "This is the procedure and it must be followed to the letter. Your mother must drink at least a pint of water every hour. If she is asleep, you will have to wake her up. You can do that by shouting or clapping your hands or making a loud noise. Remember what I just said. You cannot touch her face or the bedclothes. If you can't wake her up, you come and tell me. I will go in and wake her myself."

Mrs Farley had raised her children well, and the girls quickly learned to follow the colonel's orders. During the first few hours, the colonel brought the water to the bedside, accompanied by the girls, so they would know exactly what to do. Once he had their full cooperation, he sent in Grace or

Harriet to wake up their mother every hour, while he poured the boiled water into a cup for the girls to carry to the bedside.

The colonel sat in the kitchen drinking whisky and watching the clock until Grace and little Harriet had grown too tired to continue. He took over for a couple of hours and let them sleep on the cot in the kitchen.

It was touch and go until sunup, when he woke up Grace and Harriet, so they could give him a hand.

Sixty-two

By ten o'clock in the morning, the white-haired colonel was drunk and snoring loudly in a rocking chair in the parlour. It had been a long, exhausting night.

"Colonel," Harriet tugged on his sleeve. "Mama is awake. She's calling for you."

"Okay, Harriet. I'm coming."

He staggered to his feet and followed the young girl into the bedroom. Grace was standing by her mother's bedside waiting for his prognostic. Mrs Farley looked better. Her colour had come back a bit, and she seemed to show some positive signs.

"Colonel," Mrs Farley said in a weak voice. "I can't thank you enough. If I don't make it, will you?"

"Don't worry, my dear. I'll look after the girls. They've been wonderful, a great help during the night."

The poor woman then began vomiting again. The colonel realized she was not yet out of danger. It was no time to let down his guard.

"Harriet, get some water!" said Grace to her sister.

Harriet ran into the kitchen just as there was a loud knock on the front door. Colonel Butler hurried past Harriet and opened the door to a well-dressed gentleman, Mr Ackerman, the owner of the house and Mrs Farley's landlord.

"I've come for the rent," Ackerman said brusquely. "Tell Mrs Farley, she's overdue."

"Mr Ackerman, Mrs Farley is sick," Butler said. "She's got the cholera."

"I don't care, I want her out. She owes me a month's rent."

"Go away," croaked Mrs Farley from the bedroom. "I ain't payin' you a twopenny, you lousy bastard."

Ackerman's face reddened in anger.

"Okay, boys," he called over his shoulder to two young men waiting near a wagon. "We're gonna have to move the bitch. Haul her stuff out of there."

Colonel Butler slammed the door in Ackerman's face. He locked it and turned to see Grace and Harriet watching him.

"Grace, dear," he said calmly. "I want you to run over to the jail and get Constable Riley. Can you do that?"

"Yes, sir."

"Harriet, go with Grace."

Ackerman was pounding on the door and shouting, but the colonel was unperturbed. He had faced down armed sepoys and rebellious natives in the Indian subcontinent, so a runt like Ackerman didn't frighten him. He smiled reassuringly at the girls.

"Don't you worry, now. I'll look after your mama. Go now."

The two girls ran out the back, and the colonel opened the door to Ackerman.

"I don't advise you to come in here, Mr Ackerman. Mrs Farley's got the blue death."

"We just want to be paid, Colonel, that's all."

"I understand, Mr Ackerman, but Mrs Farley is desperately ill, and this is no time to be harassing her about money. You're a respected businessman in this town," said the colonel, failing to keep the sarcasm out of his voice. "Are you telling me you can't afford to give this woman a few days to get back on her feet?"

"It ain't a question of what I can afford," Ackerman growled. "If I go easy on her, all my tenants will want the same thing."

"Do all your tenants have the blue death and two little children to feed?"

"It's tough times for everybody, including me," Ackerman snapped. "Besides, it's the principle of the thing."

"Yes, of course, the principle," Butler nodded sagely. "I wasn't aware you had any."

That was too much for Ackerman. He turned back to his men.

"Don't just stand there!" he bellowed. "Go in there. If he closes the door again, you break it down."

The colonel had used the distraction to rifle through the kitchen drawers. By the time Ackerman turned back to the door, Colonel Butler was standing there with a butcher knife in his hand.

"Nobody is coming in here," Butler shouted, brandishing the knife. "Mr Ackerman, you get the hell off this property right now. The poor woman is fighting the cholera, and she doesn't need you screaming at her from the road."

"Now listen here, Colonel," Ackerman said as he pulled a pistol from his coat and pointed it at Butler. "This is my property and you ain't got no right to be ordering me about."

"No, he doesn't," Constable Riley told him, forcing his horse between Ackerman's men and riding up to the house before he dismounted. "But I do. Now put that gun away before you shoot someone and tell me what's going on here."

"I'm evicting Mrs Farley 'cause she refuses to pay the rent," Ackerman said, hastily putting his pistol back in his pocket.

"She's sick, and this bastard wants to turn her out of her home," Butler said scornfully.

"It ain't nothin' like that, sir," said Ackerman. "She pays the rent. She can stay all she wants."

"I've already told this man," Colonel Butler gestured disdainfully at Ackerman, "that Mrs. Farley is ill with cholera and she is not in a position to pay him anything. She has two little girls to support."

"I see," said Riley as he turned to look at Ackerman's men who stared back at him for a moment. Then one of them shrugged and they both climbed back on their wagon. They whipped the horse and the wagon took off down the street.

"Hey, come back here!" Ackerman yelled.

Grace and Harriet arrived, breathless from their run to get the constable. Riley watched the girls as they went inside, then looked reproachfully at Ackerman.

"How much she owin' you, Mr Ackerman?" he asked.

"Why one pound, two shillings and sixpence for the month, sir."

"Constable, I ain't gonna pay nothing to that old fart," croaked a weak voice from the bedroom.

"I'll give you ten shillings, Mr Ackerman," said Riley, stifling a smile. "That's almost half of what you're owed to clear the debt. Think about it. That's a good deal 'cause you may get nothing if Mrs Farley doesn't recover."

"That's not fair, Constable."

"Life ain't fair, Mr Ackerman, but sometimes you just gotta take what's on the table."

"Constable, I don't have to accept your offer."

"No, you don't, sir, but it's better than nothing. You come by the office tomorrow and collect your money."

Ackerman started to say something but apparently thought better of it. Instead, he gave Riley a curt nod and mounted his horse. Riley and the colonel watched as Ackerman rode away.

"That was very generous of you, Constable," Colonel Butler said.

"Not a problem, sir. We'll take it from our housekeeping budget at the jail. Anything else I can do for you, Colonel?"

"No, but thank you."

"She gonna make it, Colonel?"

"I ain't dead yet," croaked Mrs Farley as the girls stood in the doorway. "Grace and Harriet, say thank you to the constable."

"Thank you, sir," chorused the two girls.

"Girls, your mum's sounding better," said Butler. "I think she's going to be all right."

Grace and Harriet beamed wide smiles at the colonel.

"Good luck, Colonel," said the constable, tipping his hat, and climbing back on his horse.

Sixty-three

"It's not far now," Emily said. "My aunt bought it years ago to be close."

Paolo and Emily drove the calash down to the lake with Fuller's horse trailing behind them.

"Your aunt lives alone?"

"She died from heart failure the same year Daphne was sent away."

"I'm sorry."

"Don't be. Smiley lives nearby and takes care of the house. You'll be safe there. I'll be back tonight if the constable doesn't throw me in jail."

They pulled up near the lake cottage and stepped down. Emily climbed to the porch, looking around while Paolo tied the horse to the railing.

"Smiley!" called Emily. "Smiley!"

Paolo joined her on the porch. The sun glittered off the water in the distance. He spotted a boat dock and a sandy beach along the shore near some grassy marshland. Behind the cottage, he noticed a barn. They waited, but there was no sign of Smiley.

"Where's the wagon?" Paolo asked.

"In the barn, I think."

They walked down to the barn and took a look inside. As he entered the barn, Paolo instantly recognized the baker's wagon from York. It was the same wagon that he and Daphne had used to get to St. Francis. He heard a horse munching feed grain in a nearby stall and went to have a look.

"It's the same wagon and horse, Emily."

There were numerous bridles, saddles, and leather whips hanging from pegs on the wall. Long ago, the lake cottage had been an active farm. As they walked around the wagon, they noticed traces of blood on the bales of hay in one corner.

"There's some blood over there," said Paolo.

"You think Daphne came in here?"

"It looks like it. You hit her on the head, so she must have bled some. How did she leave?"

"I don't know. After she ran off, I left almost immediately for the manor and picked up Mrs Henderson on the way."

Paolo wondered how Daphne had left without a horse or a wagon. It would be a long walk to town. Maybe she had friends in the area.

George Benton saddled a chestnut mare in the barn and walked it out into the morning sunshine. He was about to ride away when Ginny appeared near the house, dumping the slops into the pig trough.

"When you comin' home, George?" she asked.

"Not too late," George said. "Why, what's wrong?"

Ginny looked exhausted by the hard work around the house. She came from a large family and never had to do much housework.

"You sure this is gonna work, George?"

"Sure, why not?"

"The neighbours are talkin', I can feel it."

"Don't matter one bit. They're always gossiping for no good reason. Juss ignore 'em, that's what I say."

"You know those kids across the street, Gerty and her brother? They came a-calling yesterday. They were looking at the hole in the door. She knows. I can tell."

"You shouldn't have let them in."

"I didn't. They just walked in behind me. They were there to pick up their mother's darning."

"Ah, don't worry," said George reassuringly. "They're just kids."

"You could try to talk to them."

"Talk to them? Nah, Gerty works at the estate. She's off at the moment 'cause of the murders."

"She might try to tell someone," Ginny persisted.

"She's just a scullery maid," said George, looking annoyed. "Ain't nobody gonna listen to her."

George got up on his horse. He'd had enough nagging for one morning. He kicked the horse and rode off to work.

Sixty-four

"I got away yesterday, sir," said Emily, sitting down opposite Constable Riley in his office at the town jail.

"So you snuck away on foot?"

"Yes, sir."

"So where is Morelli now?"

"He must be near St. Clair. He planned to slip across the river into the States."

The constable had hoped to rid himself of the Morelli case. Now that Miss Emily had returned, he was back in charge of the investigation and was going to have to charge her. There were still a few things in the case that gnawed at him.

"I appreciate you turning yourself in like this, Miss Grenville. I'm sure the judge will be lenient with you."

"Thank you, sir."

"I don't quite understand why a dangerous fugitive like Morelli would let you go. He's a smart man. Why would he tell you where he's going?"

"He didn't let me go, sir. It was the uncle who suggested going to St. Clair. He was told to avoid crossing at Detroit, but to go north and slip across at St. Clair."

"Well, that's a useful piece of information. I'll pass it along. I heard that Morelli confirmed your innocence to Mr Fuller in rather distressing circumstances."

"Fuller tried to drown Morelli, sir. It was outrageous."

"I'm very sorry that it happened, miss. Morelli said you were innocent, but there is something that puzzles me. He said that he wanted to be buried in a coffin with a brass burial reed like Daphne's. Why would he say something like that, miss?"

"He would know about the burial reed, Constable. He was the remembrance man who resuscitated my sister. He heard her voice calling in the night."

"You think he was trying to tell us something?"

"I don't know, sir."

"When we exhumed Daphne's body, I didn't notice any burial reed in her coffin. So someone has been tampering with her remains."

"I think Daphne is alive, sir."

"That's certainly what young Morelli has been saying all along. We've never had a case of resuscitation before in St. Francis. So was it Lionel, who paid for the remembrance man?"

"Yes, sir."

The constable mulled this over.

"After your ordeal with my deputy, I don't think it will be necessary to put you in jail again. I only need for you to guarantee your appearance in court at the hearing. You'll have to sign a statement to say that you were forced to go with him, but managed to run away."

"Thank you, sir."

Sixty-five

Eleanor and young Virgil accompanied sister Clara as she made a circuit of the Smythe estate in the wagon. They came to a pine forest at the end of the pasture and stopped.

"This will make a nice shady area for the camp meeting," Clara told them, getting down from the wagon. "It will be cooler under the trees."

Eleanor and Virgil climbed down and followed Clara to a large tree in the centre of the grove.

"We can put the wagon here for the reverend to stand on, and over there we'll put the mourner's bench."

"What's a mourner, Mama?" asked Virgil.

"It's someone who has lost a loved one," said Eleanor.

"Sometimes we call it the 'crying bench', Virgil," said Clara. "The people on the bench are sinners and they often cry out during the meetings."

"Why do they cry?" asked Virgil.

"They're unhappy, son," said Eleanor.

"They cry because they love the Lord," said Clara. "They want to be saved."

"So where will the people sit?" Eleanor asked, eager to change the subject. She was not in the least bit religious, but she didn't want Virgil to hear any more about sinners and bad people and crying benches.

"Over there on the grass, my dear," said Clara. "Yes, I think this is a fine place for our meetings."

"How many camp meetings are you planning?"

"Maybe three, maybe four, depending on the interest."

They watched as Clara marched from the large pine tree to the end of the grove of trees, taking time to count the number of paces.

"What's she doing, Mama?" Virgil asked.

"She's counting out the distance, Virgil."

Clara returned, looking satisfied.

"The reverend will like this place. We can easily sit eight hundred people here in the shade. The food will be served over there to the right."

"Eight hundred, isn't that a lot?" asked Eleanor in astonishment.

"I don't think so, my dear. We've had over a thousand in some places."

"How will you feed them all?"

"The good Lord will provide, as he always does."

The Second Great Awakening had arrived in Western Ontario and was very popular in the towns and farming communities of the region. Religious revivals were attracting hundreds of converts to various Protestant denominations, including the Methodists, the Baptists, the Adventists, the Shakers, the Congregationalists, the Disciples of Christ and others.

Ardent evangelists set up missionary societies to evangelize the people. Volunteer women ran the revivals, helping men and women during their conversion experience, relaying testimonials about the conversion experience, and performing hundreds of other tasks, but all the leading ministerial positions remained in the hands of men.

Mothers were seen as the moral and spiritual foundation of the family and were put in charge of the religious upbringing of their children. What had often started as women's prayer groups soon metamorphosed into moral reform societies run by women. The Female Missionary Society and the Evangelical Maternal Associations of upstate New York were well organized and spilled out into the surrounding states and Upper Canada. They were joined by The Temperance Movement and Abolitionist groups, who believed that people could be reformed through social activism.

Sixty-six

Daphne sat between young Reuben and Thaddeus on the wagon as they made their way to the cemetery. Wilbur hung on to the back, as far away as possible from the dead bodies. It was quiet as they passed the gates and headed over to the mass grave at the back.

As the men unloaded the bodies in the cholera pit, Daphne walked over to look at the Grenville plot. She noticed Lucille's headstone immediately, then looked curiously at her own headstone on a nearby grave. She flew into a fit of rage.

"The bastards," she screamed. "I'm alive, I'm not dead!"

Reuben ran over to see what Daphne was upset about.

"What's going on, miss?" he asked.

"My sister Emily is trying to get rid of me," she snarled, "but I won't let it happen. I'm gonna find that bitch and even the score once and for all."

She stormed away, leaving a stunned Reuben staring at the headstone of one Daphne Grenville and wondering who she really was.

Emily was driving the calash on her way back from town when she ran into Maloney on horseback, coming the other way.

"Well, well, Miss Emily, the constable let you go. You're lucky to be free."

"You forgot the burial reed, Mr Maloney. Daphne had a burial reed in her casket."

"Your cousin Lionel was in a great hurry, miss," Maloney said. "After he had me return Daphne to the Asylum, he wanted me to put a body in Daphne's grave. Couldn't have the neighbours getting any ideas, now could he? No one mentioned the burial reed."

"I don't want to talk about Lionel, sir."

"You know that Lionel was thinking of selling the manor. Now that you are in charge, you should consider it. There can be nothing but grief for you to live in the same house with all those memories."

"I've said enough, Mr Maloney. I'll be on my way."

"You are young, Miss Emily. A woman of means can do very well for herself in Hamilton or York. Well, you take your time now. Remember, I am only here to help."

"Good day, sir."

Sixty-seven

Gerty was down on all fours, weeding the vegetable garden. She was inching along, pulling up weeds and hauling a wicker basket behind her, when George Benton appeared on his chestnut mount in the lane nearby.

"Hey, Gerty. How are you doin', girl?"

"I'm fine, sir."

"You came by the house the other day and met my Ginny. Ginny's my cousin. Now that Elizabeth's gone, she's gonna stay and help out for a while."

"Yes, I met her."

"You still workin' at the manor?"

"Yes, sir, but they sent us all home after the murders."

"I understand," Benton nodded. "Hey, you wanna come work for me?. Ginny needs help around the house."

Gerty stood up with a suspicious air.

"I'm not sure I can, sir."

"Well," he said, "think on it a bit. Good day."

Gerty watched Benton turn his horse around and head across the road to his barn. She was stunned by the offer. The Bentons had never offered housework to her family or any other family in the neighbourhood. George Benton was a notorious skinflint who never paid for help of any kind around the house when Elizabeth was alive. He spent all his money on drink and loose women. She would never accept to work for a man who had killed his wife and was now living in a sinful relationship with a woman not much older than herself.

The baker's wagon was parked outside the lake cottage in front of Emily's calash. Smiley was standing near the wagon, impatient to be off. There was a pine box in the back of the wagon along with a supply of water, food, and blankets ready for the overnight trip. Nearby, Paolo and Emily held hands and said their final goodbye.

"Paolo, I'll miss you," said Emily, giving him a lingering kiss. "Don't forget to send me a card."

"I will, Emily," said Paolo.

"We better be off, Miss Emily," Smiley said, "if we want to catch the morning ferry in Port Stanley."

"Good luck, Paolo. Take care on the road."

"*Ciao*, Emily."

Paolo climbed onto the back of the baker's wagon and lay down in the pine box. Smiley placed the cover on top and threw a dirty blanket over it, then took the reins and whipped the horse into action.

Emily watched the wagon as it started its long trek to Lake Erie. It would take a good day and a half to get there. She felt alone all of a sudden. Paolo was gone from her life. He wouldn't be coming back for her after he got to Detroit, that was for sure. Not with all those beautiful high society ladies just waiting for him.

Sixty-eight

Mr Ackerman came by the jail to collect the rent money for the Farley cottage. Deputy Fuller was sitting in the constable's chair with his feet up on the desk.

"Come in, Mr Ackerman," said Fuller, waving him into the office.

"I've come by for Farley's rent, sir."

"Yes, sir. I have it here," said Fuller, as Ackerman sat down. He took a piece of paper and a steel dip pen from the desk and handed them to Ackerman.

"Constable Riley is away at the moment. I need you to sign the receipt at the bottom there. It says that we're paying you ten shillings for the month of August."

Ackerman laid the receipt flat on the desk and dipped the pen in the ink before scribbling his signature on the paper.

"You'll be happy to hear that Mrs Farley is better now," said Fuller.

"Yeah, I'm real happy that damned woman got away with paying less than half the rent," said Ackerman bitterly.

Ackerman stood up, ready to receive his money, when Fuller handed him another document. It looked official.

"What's this?" Ackerman demanded.

"It's a fine, sir. You are being fined for waving a gun around within the town limits and making threats."

"That ain't right, Fuller. I never done nothin' like that."

"Constable Riley said you drew your weapon on that old gentleman over at the Farley house, sir."

"I was within my rights, sir. Colonel Butler was trying to kick me off my property."

"The fine is ten shillings, sir," Fuller said, unmoved. "It's payable immediately. You pay or you go to jail."

"That ain't fair!" Ackerman sputtered.

"It ain't no skin off my nose, sir," said Fuller, picking up the pen and handing it back to Ackerman, "but I think we'll be keeping the rent money."

Ackerman stared at him, speechless with anger.

"The constable said to sign on the bottom there."

Ackerman scrawled his signature on the page and tossed the pen onto the desk.

"Am I free to go now?" he asked sarcastically.

"Yes, sir," Fuller said with a smile. "Nice doing business with you. Constable Riley said to tell you not to slam any doors on your way out. That would be disturbing the peace."

Dusk had come and gone as Smiley drove the wagon south, dimly illuminated by an oil lamp attached to the wagon upright. In the distance, he could just barely make out a wagon approaching along the dusty road.

Three dirty cholera men sat on the front seat of the wagon, with a fourth hanging off the back. As they got closer, Smiley tried to pull off the road to let the cholera wagon pass, but it turned off on the same side, blocking his passage. Then, as Smiley swung his wagon back the other way, the cholera wagon again moved to block him.

A small figure in a hooded cape jumped down and approached Smiley.

"Hey, Smiley Webb. Whatcha doin' out here in the middle of nowhere? You're a long way from home."

"Miss Daphne."

"You carrying a body in that pine casket there?"

Daphne jumped up on the wagon and put her foot on the casket.

"Who you got in here, Smiley?"

"Miss Daphne, please. Have some respect."

"White or Negro, a friend maybe? The blue death doesn't care much who the victim is, now does it?"

"It's none of your business, miss."

Paolo suddenly shoved the top of the casket off and clambered out of it, throwing Daphne off balance.

"Damn you, Daphne!" he shouted.

"Well, look who we have here! The whole town is searching for you, Paolo. You're the famous criminal, who killed all those Grenvilles."

"You've destroyed my life."

"I've seen you with my sister. Is she a good kisser?"

Daphne grinned flirtatiously and signalled to the two cholera men to come over. Reuben and Thaddeus approached as Wilbur hung back.

"Look who I found, boys!" Daphne yelled as she pulled her pocket pepperbox from her cape. "I think we've caught ourselves a killer."

Daphne pointed the gun at Paolo.

"Get down from the wagon, Paolo."

Paolo didn't hesitate for an instant. He leapt off the wagon, the shot from Daphne's pistol whistling past his ear. He landed in the bushes on the side of the road and ran off into the night.

Reuben and Thaddeus took up the chase, but Paolo soon lost them in the dark.

The silhouette of a man carrying a shovel was seen gliding from tree to tree in the mist engulfing the cemetery. The elusive figure stopped at the Grenville family plot and began to dig, dumping the soft earth on one side. After a time, his shovel struck wood, and he jumped down into the hole to clear away the remaining dirt.

He stopped for a moment to listen to the wind in the trees. He took a brass burial reed from his pocket and, with a sharp whack from his hammer, penetrated the soft pine box. The man quickly shovelled the dirt back into the hole, making sure the burial reed was visible at the surface.

"Stay where you are. Don't move," said a voice from behind the trees.

Constable Riley approached the grave, aiming two flintlock pistols at the large figure of Biggs, Maloney's work supervisor. Biggs turned and started for his gun. He froze when he saw Riley's pistols pointed at his head.

"Lovely night for grave robbing, or did you have some other reason for this hobby of yours, Biggs."

"Constable, what are you doing here?" Biggs asked, looking defeated.

"Same as you, Biggs," Riley smiled. "I was asking myself about the missing burial reed."

Sixty-nine

The next morning, Constable Riley walked into his office at the jail to find Fuller sitting at his desk with his feet up.

"Sorry, sir," Fuller said hastily vacating Riley's chair. "I got back 'bout an hour ago. We lost them, they must be in the States by now."

Riley hooked a saddlebag over the back of his chair and sat down. He looked at his unwashed, and exhausted deputy.

"You look like you need a cup of tea, Mr Fuller."

"Yes, sir. I'll get it started," Fuller said as he picked up the empty teapot from the hob. "I saw you got Biggs locked up back there. He says you caught him digging up a grave in the cemetery."

"A strange business. I think we can hold him on grave-robbing, but we still don't have the big picture. Why don't you bring him in here so we can have a talk?"

"Yes, sir."

"Don't forget to cuff him. We've had enough escapes already."

Fuller gave him a long look but did what he was told. He came back with Biggs a couple of minutes later.

"Sit down, Biggs," Riley said. "We need to talk."

"I ain't done nothin', sir."

"Grave-robbing is a serious offence, Biggs. You could go away for several years, depending on how the judge sees it."

"I was juss followin' orders, sir. Maloney told me to put in the burial reed."

"That doesn't matter, Biggs. It's still a crime tampering with the remains of the dead. Who is she?"

"She?"

"Yeah, the woman in the grave?"

"She's juss some poor woman who died of cholera, sir. Came off a cholera wagon."

"Who ordered you to put her body in the box?"

"Lionel Burke, sir. He's dead. He paid Mr Maloney to have it done."

"Why would he do that?"

"Well, sir, the way I heard it, the Morellis pulled Daphne from the grave and saved her life."

"Yes, but why put another woman back in the grave?"

"I don't know, sir, maybe to hide the fact she was alive."

"Then he had Daphne sent back to the Asylum?"

"Yes, sir. She was always crazy, that bitch."

"Okay, Biggs. I'm going to release you, but you better stay out of trouble."

"Yes, sir. Thank you, sir."

Fuller took out his key and removed Biggs' cuffs.

"I don't like your boss, Biggs. I know he has you doing the devil's work over at the cemetery, but be careful."

Emily answered the door and ushered Riley into the hall at Grenville Manor. They had to step around some wooden boxes containing books and various odds and ends sitting in the hall.

"Miss Grenville, I hope you're not thinking of leaving?"

"No, sir. I'm just getting rid of some of Lionel's things. I don't want them around anymore."

They went into the drawing room and sat down.

"I have a question for you," Riley said. "Last night, I caught Maloney's man Biggs in the cemetery. He was digging up your sister's grave."

Emily gave the constable a long look and then laughed.

"Of course he was. I saw Maloney yesterday as I was coming home. I told him about the burial reed, sir. I'm sorry."

"That's all right, miss. Biggs says the body we found in Daphne's grave came from the cholera pit. Do you want me to press charges against Maloney and Biggs for grave robbing and tampering with the dead? It's a serious charge, miss."

Emily looked away.

"No, sir. I don't want to hear anymore about this horrible affair."

"I understand, miss. You've been through a lot. I think I must inform you that your sister Daphne is very much alive and well, and she may represent a danger to you."

"Yes, sir."

"You shouldn't stay in this house alone, miss."

"I'll be fine, sir. The staff will be returning in a few days."

"Why don't you take a room at the hotel in town? You'll be safe there."

"I'll keep that in mind. Thank you."

The constable got up to leave.

"Oh. I almost forgot. You'll need to come by my office to sign your statement."

"Yes, of course."

"Good day, miss."

Seventy

Constable Riley arrived at the Smythe Manor house later that afternoon. He walked in on Clara, holding a meeting in the parlour with the sisters sitting around her on the floor. A makeshift table held a tea tray with cups and saucers. As the constable came in, the women turned to look at him.

"Sorry to be disturbing you, ladies."

"That's fine, Constable," said Clara.

"I hope the looters haven't been harassing you."

"No, sir. We're happy to have the place to ourselves," said Abigail.

"Have you seen Eleanor and Virgil?"

"They're in the kitchen, Constable," replied Clara.

"Well, carry on. I won't make any noise," said Riley.

As Riley left, the women returned to their discussions about the upcoming camp meeting.

The constable descended to the kitchen, where he found Eleanor in an apron chopping up a load of vegetables for a soup. Virgil was playing with a ball, kicking it against the wall.

"Hello, John," said Eleanor, smiling at him.

"The sisters appear to be getting on well. How are you?"

"It's very nice to have them around. Beats them looters any day."

"Yeah, I'm sure it does."

"Sit down, John. Have a cup of tea."

"Thank you."

"What happened to Red and Eugene?"

"They're in jail waiting on the circuit judge, Eleanor."

"Will they do jail time?"

"I would think so. The judge won't take kindly to these men harassing the Methodist sisters and stealing private property."

Eleanor served the tea in a tin cup to Riley, who was watching young Virgil tirelessly kicking the ball.

"Virgil is old enough to go to school, Eleanor. You gonna send him?"

"Yeah, I was thinking the same thing. There's a school on the road into town."

"I don't know whether they still have a teacher. There have been so many deaths. I can inquire in town for you if you like."

"Sure, I'd like that, John. Maybe I could do some teaching. My mum was a teacher when I was growing up."

Riley picked up the ball and returned it to Virgil.

"She was one mean teacher. She'd rap our knuckles with a ruler. When we spelled a word wrong, she had us writing it out a hundred times on the blackboard."

"So you got all the punishment, did you, Eleanor?"

"Not all of it, but my mum believed in 'spare the rod and spoil the child'. As her daughter, I was supposed to do better than the others. By the way, Clara wants me to write up the camp invitations 'cause I got such nice handwriting."

"Good for you."

"They're an interesting bunch, John. The sisters come from all over. Some of them are widows like me, others just up and left their families to follow the reverend. You know they're planning several camp meetings out here."

"Yeah, I heard."

"You ever hear of the preacher James McGready and the Cane Ridge revival?"

"Nope. I don't go to church much."

"Well, Clara's been telling me about it. Cane Ridge was the biggest revival meeting ever in the States and it was held in a log cabin church in the backwoods of Kentucky. She said they had 25,000 people there. They all came to this tiny church in the woods and marvelled at the preaching, the weeping, the groaning and the falling on the ground."

"Well, I hope we don't get anywhere near that number of people out here. It'll be a disaster."

"They converted thousands of people, John. Clara says it was the most amazing religious gathering ever."

"You gonna give them a hand preparing the meeting?"

"Yes, I am."

"Well, good for you. When you get tired of the sisters and the empty house, I'll find you some accommodation in town."

"John, that's so kind of you. Thank you."

"I'm serious, Eleanor. You can't stay out here forever."

Eleanor took off her apron and came over to give Riley a kiss.

Seventy-one

"Wake up, bitch! You're comin' with me," Daphne screamed, grabbing Emily by the hair and pulling her out of her bed in her nightdress.

"What's going on?" Emily protested. Only seconds before, she had been sound asleep and now her wild-eyed sister was trying to drag her out of her bedroom. Emily seized the door handle with her free hand and slammed the door in Daphne's face.

"Why'd you do it, Daphne?" screamed Emily. "Jimmy and Tommy were lovely boys. They were our brothers."

"Brothers, sisters, who cares," said Daphne, picking herself up off the floor. "They were nothing to me. I hardly knew them."

"How can you say that?"

"I am what I am, sister. Now, come along."

Daphne pulled and pushed her sister down the stairs.

Reuben and Thaddeus sat in wooden chairs near Lionel's desk in the drawing room, drinking whisky while Wilbur examined a pewter beer mug on a shelf. They turned simultaneously towards the door when the twins arrived. They were stunned by the likeness of the twin sisters.

"This is my sister, Emily, boys. Don't she look nice?"

"Who are these people, Daphne?" asked Emily.

"They're my new friends, sis. The handsome one is Reuben. That's his brother Thaddeus and over there is Wilbur."

"Well, you better send them away. I won't have them trespassing in this house."

"You ain't in no position to give orders, sis. Where are the servants?"

"They were sent home."

"Good, 'cause we're gonna make some changes 'round here. You were hoping that I would just disappear, right?"

"No, Daphne. I didn't send you away, Lionel did."

"Well, the bastard is dead now."

"Daphne, you realize that you killed four people, and the constable is out looking for you."

"No, he ain't. I'm buried in the cemetery. I got me a nice headstone. No one is out looking for me," Daphne said with a sly grin. "They're lookin' for Paolo Morelli."

"Paolo's gone. He's returned to Detroit. They won't find him."

"Last time I saw him, he was hiding in a pine box on Smiley's wagon," said Daphne with a laugh.

"What did you do to him?" Emily asked in shock.

"I ain't done nothing to him."

"I want to see him."

"Then you better get dressed, girl. I'll take you to him."

Seventy-two

Constable Riley found Mrs Henderson out in her garden. She was wearing a bonnet, apron, and boots. She dipped her hand into a bag of seeds and threw a handful into a row, turning the soil with her foot as she moved along.

"Good morning, Constable."

Riley dismounted and walked over.

"Good morning to you, ma'am. Sorry to interrupt your work. I've got a few questions concerning the Grenville murders."

"Poor Emily. She has had such a hard time. I heard you arrested her along with that Italian man who escaped from jail."

"She's been released, ma'am."

"Good, she's innocent. I only hope she will get over it. It's been a terrible shock for her."

"How was she when she came to collect you on the day after the murders?"

"Same as always, sir. She's a sweet girl."

"Was she disturbed, quiet?"

"She can be quite moody, you know. The sisters were very different. Daphne was the wild young thing, going off on dares and harbouring grudges against friends while Emily was always less extreme, often quiet and reserved. We didn't talk much."

Riley looked up and down the lane.

"She was coming down this way from her aunt's house on the lake and you were standing at the gate?"

"Why, yes? I was standin' by the gate waiting for her."

The constable moved away a bit, looking up and down the lane.

"Was it rainin' that morning, ma'am?"

"Yes, I believe it was. It rained during the night and we had a shower early in the morning. It was wet. I had my umbrella with me."

"You still housekeeping down at the manor?"

"I've been in once or twice since that day."

"Soil looks good," Riley said, glancing down at the ground. "You gonna have a fine crop. I'll be on my way. Good day, ma'am."

Riley walked back to his horse and mounted up. He rode down the lane a hundred yards, looking down at the wheel ruts in the soft earth. He stopped and leant down to examine the marks of a light wagon, or maybe a calash. He surmised that Emily's calash had made those marks the morning of the murders.

He rode on to the lake cottage and dismounted near the front steps. He looked down at the deep wheel ruts in the dried mud along the road before stepping through the front gate and knocking on the door.

There was no one around, so he followed the wheel ruts to the barn. He stepped inside and saw a big wagon parked there. He stepped out of the barn and went down to the lake. A black man in a waistcoat and straw hat was fishing from the wooden dock with a bamboo pole. Riley approached noisily, so as not to startle the man.

"I remember an escaped slave skulking in the bushes," said Riley, grinning. "You didn't want to come out."

"Yep, that was a long, long time ago, Constable," said Smiley. "You could have sent me back, but instead you found me a job working for Lucille. I'll always be in your debt, sir."

"That was before I became the law enforcement in these parts, Mr Webb."

"Back then, you were just a badass cowboy from Texas, but you did good up here. I know it."

Smiley pulled in his line and put another worm on his hook.

"You heard any talk about the murders?" asked Riley.

"Yep, that's all anybody talking 'bout 'round here."

The constable looked over at the weathered walls of the shed near the water's edge.

"How long you been living out here, Mr Webb?"

"Been a long time, sir. That was before Mr Marcus passed away with typhus. Going on twelve years now."

"I thought you'd moved on."

"Where am I gonna go, Constable, an old man like me? Lucille left me the shed, so I fixed it up a bit. It's my home now."

Smiley pulled on the line and felt a fish take the bait, then nothing.

"You missed a big one," Riley teased.

"I sure did," Smiley said as he set about baiting the hook again.

"You seen Miss Daphne?"

"Nope. I heard Miss Daphne died of cholera in that there Asylum in the city."

"It looks like she was nursed back to health by a remembrance man."

"Wouldn't know 'bout dat, sir. The blue death takes the best of us. It's like the blackfly, the more of 'em buzzing 'round your head, the more they drive a man crazy. A man is juss 'bout ready to give up his life for a little relief. You know what I mean?"

"I think I do."

"Folks are grievin' so bad they cain't work the farm no more, lost their pa, their ma, they cain't hardly feed themselves. A stranger comes along, offers a pittance for the farm, and takes it away for next to nothin'."

"I'm gonna ask you a question, Mr Webb. I need an honest answer 'cause I know you'll do anything you can to protect the Grenville girls."

"Sure, Constable. I'll answer the best I can."

"I found the big wagon that Miss Daphne and young Morelli took when they returned from York. The tracks lead right up to your barn over there. Can you tell me what happened?"

"Constable, I won't lie to you. I'm worried about Miss Daphne. I saw her the night of the killing. She came here alone in the wagon."

"What happened?"

"That girl was half crazy. She attacked me with a hatchet, comin' in the door. She told Emily that she'd shot Lionel and Baxter. Miss Emily was furious at her sister and ran off to check on the boys."

"So she went to the manor house?"

"She must have 'cause when she came back, she tried to kill Daphne with a clothes iron. She knocked her unconscious. We thought she had killed her sister, but then Daphne ran off and disappeared."

Seventy-three

Through the small window high up on the wall, Emily could just make out the milking staff arriving in the early morning hours and carrying out their duties in the cow shed behind the stables. Although the household staff had all been sent home, Emily had kept the farm workers on the job because the estate could not be run without a phalanx of able-bodied workers bringing in the milk and crops.

Emily was locked up in a storage room in the blacksmith's shop. The walls were filthy, covered in soot from the forge, and the small room was littered with all kinds of farm implements and slabs of molten iron.

She had tried for over an hour to call attention to her plight by pounding on the walls and shouting for help, but no one could hear or see her. She sat down on a metal plough and cried.

At the Smythe Manor house, the sisters were taking their morning tea with Eleanor in the parlour as they played blind man's buff with young Virgil. With a cloth covering his eyes, he stumbled around the room as he tried to latch on to the sisters, who darted away like schoolgirls squealing with delight.

Soon all the women were shrieking with laughter as Virgil ran around in circles. The game went on for a few moments before Virgil latched onto Juba.

"You got me, Virgil," she laughed. "You got me."

Abigail took off Virgil's blindfold and handed it to Juba.

"Virgil, do you know *Ding, Dong, Bell*?" Amelia asked.

Virgil nodded, and they started to chant the nursery rhyme.

> *"Ding, dong, bell,*
> *Pussy's in the well.*
> *Who put her in?*
> *Little Johnny Thin.*
> *Who pulled her out?*
> *Little Tommy Stout.*
> *What a naughty boy was that,*
> *To try to drown poor pussy cat,*
> *Who never did him any harm,*
> *But chased all the mice in the farmer's barn."*

"You can't catch me," yelled Virgil as Juba, wearing the blindfold, went after him. He dropped to the floor to avoid her searching hands and snuck under the table.

"Don't talk so much, Virgil," said Eleanor, laughing. "Juba will get you."

Instead, Juba turned around suddenly and grabbed Amelia, who was just behind her. She pulled off her blindfold and helped Amelia put it on.

"I can hear you, Virgil," Amelia cried as Virgil scampered out from under the table. "If I catch a naughty boy, I'm gonna put him in the well, put him in the well."

"Careful, Virgil," Eleanor warned. "Amelia is gonna catch you."

"Put him in the well, put him in the well," repeated the women as Virgil squealed with delight.

Seventy-four

Timing was everything. A landowner might resist selling a property for years, but there would come a time when selling out was the only choice. With the cholera epidemic and the scandal surrounding the murders, the Grenville estate was losing money and would soon attract the attention of the big property dealers and bankers in Hamilton and York. Loan sharks, confidence men, and other dodgy businessmen would soon descend on St. Francis and try to confiscate the estate for some unpaid tax or over a legal issue.

It was time for Maloney to make a move before the competition arrived in town. He knew better than anyone how to ruin a property owner while making a pile of money for himself. All he needed to do was to get a foot in the door, and by hook or by crook, he'd dispossess the owner in no time and make the property his own.

He arrived at the manor and dismounted, tying his horse to the railing. He climbed the steps with a confident air and knocked on the front door.

The door opened and Reuben, clean-shaven and dressed in Baxter's clothes, stood on the threshold, observing Maloney with an insolent look on his face.

"Can I help you, sir?"

"Bloody hell, Reuben. What the fuck are you doing here?"

"I work for Miss Grenville now, sir."

"That can't be right. You're nothing but an alkie and a thief."

"Would you like to come in, sir?"

Maloney barged past Reuben and headed into the drawing room, then stopped short when he saw Thaddeus all cleaned up, dusting the bookshelves.

"Thaddeus," he hissed. "You fellas are cholera boys. You're supposed to be out there collecting blue death cadavers. You shouldn't be anywhere near the Grenville Manor. What's going on?"

"Good evening, Mr Maloney," said Daphne, entering the room wearing one of her sister's dresses. "I've decided to move to town and sell the house."

"Good idea, Miss Grenville. It's a good plan. You look very lovely this evening."

Maloney went over to the drinks tray and served himself a large glass of Lionel's whisky.

"I must say, you're making a big mistake hiring this riff-raff. They'll never make proper servants. Can't you find any decent staff?"

"Oh, I don't know," Daphne said airily. "I admit they're a bit rough around the edges, but they're learning how to do their jobs. Everybody has to start somewhere, Mr Maloney."

"You know Lionel had a good life here. He got rid of your sister Daphne after she was pulled from the grave and resuscitated. He then sent her back to the Asylum. You and the bookkeeper could have done well together."

"Yeah, but I never trusted Lionel. He was a sneaky bastard. He wanted me to marry him so he could control the property."

"You'd make an attractive bride for any man, Miss Grenville. I hear the constable has decided you're no longer guilty of helping Morelli escape."

"Yes, I hope they catch that man."

"Don't you worry your pretty head, Miss Grenville. They'll get him and he'll hang."

"What is the purpose of your visit, Mr Maloney, other than helping yourself to the free whisky?"

"I was passing by," Maloney said, ignoring the sarcasm in her voice. "I thought I would stop by and have a chat with you, my dear. I want to make you an offer for the estate."

"That's wonderful news, Mr Maloney."

"You know you are not quite off the hook for Morelli. If the judge finds you guilty of associating with a known criminal, you could lose everything: the house, the estate, everything. That would be very sad."

"Indeed."

"You know your sister is officially deceased," Maloney said, drinking from his whisky. "I'll only need your agreement to acquire the property, Miss Grenville."

"Yes, I understand that. So how much are you offering me, Mr Maloney?"

"A very handsome sum, Miss Grenville. You'll soon be rich and able to move into very suitable lodgings in the city."

Daphne smiled as Maloney finished his drink and put the empty glass back on the tray.

"I have an appointment in an hour, but I'll come by this evening, if you like, with a proper offer."

"We'll be here," Daphne said, smiling pleasantly. "Thank you, Mr Maloney."

Seventy-five

Eleanor and Clara watched from the porch as Virgil played in the garden of the Smythe Manor. They were drinking tea and enjoying the cool evening air.

"So you're a widow too, like the others?" asked Eleanor.

"Well, not exactly, my dear. I left my husband 'cause he was a violent man and a devil worshipper."

"A devil worshipper?" Eleanor asked uncertainly.

Virgil threw a ball into a patch of purple clematis in full bloom and went after the ball, trampling the flowering plants underfoot.

"Careful of the flowers, Virgil," Clara stood up suddenly. "Those are clematis you're stepping on. See the purple flowers."

Virgil quickly stepped back from the clematis and crushed the flowering plants behind him.

"Careful, my boy, the yellow flowers behind you are black-eyed Susans."

"Get out of there, Virgil," ordered Eleanor.

Virgil sheepishly picked up his ball and ran off. Clara sat down and drank her tea.

"The Smythe gardener sure knew what he was doing," she said, observing the flowers. "It's sad to see it go."

"So you left your husband?" asked Eleanor.

"My husband was a bad man," said Clara. "I've always wanted to live my life in harmony with God, but with him it was impossible."

"You ran away?"

"Yes, I did after he fell sick."

"He fell sick?"

"One morning I put rat poison in his tea. It served the bastard right. He became grievously ill, couldn't stand up and sure couldn't beat me up no more. I told him to pray for forgiveness and left the house."

"Rat poison?"

"Yeah, it works wonders," Clara said coldly. "We sisters are all victims of violent men, Eleanor. Abigail killed her husband with a scythe in the garden, Lucy stabbed hers with a pair of scissors when she was darning his socks, and the others all escaped unhappy marriages."

"You never went back?"

"No, he would have killed me if he could."

"You've confessed this to the reverend?"

"Yes, I have. I was a wicked woman living a sinful life. I deserved to be cast into hell with my husband. Remember the words of Isaiah 63: "I will tread them in mine anger and will trample them in my fury, and their blood shall be sprinkled upon my garments, and I will stain all my raiment."

"So you found yourself in God?"

"Yes, I put my trust in Jesus and he cleansed me of my sins. I have my calling now."

Eleanor couldn't think of anything to say, so she sipped her tea and sneaked a look at Clara's scarred face. Eleanor had lived a hard life, but it was nothing compared to what the sisters had endured in their previous lives.

"It ain't always easy," Clara said with a smile, "but nothing good ever came from an easy life. I can't help noticing, my dear, but you've got eyes for the constable."

"Yeah, John's been real nice to us, to Virgil and me. He came to collect my husband's body out on the prairie after he died from the blue death. I almost shot him. I was crazy. I didn't want anyone messing with his body."

"You shot at the constable?"

"Yeah, but just to scare him off."

"Well, you got his attention, my dear," Clara said with a laugh.

"Yeah, I think I did. You think he's too old for me?"

"He ain't young, but he seems nice enough. How's he get along with your son?"

"Virgil likes him."

"And you?"

"Oh," Eleanor said, feeling an unfamiliar blush coming to her cheeks. "I like him all right."

Seventy-six

Through the hedgerow, the silent manor house looked abandoned. It was a time when the kitchen staff would normally be busy preparing food for the evening meal.

Paolo walked along the hedgerow and approached the kitchen through the back door. He slipped inside and had to hide behind the stove to avoid being seen by Thaddeus, who was returning a tea tray to the kitchen. Paolo noticed the piles of dirty dishes on the counter and wondered how long the kitchen had been this way. Where was Emily? What was this strange man doing in the Grenville Manor?

He snuck out of the kitchen and quietly climbed the stairs to the second floor to have a look around. Emily's bedroom door was open, and her bed was covered with dresses and underclothes. Was Daphne hiding out here and sleeping in her sister's room? He returned to the first floor, avoiding the drawing room where he could hear voices.

"That sonofabitch will be back with an offer," yelled Daphne in a loud voice.

"No, he won't," protested Reuben. "Maloney's an arsehole. He ain't got the money to buy a fancy place like this."

"Shut up! I know what I'm doing."

Paolo ran back to the kitchen and went out through the back door. Standing in the quadrangle of farm buildings, he could see the entire layout of the estate with the barn, the blacksmith shop, the cow shed and the outlying buildings. He was in the barn having a look around when he saw Thaddeus coming out the back door with a tray.

Through the high window in the storeroom, Emily could just make out the cows returning to the shed and the farm workers heading home with their lunch buckets. She picked up an iron bar with a sharp end and started to attack the frame of the heavy oak door. The frame was made of soft pine and she had already managed to gouge parts of it away. She stopped when she heard footsteps on the stone steps and a voice on the other side of the door.

"Step away from the door," ordered a man's voice.

Emily stepped back as a man walked in carrying a tray with a bowl of chicken broth and a crust of bread. He thrust the tray into her hands.

"Time to eat," he said.

"What's your name, please?"

"I'm Thaddeus, miss. Your sister wants you to eat. She cares about you."

"My sister is mad. I despise her," Emily said.

Thaddeus shrugged and left, locking the door behind him. Emily was famished and sat down to eat.

Maloney knew how to make a killing from a large estate like the Grenville's. He had done it before with smaller properties around St. Francis. Once he had the deed to the land, he would break up the estate into small thirty-acre lots and sell them to new arrivals for one hundred pounds each.

European immigrants, arriving in the new country, had little or no money and purchased everything on credit. They worked hard clearing the land and building a log house for themselves. They got credit from a local store for provisions and after a harvest or two, the storekeeper would put pressure on them for repayment, either in cash or in disposable produce from the farm. Meanwhile, the unpaid interest on the original loan would keep accumulating. The family would soon find itself poorer than when they started working the land. After a hopeless struggle to pay off their debts, the land would revert back to the former owner or be sold again to a new arrival at a higher price. It was a profitable business. sucking new immigrants dry.

It wasn't dark yet when Maloney rode up to the house. He tied his horse to the railing and climbed the steps to the front door. Reuben opened the door and accompanied him to the drawing room, where he went straight to the drinks table.

"I'll get Miss Grenville, sir."

"You do that."

Maloney poured himself a generous shot of whisky as he waited for Daphne to arrive.

Seventy-seven

"I have good news, Miss Grenville," said Maloney.

"You better have some good news before you finish that bottle of whisky," said Daphne from the hall.

Reuben and Thaddeus looked up as Daphne entered the drawing room, wearing another dress from Emily's wardrobe.

"You are looking very lovely this evening, Miss Grenville."

"Thank you, Mr Maloney."

Maloney pulled a handwritten contract on a piece of foolscap from his saddlebag and put it on the desk before him.

"I'm not interested in acquiring the manor house, Miss Grenville, just the land," said Maloney. "I'll make you an offer for the house at a later date. I figure you've got about six hundred acres of good farmland, which would be worth about six hundred pounds in good times, but now with the cholera and the depressed state of business, the land is worth a lot less."

"He's lying, miss. I'm sure you can get two pounds an acre for the land," said Reuben, who snatched the paper from the desk and started to read.

Maloney was silent for a moment, apparently unruffled by Reuben's outburst. He was surprised to see that Reuben could read since most of the cholera men who worked for him were illiterate.

"No one is buying land these days, Miss Grenville," said Maloney, "except tenant farmers from the old country. They have little or no money and they're buying on credit."

"I don't fucking believe it," said Reuben as he read the figure at the bottom of the contract. "The bastard is only offering ten shillings an acre, miss. That's hardly enough."

"When do we get the money, Mr Maloney?" asked Daphne.

"Well, if you look at the finer details, you'll see that there are certain conditions. The money will be disbursed at the end of the growing period in October."

"October. That's not good enough."

"Well, it takes time to put together such a large sum, miss."

"We need the money now. Don't we, Reuben?"

Maloney looked at Reuben with a suspicious air.

"Please, Miss Grenville. I'm dealing solely with you," Maloney glared at Reuben, "not with this feckin eejit."

"Shut the fuck up, Maloney," said Reuben as he pulled out a bowie knife from under his coat and plunged it into the desktop near Maloney's hand. "We don't work for you no more. How much are you givin' Miss Grenville on the signing?"

"If you sign the document right now, Miss Grenville," Maloney said with growing unease, "you'll have fifty pounds in your account at the bank by tomorrow noon."

"Fifty bleedin' pounds," Daphne exploded. "Are you mad? That's robbery."

"And what about the house?" Reuben asked, still brandishing the knife. "You know that if he owns the estate lands, miss, he can force you out of the house by cutting off access to it. The house has no value without the land."

"Reuben is my financial advisor, Mr Maloney," said Daphne. "I listen to his advice."

Maloney realized his mistake coming here. He had figured that he would make two thousand pounds from selling the estate in small lots over several years. In addition, he planned to sell the estate's wheat harvest in October and net some three hundred pounds or more after expenses.

He should have met Miss Grenville alone at the hotel in town and plied her with liquor. But now he had to contend with a new player, this cheeky little Reuben gobshite with his cursory knowledge of property title deeds. He remembered that the young man had worked for his uncle, a notary in St. Francis, who handled a lot of immigrant land deals.

At a nod from Daphne, Reuben grabbed Maloney by the neck and held the knife to his throat.

"Reuben doesn't say much," said Daphne, smiling, "but he is very wise in these matters."

"Please, Miss Grenville," Maloney croaked, fearing for his life. "Maybe I can improve on my offer."

"Okay, Maloney, whadda you offering?"

"I'll go to sixty pounds because I have always been a good friend of the family," Maloney said before he gasped as Reuben dug the point of the knife into his neck. "I'll pay you the rest in October when the harvest is in. That's the best I can do in these troubled times."

Daphne was not impressed. That was hardly enough to keep her out of trouble and running from the law.

"It's a hoodwink, miss," Reuben snapped. "He's gonna harvest the wheat, sell it and then use the money to buy the estate. It won't cost him a penny."

"Let's see what he's got in his bag," Daphne said.

She opened the bag and dumped some papers and a leather purse onto the desk. In the purse, there were a dozen Spanish dollars, a few gold sovereigns worth a pound each, and a bit of paper money from the Bank of Upper Canada in dollars.

"How much is your life worth, you scumbag?" asked Daphne. "Tie him up, Reuben."

Reuben and Thaddeus used a rope to tie Maloney's hands behind his back as Daphne collected the money and looked through the paper documents.

Seventy-eight

Paolo had been about to leave the barn when Wilbur staggered out of the house. He crossed the quadrangle and entered the barn. Paolo hid behind a bale of hay and watched as Wilbur struggled to harness one of the horses. He finally succeeded and hooked up the horse to the wagon. He then led the horse and wagon out through the courtyard to the front door of the manor house.

Paolo did a quick scout of the estate buildings. It was late, and the workers had all gone home. Paolo had only caught a glimpse of Thaddeus with the tray, so he wasn't sure where he had gone. Paolo checked the cow shed first, which was full of silent ruminating cows. That left the blacksmith's shop, or possibly the chicken coop.

He tried the chicken coop first and found nothing. He was still a few feet away from the blacksmith's shop when he thought he heard a scraping sound. He stopped and listened, then hurried to the door. He glanced inside, but no one was there. The sounds were louder now and coming from the storeroom. Paolo tried to open the door, but it was locked.

He lit an oil lamp and looked around the shop before he found a set of keys on a hook on the wall near the forge. The larger key turned easily in the lock, and he pushed the door open. He came face to face with Emily in the doorway holding a metal bar.

"It's me, Emily," he whispered.

"Paolo!" she exclaimed, dropping the bar and rushing into his arms. "You came. I can't believe it."

"I never made it to Port Stanley. Daphne and her gang of thugs attacked us on the road. I got away, but I don't know what happened to your man, Smiley."

"I heard. You came back. This is amazing, Paolo."

"Let's get out of here," said Paolo, taking Emily by the hand and leading her out of the blacksmith's shop.

"What's going on? I saw Daphne in the house."

"I think Daphne is trying to sell the estate. We must stop her."

They headed toward the manor house and entered quietly through the kitchen.

"Daphne has a gun, Paolo," whispered Emily. "She won't hesitate to use it. There's a pistol in a drawer upstairs. It belonged to my father."

They stealthily climbed the stairs and Paolo removed the flintlock pistol from a cabinet. He quickly set about loading the pistol. He poured black powder down the muzzle and then rammed the ball and a cloth patch down until it fit tightly in the barrel. He then poured some fine black powder into the flash pan and nodded to Emily that he was ready.

They went back down the stairs, Paolo in the lead. The house was eerily silent. Paolo motioned for Emily to stay behind him and then stepped cautiously into the drawing room, holding the pistol.

Maloney was hanging from a beam with bloody knife wounds to his torso. His throat had been cut. Paolo whirled around and managed to stifle Emily's terrified scream with a hand over her mouth. Finally, she nodded to him, her eyes wide with shock, and he took his hand away.

"Stay here," he whispered as he went in to take a closer look.

There was blood all over the floor. Maloney had been gagged, and his face was a ghastly rictus of pain and suffering.

"He's dead?" asked Emily.

"Yes. It looks like he was tortured," said Paolo.

"Watch out!" Emily yelled.

Paolo turned and nearly pulled the trigger on young Wilbur. The boy staggered to his feet, rubbing his eyes. It looked like he was drunk and had fallen asleep.

"You killed Maloney?" Paolo demanded.

"No, sir, not me," Wilbur said, his voice slurred. "That was Reuben. He's as crazy as that bitch Daphne."

"Where'd they go?"

"They're after his money. I've had enough. I'm going home."

The young man stumbled out of the room and Paolo let him go. The front door slammed shut.

"We've got to find the constable," said Emily.

"No, we don't," said Paolo. "I'm not going to jail for another murder."

"We don't?" asked Emily.

"No, the constable arrested me for killing Lionel, Baxter, and the boys. I don't need to add to my crimes."

"Then we better get rid of the body," said Emily.

Paolo quickly dragged a wooden chair over and went into the kitchen to get a knife. He climbed up on the chair and cut down the funeral director.

"I'll dump the body in the quarry, Emily. It's not far from here. You can clean up the place while I'm gone."

Seventy-nine

Gerty didn't like leaving her milking chores so late, but she'd been so busy with her mother's sewing that she'd lost track of time. Her mother was putting the twins to bed and wanted some fresh milk for the morning.

The barn was on the hill behind the family cottage. It wasn't far, but Gerty knew from experience that it wasn't an easy walk back with a full bucket of milk in the dark. The cow was agitated as Gerty sat down on the stool and felt the hardness of the udder. Gerty stripped out each teat a few times before collecting the milk in the bucket.

She liked milking the cow and whistled a tune as she worked. After she had been at it for a while, she heard footsteps approaching and looked up to see Mr Benton step into the light of the oil lamp by the door.

"Hey, Gerty."

Gerty stopped milking at the sound of his voice.

"When are you comin' to work for my Ginny?" he asked. "I ain't heard nothin' back from you."

"I can't, Mr Benton. I'm gonna be returning to the manor in a few days."

"Someone's been bad mouthin' my Ginny. That wouldn't be you, would it?"

"No, sir. I ain't said nothin' about your new girlfriend."

"She's my cousin, I tell you."

"No, she ain't, Mr Benton."

"You callin' me a liar?"

"No, sir, but the gossip says different."

Gerty didn't like to be in the barn alone with Benton. She got up and gave the cow a comforting pat on the rump before picking up the half-full bucket of milk. She was on her way out the door when Benton seized her arm.

"What they're sayin'?" he demanded.

"Mr Benton, it ain't got nothin' to do with me."

Benton tightened his grip on her arm.

"I got a right to know. What are they're sayin'?" he insisted. Ginny had been complaining about being shunned by the neighbours. They refused to talk to her, and rumours were rife in the town.

"They're saying," Gerty said testily as she pulled her arm away, "that you killed Elizabeth."

"That's a nasty lie!"

"That's what they're sayin'."

"Is that you spreading them lies, Gerty?"

"No, sir."

"You lyin' bitch."

Benton struck Gerty across the mouth with the back of his hand and she fell down, spilling the milk in the bucket.

"You are mad," she whispered, too angry to be scared. "The gossip is true then. You killed Elizabeth."

Benton went almost purple with rage, and Gerty knew she'd gone too far. He took a riding crop off a wall hook and struck her on the arm with it as she made a break for the door.

Benton wanted to chase her down, but he knew he'd never catch her. He watched her race down the hill, so he headed up over the rise to collect his horse. Now the rumours would be even worse.

The house was quiet when Gerty opened the door and then locked it behind her. Her mother was exhausted and had gone to bed. Alfred was whittling a piece of wood by the fire.

"What happened to you, Gerty?" asked Alfred.

"Quiet, Alfred. I don't want you to wake Mama," Gerty whispered as she glanced down at her arm and saw the ugly red welt from the riding crop. "That bastard Benton attacked me while I was milking."

"What?" Alfred asked, his eyes wide.

"Mama won't be happy. I spilt the milk."

"Is he gonna come after us?"

"I don't know what he's gonna do, Alfred. He hit me with a riding crop. He killed his wife. He's gone mad."

"I'll get the musket," Alfred said, jumping up and running to the hall closet.

"Leave it, Alfred," Gerty said, exhausted. She had to stifle a smile. The old musket was bigger than he was.

"I'll shoot 'im if he comes in the door."

"He ain't gonna attack us at home, Alfred."

"You sure, Gerty?"

"Don't worry. Now put that away and go up to bed."

Alfred reluctantly put down the musket and started up the stairs. He stopped, fighting back tears, and looked at his sister.

"I don't want nothin' to happen to you, Gerty."

"Ain't nothin' gonna happen to me, dear brother. Go on up with you. I'll be up shortly."

Gerty didn't feel half as confident as she'd tried to sound with her brother. She wanted to talk to her mother, but her mother had her own problems. Her dad had died from an accident at the sawmill when Gerty was younger and her mother struggled to keep the roof over their heads.

Eighty

In the moonlight Reuben fumbled with Maloney's keys, trying to open the door. He finally got it open and led them inside. Daphne wordlessly held out her hand for the keys and he handed them over. Reuben knew Maloney's building well, but it was pitch dark inside and he lit a match so he could see better. He heard Daphne gasp in surprise. The feeble light of the match had revealed a row of coffins lining the wall.

"Carpentry shop," he grinned. "The office is upstairs."

Daphne glared at him, embarrassed, then followed Reuben and Thaddeus up the stairs. There were two large rooms on the second floor, an office belonging to Maloney and another for staff. Maloney's office had a large table in the middle of the room, an old roll-top desk and a tall drinks' cabinet along the wall next to a filing cabinet. While Reuben lit the oil lamp on the table, Thaddeus drew the curtains. Daphne brushed past Reuben and sat down at the roll-top.

"This is where we get rich, boys," said Daphne, her eyes gleaming with anticipation in the dim light.

Reuben and Thaddeus had already started searching the office as Daphne went through Maloney's keys until she found one that fit and unlocked the first drawer. She rummaged through the contents but found only loose papers, not even a cash box. Reuben had given up looking for a wall safe and was going through the filing cabinet while Thaddeus had pulled up an old rug looking for a cache under a loose plank. Daphne thought she heard footsteps and ducked behind the cabinet just as Biggs appeared in the doorway.

"Don't move, you gobshites," said Biggs, standing in the doorway with two loaded flintlock pistols in his hands. "What makes you arseholes think you can come in here and steal us blind?"

Daphne came out from behind the cabinet and aimed her pocket pepperbox at Biggs' head.

"Well, well," he sneered, not the least bit surprised. "If it isn't Miss Daphne back from the dead? I liked you better lying in a pine box in the cemetery."

"Maloney's dead," Daphne said. "We figure he's got money hidden away."

"Dead? I don't believe it. That man's got nine lives."

"We kill't the bastard," Reuben said. "Now where you keepin' his money?"

"See, you nitwits don't know nothin'. Maloney never kept any money 'round here, what with the workmen comin' and goin'. I don't know where his hidey-hole is, but it sure ain't in here."

"Well, where the hell is it?" asked Reuben. "All we want is our share."

"Your share? What makes you think you got a share coming, a gobshite like you?"

"Come on, Biggs," Thaddeus whined.

"You're nuts, comin' in here," Biggs said. "Would you put that gun away, Miss Daphne?"

"You first," said Daphne.

"Get the hell out of here, all of you!" Biggs shouted.

Reuben and Thaddeus marched silently past Biggs while Daphne lowered her gun and waited. Biggs sat down at the table, laying the pistols in front of him near a pile of files.

"You know something, don't you, Biggs?" asked Daphne. "Suppose I give you thirty percent of everything we find?"

"Thirty, no way," said Biggs with a laugh.

Daphne sat down on the edge of the table.

"Fifty and maybe I'll give you something else to remember me by," said Daphne with a smile.

"Miss Daphne, you know that Maloney was after your estate. He was always trying to buy up property on the cheap. If he couldn't get it one way, he'd steal it another way."

"Where'd he live?"

"That's easy. He lived at the hotel in town. He had a room on the top floor. He did his bizness in the bar next door."

"Maybe he left his money in the room?"

"Impossible. Too many people around, not to mention the chambermaids. No, Maloney would hide his money where none could find it."

Eighty-one

Paolo silently led his horse around the perimeter of the quarry in the moonlight. Maloney's body was draped over the saddle. The land near the edge was unstable and dropped away into the quarry some fifty feet below. The horse was skittish, with the smell of blood in its nostrils, and it was all Paolo could do to keep it under control while he cut the ropes that secured the body to the saddle.

Paolo pulled Maloney off the horse and rolled his body to the edge, then shoved him off the cliff. He heard a dull thud as the body struck the bottom. He led the horse away from the edge before he mounted it.

That was when he decided to go after them. Daphne and the others had tortured Maloney for a reason, and it had something to do with money or the estate or both. If they'd already got what they wanted, they'd be long gone. The only place he could think of looking was the carpenter's shop.

"It ain't gonna be easy to find his hidey-hole," said Biggs after he had poured himself a drink. "You know, the first place I'd go is the cemetery."

"What?"

"You heard me. He was an undertaker. He was over there all the time and the Maloneys have a plot in the cemetery."

"You think he hid his loot in a grave."

"Sure, why not? He could dig all the holes he wanted over there, day and night, and nobody would say a word."

"Okay. Good, we better get going," said Daphne, who stood up and was about to walk out of the office.

"Cian Maloney."

"What's that?"

"The father's name. He's buried in the southeast corner."

Daphne walked out and joined Reuben and Thaddeus in the wagon parked near the front door. Reuben whipped the horse, and the wagon took off along the rutted track.

Hiding in the trees, Paolo observed the scene. He wanted to follow the wagon, but was curious as to who Daphne was meeting in the middle of the night. There was a thin glimmer of light showing between the drapes of an upstairs window. He thought he would have a quick peek inside before following Daphne's wagon to town.

He led his horse down towards the carpenter's shop and tied it to the railing. He entered the shop as silently as he could in his leather boots. The loose stone on the cement floor made scraping sounds as he walked past the upright coffins and the cutting table. He arrived at the staircase leading upstairs and could see Biggs in the office pacing back and forth. He backtracked and slipped into the viewing room on the shop floor. He unlocked a window leading to the back of the building and left.

Reuben searched the Maloney plot in the cemetery while Daphne and Thaddeus waited in the wagon. It was too dark to see much with the moonlight filtered by the branches of trees. Reuben went from headstone to headstone with an oil lamp, trying to find a loose stone with a cavity of some kind.

"It's too fuckin' dark to see anything," complained Thaddeus, sitting with Daphne in the wagon.

"We better come back in the morning," said Daphne.

"Gimme a minute," said Reuben. "Just a couple more to go."

Reuben ran his hand over the last headstone with the Maloney name. The headstone suddenly broke apart, revealing a deep cavity in its base. He held up the oil lamp.

"Hey, I got something here," he yelled.

Daphne and Thaddeus jumped down off the wagon and ran over.

"What you got, Reuben?" Thaddeus asked eagerly, picking up the oil lamp.

"Ah, shit. It's just some animal been diggin' in here."

Thaddeus knelt beside Reuben.

"Let me look," said Thaddeus, who stuck his hand in the hole and came up with sand and bits of dirt.

"That sonofabitch!" Daphne exclaimed angrily. "Biggs sent us out here for nothing."

Daphne and the cholera men gave up and climbed back on the wagon. They drove back to town..

Hidden in the bushes, Paolo had observed them searching for something near the tomb of a member of the St. Francis gentry. It had taken him no time to catch up with their wagon on its way to the cemetery. He had followed the wagon at a slow pace, careful not to make any noise, then hidden his horse in the trees in the new part of the cemetery.

He waited until he could no longer hear the horse's hooves on the road before he approached the tomb in the dark. He lit a match near the name of Cian Maloney, and it became clear to him. They had killed the man's son, but it was his loot that eluded them.

Eighty-two

It was almost dawn by the time Paolo returned to the carpenter's shop. The front door was locked, so he crept into the building through the viewing room window. It was deathly quiet as he climbed the stairs to Maloney's office. He slipped inside and lit the oil lamp on the table as he looked around. The drawers of the roll-top were open and someone had been searching through them. He went to the cabinet and looked inside at the bottles of whisky and gin. The filing cabinet nearby was full of old files gathering dust, which held little or no interest for him. He returned to the fine old English writing desk, simple in design, with carved wood trim and decorative pilasters on the front. Paolo brought over the oil lamp and sat down to admire the workmanship. Maloney had good taste. The roll-top was a beautiful piece of work with a unique design.

Paolo's dad was a carpenter who had built several old writing desks with hidden drawers, so Paolo had a deep appreciation of the workmanship. They were popular in Genoa with the aristocracy and very expensive to produce with their intricate design. He squatted down and inspected each pilaster. He pulled out one pilaster to reveal a small tray behind it. The tray was empty, but Paolo discovered a moveable separator which, when he pulled it out, revealed a large drawer in the back of the desk full of documents including deeds to land holdings, bearer bonds, contracts, and stacks of banknotes.

Emily sat alone in the drawing room, waiting for Paolo to return. She had washed up and put on some clean clothes after her time in the sooty blacksmith's shop. She was exhausted and worried. The quarry wasn't far away, and Paolo should have been back by now. Where was he? Had he gotten rid of Maloney's body? He was supposed to return as soon as he had dumped the body.

She had removed all traces of Maloney's visit and carried the dirty glasses used by Daphne and her crew out to the kitchen. The room looked a lot cleaner and more respectable. She had turned down the oil lamp because she didn't want to attract attention from passers-by as she watched the road through the window.

She fell asleep on the daybed and was awakened at dawn by a voice calling from the kitchen. She got up and went to have a look. The house was empty and silent as a tomb. An anxious voice was calling from behind the kitchen door.

"Miss Emily, please open the door. It's me, Gerty."

"Gerty? What are you doing here?" asked Emily as she opened the door and Gerty fell into her arms.

"Are you all right?"

"Lock the door, miss! There's someone after me."

Emily let go of Gerty and looked out at the pasture. Daylight was just coming up in the east, and the grass was wet with morning dew. She craned her neck out the door, but couldn't see anyone.

"Please, miss!" Gerty said as she grasped her arm and pulled her back inside.

She slammed the door shut and turned the knob to lock it.

"What's going on, Gerty?"

"It's a long story, Miss Emily. Please, let's go into the drawing room. There's a man after me. He followed me out here."

"Who is this man?" asked Emily as Gerty led her out of the kitchen.

"Wait," Gerty said. She rushed back into the kitchen and emerged a moment later with a butcher knife. "Just in case he gets into the house."

"Gets into the house?" Emily asked, struggling to keep up with what was happening. "What man? What are you talking about?"

Eighty-three

"It's Mr Benton, miss. He killed his wife and now he's after me."

"Gerty, this is mad," Emily said as they sat down on the daybed.

"I knew his wife Elizabeth," Gerty said, her eyes on the windows. "She lived across the road from our house. I heard a gunshot the night she died. I think he killed her so he could marry Ginny. She ain't his cousin. She's just a cheap hussy."

"A cheap hussy! Really, Gerty. That's not a very nice thing to say about her."

"Well, if you saw her, miss, you would have no doubt."

"Gerty, what kind of pickle have you got yourself into?"

"There!" Gerty pointed out the window.

A man on horseback appeared on the road from St. Francis. The rider trotted along the hedgerow and then turned his horse into the estate. Emily and Gerty went from window to window, following his progress as he dismounted near the kitchen door. He tried to open the locked door by kicking at it. It was a solid oak-framed wooden door with cross battens. Finally, he stepped back, enraged.

"Gerty, come out," he bellowed. "I know you're in there."

"I told you he was crazy, miss," said Gerty, looking terrified. "Do you have a gun?"

"Yes, it's over there on the table. Be careful, it's loaded."

"Good."

Gerty went to fetch the flintlock pistol and returned.

"Do you know how to use it, Gerty?"

"Sure I do. My mama taught me."

Outside the kitchen, Benton gave up on the door and went around the house to the stables in the back.

"Is the back door locked?" asked Gerty.

"Yes, it is. Don't worry, Gerty, there is no way he can get in here."

Emily was wrong. Benton had no intention of giving up. He soon found an axe in the barn and returned to attack the kitchen door. The axe cut cleanly through the oak planks and fractured the cross battens that held the door in place. Emily and Gerty ran into the kitchen and stared, horrified, as Benton swung a second time with the axe. Gerty recovered first.

"Hurry," she shouted, putting the gun and the knife on the kitchen counter, and running over to a heavy armoire near the wall. "Let's block the door."

Together, they pushed the armoire in front of the door, just as another blow of the axe shattered an oak plank. Benton could now see the two women through the holes in the door.

"Come out, Gerty," Benton said impatiently. "I just wanna talk."

"You killed Elizabeth, Mr Benton. Now you want to kill me, too."

"I won't hurt you, Gerty."

"Go away, Mr Benton," ordered Emily. "This is Emily Grenville, this is my house, you have no right. Go away."

"I can't, Miss Emily. I won't go without Gerty."

He swung the axe again. The impact collapsed a batten, producing a hole at chest level. Benton snaked a hand through the hole and tried to seize Gerty by the throat, but she grabbed the knife and slashed at his arm. He quickly removed his arm.

"He's gonna be through that door any moment," screamed Gerty as they pushed with all their strength to hold the armoire in place.

"Get the gun, Emily," cried Gerty, holding the knife. "I'll cut him if he tries to put his arm through again."

Emily grabbed the flintlock pistol from the counter as Benton charged the door. The armoire rocked backwards, and Benton came at the door again. Emily aimed the pistol through the hole in the door and waited for Benton to appear in her sights.

"Shoot him, miss, shoot him," yelled Gerty.

Benton gave a huge kick to the door, and the armoire slammed into Emily just as she pulled the trigger. The sound of the shot was thunderous in the room. A cloud of acrid, sulphuric smoke obscured their view of the door and then, there was silence.

"Did you hit him?" Gerty asked.

"I don't know."

They pushed the armoire back against the door and waited for Benton to mount another attack. Finally, Gerty stood on tiptoe and risked a peek over the armoire.

"I can't see anything from here, miss. Maybe you scared him off. Stay here and I'll take a look from the front room."

Gerty ran back through the drawing room. After a moment, she returned.

"He's on the ground, Miss Emily. I think you killed him."

Emily and Gerty pulled the armoire out of the way and opened the door. Benton lay on his back on the grass, bleeding from a chest wound.

"You kill't me, miss. Why'd you do that?"

"'Cause you deserved it, you bastard," said Gerty.

"You were trying to break into my house, Mr Benton," retorted Emily. "That's why I shot you."

Benton was losing blood fast and struggling to breathe as Emily rolled up her shawl and put it under his head.

"Please, Gerty, get me some sheets or dish towels. We need to stop the bleeding."

"He ain't gonna make it, miss," said Gerty. "Let him die, I say. Good riddance."

"Please, Gerty."

Reluctantly, Gerty returned to the kitchen while Emily tried to stop the bleeding by putting pressure on the wound with bits of Benton's shirt.

Eighty-four

Emily sat quietly in the drawing room, wrapped in a blanket. There was blood on her hands and blouse.

Gerty came in from the kitchen with a tea tray.

"He's dead, miss. There was nothing you could do for him."

"Yes, I know," said Emily, looking exhausted and in a state of shock from the incident.

"Are you hungry, miss? You look rather pale. I can fix some eggs and toast."

"That would be lovely, Gerty, but first let's have a drink."

"A drink, miss?"

"See that bottle of brandy in the cabinet?"

"The one on the top?"

"Yes, that's the one."

Gerty hesitantly picked up the bottle and two crystal whisky glasses that had belonged to Emily's father. She poured one for Emily and a small one for herself.

"I don't drink much, miss," said Gerty, "but this sure is one special occasion. You saved my life."

"It's not every day that I kill a man, Gerty."

"You did the right thing, miss. Mr Benton was crazy."

"I don't regret it, Gerty," said Emily, sipping the brandy and smiling as she thought of her parents.

"The drink will take the edge off. My father used to say that a lot. It always infuriated my mother. She'd ask him what edge was that? What did he ever have to complain about?"

"I'm sorry about your mother, miss."

"I am too, Gerty," said Emily with tears in her eyes.

They sat in silence for a long moment.

"My mother was a shrew, Gerty," said Emily. "She was always fussing and was not an easy person to live with."

Gerty tried her brandy and coughed as the hard liquor hit her throat.

"Take it slow, Gerty."

"When do you think we'll be getting back to work, miss?"

"I don't know. Soon, I hope," said Emily. "Let's eat. Then we have to go to town to find the constable."

Fuller was napping with his feet on the desk in the office. He jumped when he heard Riley come in the door.

"I thought you weren't coming in until later, sir," Fuller said.

"I can see that," Riley said, mocking his deputy. "Let's get Buckley and Pullman ready for the show. Then I have to go to the hotel to meet with the witnesses."

"Yes, sir."

"Bring 'em out one at a time so we can put the chains and shackles on them."

As Fuller went off to fetch the two looters, a young boy entered the office.

"Constable," said Alfred, looking very agitated.

"Hello, Alfred," said Riley. "How's your mum doing?"

"She's fine, sir."

"What can I do for you?"

Eighty-five

Constable Riley was drinking tea in the hotel dining room as he waited for Eleanor and Clara to arrive to testify in court. He was confident that the Red Buckley case would go well. His only fear was that the judge might not accept Eleanor's self-defence claim when she fired her musket at the man, but he figured the worst she risked was a fine. The judge liked to collect fines to pay for his services and those of the court. He noticed the familiar profile of Biggs coming into the hotel lobby and heading up the stairs. He paid the waiter and followed Biggs.

Riley climbed to the top floor landing and watched as Biggs fiddled with the lock on the door of a room at the end of the hall. It was too early for the maids to be cleaning the rooms, and the hallway was deserted. Biggs got the door open and went inside, closing the door behind him. The constable headed down the hall and listened outside the door. It sounded like Biggs was moving furniture.

Riley frowned and opened the door a crack. There was a chest of drawers along one wall with clothes dangling from them. The contents of the bedside table had been dumped on the bed.

"What are you doing here?" Riley demanded, stepping into the room.

Biggs stood up with a guilty expression.

"Nothing, Constable."

Riley almost laughed but reminded himself to be vigilant. Biggs was a dangerous man.

"I believe this room belongs to your boss," Riley said. "Did Mr Maloney give you permission to come in here?"

Biggs remained silent.

"Mind telling me what you are looking for?"

"It ain't none of your business, sir."

"You're right, Biggs," said Riley. "It ain't none of my business, but I'm warning you. Be careful where you tread, my friend."

Riley turned and left the room.

Since courthouses were scarce in Western Ontario, the proceedings took place in the guildhall near the hotel. The looters Red Buckley and Eugene Pullman were being tried for theft and assault at the Smythe Manor. Judge Waters with his baldpate, side whiskers and thick spectacles, sat on the bench, reading the constable's report and asking questions of the witnesses. Clara Torrey stood nervously next to Eleanor Ross, sitting in the front row while Constable Riley sat several rows behind them.

"Mrs Torrey, please tell us what happened when you and the sisters arrived at the manor house?"

"We were attacked by Mr Buckley and Mr Pullman. They were looting the house, sir. Buckley smelled of whisky and was holding a pistol when he came out of the house and threatened us."

"What did he say?"

"He told us to leave immediately, but then he changed his mind. He said he would hold two of our group hostage, sir. He held the pistol to my head."

"Why did he want to hold back two women?"

"He wanted to have some fun with them. Those were his words, sir."

Eighty-six

Judge Waters smiled at Clara and looked over at the two looters in shackles guarded by Deputy Fuller. Buckley looked red-faced and angry as he listened to the testimony.

"You can sit down, Mrs Torrey."

"Now, Mr Buckley, please stand up."

Deputy Fuller kicked Buckley, who struggled to stand up with his fettered arms and legs.

"Mr Buckley, you say in your defence that you have done nothing wrong, but were you not holding a pistol to Mrs Torrey's head and making threats?"

"No, sir. That is not true. I never had a pistol, so I couldn't have threatened anyone."

"The pistol was not yours?"

"No, sir. It belonged to the sisters."

Clara gasped at the barefaced lie. She was about to protest when Eleanor whispered to her to keep her mouth shut.

"So how did it get into your hands?" asked the judge.

"I took it away from her, sir. She's the one who had the pistol."

"You mean that Mrs Torrey had the pistol, and you took it away from her?"

"Yes, sir. She was threatening me with it, sir."

"And why would she threaten you?"

Buckley was getting more and more confused by the questions.

"I think she wanted to steal our things, sir."

"Thank you, Mr Buckley. You can sit down."

The judge turned to Clara.

"Now Mrs Torrey, what happened next?"

"Eleanor Ross came up on the porch with a musket and told Buckley to stop, but he refused, so she shot him."

"Mrs Ross, why did you shoot this man?"

Eleanor stood up nervously and addressed the court in her usual matter-of-fact way of talking.

"I could see Buckley was a mean sonofabitch, sir," said Eleanor. "He was drunk and red in the face and sweating like the disgusting pig he is. You could tell by the way he was treating the sisters, he was gonna fire the pistol at Clara at any moment out of sheer spite. I couldn't take a chance, so I shot him, plain and simple, the way I'd shoot any kind of varmint."

"You claim you shot Buckley in self-defence?"

"Yes, sir. I had no choice. That fat bastard was turning the pistol on me when I shot him."

"Thank you, Mrs Ross. You can sit down."

The judge poured whisky into his cup of tea as he reflected on the case. He turned to Constable Riley to ask a question.

"Constable, can you tell me how much money these men were carrying?"

Constable Riley stood up to answer.

"They had twelve pounds in cash, sir, and a wagon full of stolen goods. The goods have been auctioned off for a sum of four pounds, five shillings."

"Very good. Are the funds here?"

"Yes, sir."

"Thank you, Constable."

The judge drank his tea and lit a cheroot. Buckley and Pullman squirmed uneasily in their chairs as he stared at them for a long moment before taking out a pen and writing on the paper in front of him. He finished writing and then looked up at the witnesses.

"Everyone stands for sentencing."

Deputy Fuller kicked Buckley to get him back on his feet as the women and the constable stood up for the verdict. Eleanor was worried that Red Buckley might be let off and would come after her. She knew the type, holding grudges and beating up women whenever he got a chance.

"I find Mr Buckley and Mr Pullman," said Judge Waters clearing his throat, "guilty of looting and theft for which they will forfeit the value of the goods and pay a fine of ten pounds and court fees to the amount of six pounds five shillings. I find Mr Buckley guilty of assault on Mrs Torrey, for which he will be remanded to the prison in Hamilton for a sentence of three years of hard labour. Mr Pullman is free to go. Thank you, ladies and gentlemen. Good day."

Eleanor and Clara exchanged a look of relief. They were filing out when Riley joined them.

"Well, ladies," he smiled. "Congratulations! You did very well. You can testify in my courtroom any day."

"Your courtroom?" laughed Eleanor.

"Let's have a drink to celebrate," said Riley, smiling. He was also happy to empty out his jail and rid himself of that whiner Buckley.

"We don't have much time, Constable," Clara said. "We need to get back."

"Oh, I'm sure you do," Riley said with a smile, "but maybe you'd like a cup of tea before riding out there in the heat."

"Come on, Clara," Eleanor implored. "We have time."

"Very good," said Clara, nodding.

They were going out through the doors when they heard a ruckus behind them. Buckley had swung a length of loose chain from one of his shackles and had hit Pullman hard in the face. He was about to swing it again when Deputy Fuller hit him with a billy club, knocking him down. Riley turned back to Eleanor.

"I reckon he didn't like the verdict," he grinned.

Red was furious that Eugene had got off scot-free while he was going to prison. *The judge had stolen his loot, and now he would have to wait three years to teach the musket bitch a lesson. The world was so unjust.*

Eighty-seven

Daphne and the cholera men returned to the Grenville Manor in the afternoon to find a dead man lying near the fractured kitchen door. Reuben stepped down from the wagon to get a better look at the man.

"It's Benton from the sawmill, Miss Daphne. What's he doing here?"

"I don't know. Better check inside."

Reuben stepped into the kitchen through the broken-down door, followed by Thaddeus and Daphne.

"Hey, Wilbur. Where are you, my man?" yelled Reuben.

"He's gone," said Thaddeus.

"Wilbur, you lazy son of a gun. Where you at?"

"He's taken off, probably gone home."

They entered the drawing room, and Daphne immediately noticed the disappearance of Maloney's body.

"Where's Maloney?" asked Daphne.

"What happened to the body?" asked Thaddeus.

"Shit, if I know," said Reuben. "The old bastard didn't walk out of here all by hisself."

"We better search the house," said Daphne.

As the men went about searching the premises, Daphne climbed to Emily's bedroom on the first floor. She suddenly had a thought and ran back downstairs.

"Thaddeus, go check on Emily."

As Thaddeus left the house through the back door to go to the blacksmith's shop, Reuben returned from the kitchen.

"There's no one around, Daphne."

Emily and Gerty were in the stable, harnessing a horse to the calash when they heard the back door slam. They ducked down as Thaddeus crossed the quadrangle on his way to the blacksmith's shop. They finished hooking up Emily's favourite horse, a white gelding, to the calash when Thaddeus came running back to the house.

"She's gone, Daphne. She ain't there no more," Thaddeus yelled as he entered the house.

Emily and Gerty led the horse and calash silently out of the stable and through the back of the estate to the farmland beyond.

Riley was having his lunch in the hotel bar after Eleanor and Clara left for the Smythe Manor. The place was almost empty except for Judge Waters and a rather plump, red-lipped woman who were carrying on at a far table.

"Judge," she smiled, tugging at his arm, "let's go upstairs."

"What?" Waters laughed. "You think I can't stand up?"

"No, I never said anything of the sort. I said, let's get a room upstairs."

"I already got a room upstairs, miss."

"Okay, sir, let's go."

The woman helped the judge get to his feet, and they stumbled out of the bar together. The judge recognized the constable and nodded briefly before leaving.

"He's in his cups again," said Eddy, the barman. "Judge Waters comes in every couple of Thursdays after doing his business over at the guildhall, eats a steak dinner and gets drunk."

"You should see him in court," Riley said, grinning at the barman. "He's always got a flask of whisky going behind the bench."

"How'd it go with fat arse Buckley?" Eddy asked. "What's he getting for looting the Smythe Manor?"

"Three years for assault. He threatened a woman with a pistol. Judge Waters doesn't like violence towards Christian women."

"Damn, I never would have thought. What about his buddy Pullman?"

"Got off with a fine."

"I don't know, sir, but Pullman can be worse than Buckley. He right disfigured a quarry worker he didn't like."

"Did he now?" asked Riley. "I better keep an eye on him."

Riley paid and got up to leave.

Eighty-eight

Riley returned to the jail and found an old poor box that churches used to collect alms sitting on his desk with his name on it. Fuller had gone out to look into a farmer's complaint and was not back yet. The box was not locked, so he slid off the cover and found it filled with documents and cash. There was a handwritten note on the top. It read:

MALONEY IS DEAD,
DAPHNE HAD HIM KILLED

Riley looked inside the box. There were numerous deeds to property that had been signed over to Maloney during the outbreak of cholera and before. He knew some of the names. They were mostly 'deathbed deeds'.

Obviously, Maloney had made it his business to keep an eye on the property owners in his district. If someone came down with cholera, he would swoop in and provide some kind of last-minute service to the family, who then made him a gift of property on the condition of death. A deathbed gift or *Donatio Mortis Causa* was perfectly legal and had existed since Roman times. Of course, if the donor did not die within a short time, the deed became null and void.

Among the papers, there were loan documents for small amounts with exorbitant interest rates payable each week. Maloney was St. Francis' own Shylock, exploiting both the rich and the poor. In the bottom of the box, Riley found stacks of banknotes and a bag of gold sovereigns.

Someone had killed Maloney for this box. Who was the good Samaritan who had delivered Maloney's riches to his doorstep? It wouldn't be Biggs doing him a favour, although Biggs did have access and had been searching for something in the man's hotel room. Maybe it was someone working at the carpenter's shop or quarry.

"Have you seen Mr Maloney, James?" Riley asked, standing in a small cubbyhole off the front desk of the hotel.

"Nope," said the hotel manager, preoccupied with the tally of the week's receipts. "I ain't seen 'im for a day or two."

"I need to get into his room. Do you have a key for me?"

The manager hesitated a moment and then acquiesced to the constable's request.

"I won't touch anything. It'll only take a moment."

"Five minutes, sir. No more. Mr Maloney won't be pleased if he catches you in his room."

Riley nodded and headed up the stairs.

On the top floor, a cleaning woman was finishing up her work with a pail of soapy water and a mop. The constable tried the key to Maloney's door, but it was not locked. He entered the room and found it in the same disorder as Biggs had left it. As he was looking around the room, the door opened and the cleaning lady appeared on the threshold.

"Sorry to bother you, sir. I thought you were Mr Maloney."

"Have you seen him, ma'am?"

"No, sir. He's usually gone when I make my rounds. He don't like me coming into his room when he's not here, but I gotta clean sometime."

"Well, thank you, ma'am."

The young woman turned around and shut the door. Riley ran his hand under the horsehair mattress but found nothing. He pulled out his watch chain to look at the time and then left the room, locking the door.

Eighty-nine

It was getting late as Smiley drove Emily and Gerty into town in the calash. They had gone out to the lake cottage to look for Smiley after Emily expressed her fear of circulating on the roads with Daphne on the loose. The two women disembarked in front of the jail and went in to see Constable Riley.

"Miss Emily, I wasn't expecting you," Riley said as he poured himself a cup of tea.

"I have some news," said Emily, "but first Gerty has something to tell you."

"Miss Gerty, your brother Alfred came by this morning and said you hadn't come home yesterday," said Riley. "Your mother is worried about you."

"It's Mr Benton, our neighbour," said Gerty. "He chased me out to the Grenville Manor this morning."

"Benton? Young Alfred said you think he killed his wife."

"Yes, sir," Gerty said. "He's a violent man and..."

"... and a dead one," said Emily. "I had to shoot him when he tried to force his way into the manor."

"You shot him, Miss Emily?" Riley asked, astonished.

"Yes, sir. She shot him real good, right through the door," said Gerty. "Miss Emily is my hero."

"He was trying to get in," Emily said. "He chopped down the kitchen door with an axe, sir."

"Miss Emily, you seem to get into a lot of trouble. I better go out there and have a look. Where's the body?"

"You can't miss it, sir. It's just outside the kitchen," said Gerty.

"You ladies have been through a lot. Can I offer you a cup of tea, perhaps?"

"Yes, please. It was a long ride into town," said Emily, looking exhausted.

As Riley took the pot off the hob and started to pour the tea into tin cups, Gerty stood up to pour the milk.

"I have some news of my own," Emily said, accepting a cup of tea from Gerty. "It's about my sister Daphne."

"You've seen her?" said Riley, sitting down.

"She's travelling with three cholera men who are doing her bidding. They locked me up for two days in the blacksmith's shop at the estate. Daphne has been trying to sell the estate to Mr Maloney for some easy money."

"How did you free yourself, miss?"

"Paolo Morelli is back, sir. He came to the manor yesterday and set me free."

"Morelli is back? I thought he went to Detroit."

"He's innocent, sir. He didn't kill anyone."

Emily burst into tears at the thought of her dead brothers. Gerty put a comforting arm around her.

"I haven't seen him since yesterday evening, sir. He went after Daphne and the cholera men. He promised to come back, but he never did. He's disappeared."

"It's that sister of yours who seems to be behind all this mischief. I was out at the lake and I had a talk with Smiley Webb, your houseman. He and I go way back, you know."

"He told you everything?"

"Yes, miss, but he didn't give it up easily. You know that he would do anything to protect you and your family. You could have saved me a lot of trouble if you had come right out with it."

"I'm sorry, sir. She's my sister, but she has gone from bad to worse. I just don't understand what is going on inside her head."

"And you think Morelli is innocent?"

"Daphne stole Paolo's gun and used it to kill them."

"Where is she?"

"She was at the manor a while ago. We got out of there just in time."

"We better get after her," said the constable, standing up and calling to his deputy. "Fuller, we're gonna run out to the estate."

The constable took his hat off the peg as Fuller walked into the room.

"Get the horses," Riley told him.

Fuller nodded and left for the stable. Riley turned to Gerty.

"Why don't you go along home, Gerty? Your mama must be in a terrible state, worrying about you."

"Yes, sir," said Gerty, hugging Emily. "I'll come by later to give you a hand."

"Thanks, Gerty."

"Miss Emily," Riley said as Gerty left. "It's probably best that you stay here for your own safety."

"I appreciate your concern, Constable," Emily said firmly, "but I need to get back. I've got to bring back the staff and get the place cleaned up."

Ninety

As Smiley waited with Emily in the calash, Constable Riley stepped out of the jail carrying two flintlock pistols and his Nock six-barrel musket. He gave a pistol to Smiley and the other to Deputy Fuller, who arrived with two horses. They mounted their horses and followed the calash out of town.

As they passed the hotel, the manager ran outside, calling to the constable from the wooden sidewalk.

"Constable Riley, Mr Maloney still hasn't returned, and he has a client waiting for him in the lobby."

"Sorry, I can't help you now, sir."

With that, Riley spurred his horse on to catch up with his deputy and the calash. The manager watched them go and then walked reluctantly back to the hotel where an irate client was waiting for him.

"Smiley, you and Miss Emily stay out of sight behind the cow shed," Riley said. "Stay there until I come back for you."

"Yes, sir," said Smiley.

Emily remained silent with an interrogative air.

"You stay out of sight, both of you," said Riley, giving Emily a stern look.

She had been looking forward to confronting her sister. *She wanted to tell her what she thought of her vile behaviour, but Riley wasn't going to brook any arguments about her safety. Daphne and the cholera men were dangerous and might come out shooting.*

They had worked their way to the back of the estate and approached the manor through the fields, waving silently at a dozen farm workers heading home with their lunch baskets. They arrived at the cow shed and Smiley pulled up in the calash while they waited for the police constables to make their approach.

Riley and Fuller walked their horses over to the stable, keeping their eyes on the windows of the manor house. There was no sign of life at the house, so they left their horses in the stable and started towards the kitchen.

Benton lay sprawled on his back near the shattered door, a blood-caked stain in the centre of his chest. Riley had seen enough bullet wounds to know that this one would have been fatal within minutes. Miss Emily was a force to be reckoned with, killing a man in his prime like Benton, thought Riley.

The constables snuck into the house through the broken door with guns drawn. They ran into Thaddeus hidden behind Lionel's desk. He fired wildly at the constables and then ran out of the drawing room, disappearing through the front door. Fuller got off a shot with his pistol, but Riley was too slow bringing the big musket to bear.

"Go after him!" Riley ordered his deputy. "He can't have gone far."

Fuller went out the front door in pursuit of Thaddeus while Riley stepped into the foyer. He just had time to see Daphne and Reuben at the top of the stairs when he felt a hammer blow to his arm. He dropped the musket and was vaguely aware he'd been shot when Daphne and Reuben dashed down the stairs towards him. He had expected one of them to stop and finish him off, but they kept going through the foyer and out the back door. Riley forced himself to his feet, grasping the musket in his other hand, and staggered after them.

Daphne and Reuben stole the horses belonging to the constables and burst out of the stables on horseback just as Riley appeared in the courtyard. It was too late to get off a shot with the heavy Nock musket as the fugitives disappeared around the side of the manor house.

Near the road and hedge, Fuller appeared out of nowhere, running full out after Thaddeus. He was gaining on him when Reuben took up the chase and veered off, slamming his horse into the deputy and knocking him flat in the tall grass. He extended an arm to Thaddeus and swung him up into the saddle behind him. Together with Daphne, they galloped off in a westward direction along the road.

Ninety-one

Paolo on horseback had followed the creek bed several miles into the hills north of St. Francis. He knew that Daphne and her boys were holed up somewhere and they would need water to make a camp. Of course, it was a long shot, but he figured they wouldn't be staying with any local farmers because they couldn't be counted on to keep their mouths shut.

The creek wound its way west and Paolo noticed a camp with a fire pit down near the water. There was no one around, so he rode down to take a better look. There was a man's shirt drying on a branch, evidence of chicken bones in the sand near the fire, and several empty bottles of whisky lying about. He stepped closer and noticed that the embers were still warm, so he reckoned that Daphne and her boys had probably spent the night there.

Paolo was dead tired after a long night and several days on the road. He looked for a good place to set up an observation post and maybe rest up for a couple of hours. He left the camp and rode to the top of the hill.

Riley sat in a chair in the drawing room as Emily washed the wound with hot water from the stove. The injury was superficial. The small calibre ball had penetrated the skin and muscle tissue of the upper arm and exited through the back. Fuller poured Riley a glass of gin and handed it to him.

"Drink this, sir."

Riley had just taken a small sip when Emily snatched the glass out of his hand.

"That's enough of that, Constable," she said tartly, pouring the rest of the gin into the wound.

Riley gasped as the sting of alcohol hit him.

"Damn, that hurts."

"It's meant to," she said, motioning for Fuller to top up the glass. She then turned Riley's arm so she could pour the gin over the exit wound.

Riley winced again from the pain, but knew better than to complain. Emily handed the glass back to Fuller and started to bandage Riley's arm as Smiley came into the room with a tea tray.

"Where do you think they've got to?" asked Fuller.

"They could be anywhere. As soon as we're ready, let's take the wagon and run over to the quarry. It appears that Maloney has disappeared."

"Disappeared?" asked Fuller.

"He hasn't returned to his hotel room, and he missed an appointment this morning. Something's happened to him."

Emily looked alarmed and glanced at Riley as she cleaned up the mess.

"You better stay here with Smiley, miss," said Riley. "He'll protect you if they decide to return."

Emily nodded in agreement as the constable put on his shirt over the cloth bandage. She left Smiley to serve the tea to the constables and quickly disappeared into the kitchen with the bucket of bloody water and compresses.

Emily pushed the broken door aside and stood in the open doorway, looking out over the pasture. Fuller had used Reuben's wagon to remove Benton's body from the grassy patch near the door. Emily was delighted by the reversal of her situation. A great weight had been lifted from her shoulders. She was no longer a suspect in the eyes of the law and no one would ever know that Maloney had died at the manor and they had moved the body. She just hoped Paolo would return from Detroit or wherever he had gone.

She needed to go back to work. After all, she was her mother's daughter and a Grenville. This was no time for slacking. It was time to clean up the house and get the estate back on track. If her mother were to see the sorry state of the house and its finances, she would be shocked.

With their horses gone, Riley took Reuben's wagon and borrowed a horse from Miss Emily for Fuller. They set out west with Riley driving the wagon.

Near the quarry, they slowed as they saw several men with a dusty wagon talking loudly among themselves in the trees near the entrance. Fuller rode over to see what the commotion was all about. After talking to the men, he raced back to the wagon.

"Sir, they've found Maloney's body."

Riley quickly turned the wagon towards the entrance and headed over to talk to the bearded quarrymen in their long, dusty smocks. They had found Maloney's bruised and bloody corpse during the morning shift, after one of the men had noticed several carrion birds circling overhead. By the time they got over to the cliff face to investigate, the birds had already been at him. His eyes and lips were mostly gone, and much of his face was unrecognizable.

Riley climbed up on their wagon to have a look at the body. Even with all the grisly damage done by the birds, he could see the bloody tracks left by the knife wounds.

"We need to get him to town so he can be examined by a medical practitioner if we can find one," said Riley. "Can you men put him in our wagon?"

"Yes, sir," said the oldest of the group, a grizzled white beard wearing a tuque.

The quarrymen hauled the body over to Reuben's wagon and laid it next to Benton's body under a canvas sheet.

"Who's dead?" asked the white beard.

"That's Benton from the sawmill," said Fuller. "He was shot dead by Miss Grenville."

"Miss Grenville shot him?" asked a younger man.

"Yep, he was trying to break into the kitchen at the estate."

"Well, she's a Grenville, so she don't take guff from nobody," added the white beard.

"That's enough, Fuller," said Riley, who didn't want to feed the local gossip about the Grenvilles.

"What's gonna happen to our jobs?" asked another man.

"I don't know," said Riley. "I suppose Maloney's family will keep you on. Where's Biggs?"

"I saw 'im at the office, sir," said another old-timer.

Ninety-two

It was hot on the hilltop overlooking the camp. Paolo was lying in the tall grass in the shade of an oak tree. Nothing was moving down below. His plan had been simple enough: find out where Emily's sister was hiding out and alert the constable to her location. He would remain a fugitive from justice as long as Daphne was not behind bars. He knew the constable had let Emily go free, so he must have his suspicions about Daphne's involvement in the murder of Maloney and the Grenvilles. But the heat and his fatigue had gotten the better of him and he had quickly succumbed to sleep.

When he woke up, he was looking into the barrel of Reuben's pistol. Thaddeus kicked him and then pulled him to his feet. He looked around and saw that Daphne was leading his horse down the hill to the camp.

"Go on, follow her," ordered Reuben.

"You won't be getting away so easy this time," said Thaddeus with a grin. "Daphne's got plans for you."

Paolo set off after Daphne followed by the cholera boys.

Carpenters and quarrymen were congregating around the door to the shop as Riley and Fuller arrived. They climbed down from the wagon and approached.

"Constable, you heard the news?" said a man in a dusty apron. "Maloney's dead. Who's gonna pay us for our work today?"

"I'm sure Mr Biggs can handle it. Let us through, please."

Riley and Fuller pushed their way through the gauntlet of distraught employees and stepped inside the shop. They looked around at the coffins leaning up against the walls. Some were for small children. Some were varnished and well made, some were only cheap wooden planks nailed together to hold the lid in place and to support a cloth covering.

They moved on past the cutting table and up the stairs to the offices. Riley knocked on the door before entering and surprised a man writing entries in a big ledger with a steel dip pen. He looked up as they came in.

"Gentlemen, can I help you?"

"Thank you. Mister?"

"Jennings. I'm the bookkeeper for the quarry and the carpentry shop, sir."

"I'm Constable Riley and this is Deputy Fuller. Is Mr Biggs around?"

"There's been a terrible tragedy, sir. Mr Maloney is dead, but I think you must know that already."

"We need to speak to Biggs. Where is he?"

"He's stepped out. The men are worried about their jobs and want their pay."

Jennings pointed to the back door and returned to work as Riley and Fuller left the building. They found Biggs sitting on a bench in the shade and smoking a clay pipe.

"Mr Biggs, there you are," said Riley.

"Maloney's dead. That's all anyone is talking about around here."

"You didn't kill him, did you?" Riley asked.

"No, sir," Biggs snorted. "He's my boss. Why would I kill him? Someone dumped his body in the quarry. That's all I know."

"You were searching his room at the hotel. I think you know something."

"I can't talk about that, sir."

"Mr Biggs, you've been holding out on me ever since I caught you grave-robbing. It's about time I heard the truth."

"Constable, I cain't help you right now. I gotta find the money to pay the men before they tear the building apart."

"Biggs, I've had enough of your lies," Riley said in a foul mood as he nodded at Fuller. The deputy drew his pistol and aimed it at Biggs.

Riley moved fast, grabbing Biggs and yanking his arms behind his back before he cuffed him.

"You're under arrest. Fuller, go get the wagon."

"But, Constable," Biggs protested, "what about the men?"

"I'll talk to them. I'm sure Mr Maloney has the funds to pay them. Let's go."

Ninety-three

Paolo Morelli was dressed in a fashionable new frock coat and vest as he entered the noisy café on bustling Woodward Avenue in Detroit. His family was happy to have him back and, now that the cholera epidemic was starting to recede, he would have a great life in the city. No more digging graves out on the windy prairie in Upper Canada. He didn't need that. He was going to get on with his life.

The city was booming. Along with Chicago and St. Louis, Detroit sat on the western edge of civilization for most Americans, and large fortunes were being made every day. The good people of Detroit society were out and about, and Paolo quickly spied two very attractive young ladies sitting at a table in the back. The band was playing as he went over to their table to have a word and, to his surprise, he was immediately invited to join them. Paolo was a handsome young man, and he had a suave, confident look about him. He wasn't rich, but he didn't need to be if he could find the right woman.

All eyes were on him as he danced with one young beauty to Edward Fitzball's song *My Pretty Jane* accompanied by a soprano on stage.

"My pretty Jane, my pretty Jane
Ah! never, never look so shy

But meet me in the evening
While the bloom is on the rye
The spring is waning fast, my love
The corn is in the ear
The summer nights are coming, love
The moon shines bright and clear."

The young lady was openly flirting with Paolo and he was smiling, enjoying the attention as she swirled around him. At that moment precisely, Emily woke up in a cold sweat. It took her a moment to realize that she was in her own bed at the manor and no one was dancing with Paolo. She struggled to sit up as she recited the lines of the song in her head.

She put on a robe and went downstairs. The house was deathly quiet as she looked at the clock in the hall. It was three o'clock in the morning. She entered the drawing room where she found Smiley sitting at the desk drinking tea with two pistols and a flintlock musket laid out in front of him. Smiley had offered to guard the manor in case Daphne came back with the cholera men.

"I can't sleep, Smiley. I had a dream."

"Dreams will do that to a person. Would you like a cup of tea, miss?"

"Yes, please."

Smiley got up and went to the kitchen to get a cup and saucer. He returned and poured the tea, handing the cup to Emily, who sat on the daybed wrapped in a blanket.

"I'm often up in the early morning, miss. I go fishing an hour before sunup. It's the best time of day to get a bite out at the lake."

"It must be nice out there. How'd it go yesterday with the staff?"

"They're all happy to come back to work, miss."

After Riley and Fuller had left the day before, Emily had wasted no time sending Smiley out to announce the return to work at the manor.

"I'm going to have a look at the books, Smiley. I have the farm workers to pay."

"Of course, miss. Mr Burke kept them in the cabinet."

"Do you think I can do this?"

"Sure, you can. Anything Lionel Burke could do, I'm sure you can do better."

"I mean, do you think I can be as tough as my mother? I've heard people say she ran the place with an iron fist."

"Your mother was an exceptional woman, miss. She always treated her staff fairly. Sure, you're gonna make some mistakes, but over time, you'll get the hang of it."

In the morning, the staff arrived in dribs and drabs. Soon the Grenville Manor was bustling with activity. The housemaids were pulling sheets off beds, collecting chamber pots and sweeping the floors, while the scullery maids were busy cleaning up the kitchen as the cook prepared the midday meal.

Smiley entered the kitchen dressed in a black waistcoat and a loose-fitting regency shirt to welcome the staff back.

"Nice to see you all back at work," said Smiley as he put down a tray of empty glasses.

"Ain't that so, Mr Smiley," said the new cook, a skinny woman in her fifties, who was chopping up vegetables to make a soup. Gerty was pushing a mop while the other scullery maids washed down the counters and cleaned the pots and pans.

"You're looking very smart, Smiley," said Gerty.

"Thank you," said Smiley. "Miss Millie didn't come in?"

Gerty stopped pushing the mop and turned to Smiley while the others observed an awkward silence.

"Sorry, sir, but Miss Millie caught the blue death the week Miss Emily was in jail."

"Oh, I'm so sorry to hear that," said Smiley.

"She left her husband with a small child, sir."

"That's a terrible loss," said Smiley, making the sign of the cross. "Miss Millie was Lucille's maid for a very long time. She was much loved."

"She'll be missed, sir," said Gerty, "but she ain't alone. Claudette and Marjorie caught it too, and won't be comin' back."

Smiley nodded sadly. Although he didn't know all the scullery girls, the Grenville staff were all family to him, and he would feel their loss for a long time.

"I'm gonna have to repair that door," he said finally. "I see somebody decided to chop it to pieces."

"That was Benton's work, Mr Smiley," said Gerty.

"That's the man Miss Emily shot dead?"

"Yep, the missus ain't afraid of nothin'. She shot 'im dead in the blink of an eye, right through that door."

"Hallelujah," said the new cook with a laugh.

"Praise the Lord," said the scullery maids, raising their voices in support of the young mistress of the house.

The rain started later that day. Smiley in oilskins drove Emily out to the lake cottage in the calash. Sheltered in the back of the calash under the folded carriage top, Emily was desperate for news about Paolo. She had tried to console herself with all kinds of reasons for his absence, but the longer he was gone, the more upset she became.

They pulled up at the lake cottage, and Emily descended from the calash in the rain. She climbed the front steps and entered the parlour and kitchen, calling out to him several times. There was no answer. After going through every room, she had to admit to herself he wasn't there. There were tears in her eyes as she closed the front door behind her and hurried back to the calash.

"Where can he have gone?" she sobbed.

Smiley turned in his seat to face her.

"If you don't mind my saying, miss," he said gently, "it doesn't make sense to me that he would just disappear like that. After all you've been through together, people take the time to say goodbye. They don't run off without a word."

"I know, Smiley," Emily said, trying to remain calm, "but it looks to me like he has."

Smiley thought of all the people he'd lost on his desperate journey north, brothers and sisters who'd become the victims of slave catchers and misadventures.

"I don't want you to worry none, but he might have had an accident. A fall from a horse, a broken leg, it could be anything."

"You're right."

"Sometimes, misfortune happens to people and they can't get back, no matter how much they want to."

"That's it, Smiley."

Emily looked wistfully out at the lake for a long moment.

Ninety-four

On Sunday morning Miss Emily drove the calash with Gerty and two women from the kitchen staff to the camp meeting at the Smythe Manor. They followed a motley collection of wagons, calashes, and two-wheeled buggies along the rutted track, all of them crammed with families in their Sunday best. At last, they arrived at a wooded area near the house and climbed down from the calash, tying the horse to a tree.

It was another hot day. They were soon perspiring in the heat and slapping away mosquitoes as they walked around the perimeter of the large crowd of farmers, quarry workers, frontiersmen, and townsfolk. The people were watching Reverend Wigan in a frock coat and top hat address the camp meeting from the back of a wagon.

"Keep your eye on the crowd, Gerty," said Emily. "Paolo Morelli may be here somewhere."

"Of course, Miss Emily. I'll recognize him if I see him."

They surveyed the crowd for several minutes before finding a spot to watch the show. Gerty spread a blanket on the grass and the other women waited for Emily to sit before sitting down themselves.

Entire families sat in the shade listening to the skinny reverend with his long beard and small black eyes. A lot of women were holding parasols to keep the sun off their heads.

Five men and women sat on the mourner's bench near the wagon, facing the crowd under the trees. Several of the women were crying and in a state of extreme emotion.

"We have seen a pestilence sweep across our land," said Reverend Wigan, his piercing gaze sweeping across the crowd. "The blue death has cut short many lives, ruined families, and disrupted lives. I have travelled over the roads and seen our brethren abandoned in ditches to die alone — children, grandmothers, grandfathers, men and women of all ages!"

Wigan paused for a dramatic moment and then pointed his bony finger at the people on the mourner's bench, who cringed in fear.

"Before you today," he shouted to the crowd, "sit the wicked men and women who have abandoned their brothers and sisters in a time of need. The Lord protects those of you who nurse the sick, help the infirm, and believe in His power. These heartless men and women deserve to be cast into hell."

There were terrified gasps from the bench and one woman began to rock back and forth, her chin buried in her chest.

"Sin is the one thing that God most hates. There is no want of power in God to cast wicked men and women into hell at any moment. The strongest have no power to resist him, nor can any be delivered out of his hands. The wrath of God burns against them. Their damnation cannot wait. The pit is being prepared, the fire made ready, and the flames rage and glow. The glittering sword is whetted and swings in its deadly arc over their heads, and the pit has opened its mouth to receive them."

"And who stands ready to fall upon these men and women and seize them as his own? The devil, of course. He watches and waits for them like a hungry lion, seeking his prey, but is held back. If God should withdraw his restraining hand, the devil would swoop down on their poor souls in an instant. The old serpent opens its mouth wide to receive them and, if God should permit it, they shall be hastily swallowed up and lost."

Under the trees, a woman cried out and collapsed as her husband and child watched her in dismay. Sister Clara and Juba ran over to her and took her in their arms.

"Leave her alone," shouted the husband as the attention of the crowd was focused on the couple.

"Who are you, sister?" asked the reverend in a loud voice.

"Her name is Constance, sir," said the husband. "She weeps for the loss of our child."

"Well, Constance. I think it is high time you stood up and joined our happy family here on the mourner's bench."

Clara and Juba helped her stand up and brought the weeping woman forward through the crowd of onlookers. They sat her down on the bench and withdrew.

"So, dear Constance, please tell us what is causing you such distress? What have you to say for yourself as you sit among these sinners? Our community is in peril because of the bad lives of these people."

Constance was a small woman in her late thirties with dark hair and a weathered face.

"I lost a child, sir. A little boy."

"So your son died from the cholera like so many children of the Lord?"

"Yes, sir, but I was not there when he died," said the distraught woman, who broke down in tears.

"I fear you are not telling me the whole truth, my dear."

"I was not there when he died, sir."

"You cast the child aside? You abandoned him in his hour of need?"

"My husband took him away, sir. I never saw him again."

The reverend glared at the husband for a long moment while the man became increasingly agitated.

"You say that your husband took the child from your breast," said the reverend, "and left him to be feasted on by devils and wild animals."

Constance let loose a piercing shriek, putting her hands over her ears as the reverend continued, unwavering with his harsh words.

"You poor unconverted creatures," Wigan said. "Your wickedness makes your bodies as heavy as lead. You will sink with great weight and pressure towards hell. If God lets you go, you will plunge into the bottomless gulf, and your healthy constitution, your prudence, and all your righteousness will not save you any more than a spider's web can stop a falling rock."

Constance fainted and her pain was picked up by another woman on the bench, who was shaking from head to toe and soon collapsed on the ground.

"You must confess your sins to God," he bellowed, pointing at Constance, "and then perhaps he will save you and your husband from the fires of hell."

Emily watched, horrified at Wigan's unrelenting cruelty. He seemed to be building himself into a frenzy as Gerty and the scullery maids stared in rapt admiration.

Wigan jumped down from the wagon and scattered the sinners on the mourner's bench by waving his arms like a madman. He removed his hat and stripped off his shirt before jumping up onto the bench. His eyes were wild, and he began to recite an incantation, his voice building in volume.

"The war goes on, the fight goes on, the devil goes down, the devil goes down."

He repeated the incantation, and the crowd took it up: "the devil goes down, the devil goes down."

Wigan looked like a madman, pulling at his hair and jumping up and down on the bench, thought Emily. She watched him jump down from the bench and, still chanting, stalk the families sitting under the trees.

"The devil goes down, the devil goes down," chanted the crowd.

The people seemed hypnotized and afraid all at the same time. Some of them even bowed down before him as he passed. Meanwhile, Clara and Juba had climbed on the wagon, and as soon as the half-naked reverend had disappeared into the trees, they began to sing. Hesitantly, the crowd joined them in song.

"Come, saints and sinners, hear me tell
The wonders of Emmanuel
Who sav'd me from a burning hell
And brought my soul with Him to dwell
And gave me Heavenly Union."

Nearby, Emily sat wide-eyed and aghast at what she had just witnessed. She was not impressed as she turned to Gerty and the maids who appeared to be captivated by the performance.

"I have to leave, Gerty," Emily said, suddenly getting up.

"Did you see that, miss?" Gerty looked at Emily, her eyes shining. "What a wonderful man, so close to God."

"I suppose he is," Emily said curtly.

Ninety-five

Emily stepped down from the calash near the carpenter's shop. The whole town was over at the camp meeting and the shop was silent as a tomb. She knocked on the door but got no answer. She turned the knob and found the door unlocked. She went into a large room with tables full of half-finished coffins. There was a coat of sawdust over everything. She examined her brother's headstones propped up against the wall. She read:

Here lyes buried
the Body of James Grenville,
Born 1824, Dyed 1832

Emily brushed the dust away from Thomas' headstone leaning against the wall nearby.

Here lyes buried
the Body of Thomas Grenville,
Born 1827, Dyed 1832

Emily shed a tear for her brothers and then moved on to the viewing room at the back. It was empty except for a long table draped in black and a chair in the corner. Emily walked around the table and something on the floor caught her eye. It was a

Spanish dollar, almost hidden from view by the table leg. She quickly dropped to a knee to collect the coin. It was a piece of eight identical to the one that Paolo had received from Lionel, worth eight Spanish *reales*. Paolo had shown it to her when they were bathing out on the prairie.

There was an uncomfortable stir in the crowd as Juba stepped up to address them. Most people in Upper Canada had not seen many black people, and Juba was very black. She had round shining eyes and woolly braided hair. There was something childish about her as if she had never grown up.

"When I was younger," she said with a smile, "I milked cows for white people. Now it ain't often that coloured people get to milk cows, ain't that the truth?"

A few people in the crowd laughed and more joined in as she flashed her brilliant white teeth at them.

"White people always sayin' that the Negro ain't clean and always spitting on his hands when he's working on the farm, but nobody never complained about me doin' the milking. So I was out in the barn one morning doin' the dairying when I had this here epiphany.

"See, I ain't never had no epiphany 'fore. My daddy told me that he had an epiphany when he became a freeman in the backwoods of Mississippi. The day before, he'd seen a family of baby geese in the cornfield waiting for their mama, who was stuck in the swamp 'cause its foot was caught in a trap for wild hogs. My daddy was scared of geese, same as me..."

A laugh broke out in the crowd.

"You don't believe me?" Juba said with a wide grin. "Geese can hurt you real bad, so he was careful when he freed the bird. It ran off and later that day he saw the same mama goose with her babies flying north. So the very next morning, my daddy got up before it got light and started walking north, walkin' and walkin' all the way out of slavery. It took him three months of sore feet to get to the north. That's my daddy's epiphany, folks!"

There was a burst of happy applause. The crowd was with her now, and Juba waited for the hooting and yelling to die down a bit. When she spoke again, her tone was softer and more earnest. People leaned forward to listen.

"Well, I was telling you about me milking this cow in the shed one day. It was freezin' and I was singing this song on a cold winter's day to pass the time. It gets real cold in New York State in the winter, you know. When I looked up from my milking, I saw this tall, white-robed man with long hair approaching me in the sunlight. He held out His arms and waved me to come to Him."

Juba started to sing a song by John Leland.

> *"Oh, when shall I see Jesus,*
> *And reign with Him above,*
> *And from the flowing fountain*
> *Drink everlasting love?*
> *When shall I be delivered*
> *From this vain world of sin,*
> *And with my blessed Jesus*
> *Drink endless pleasures in?"*

The crowd watched, charmed by the young woman as she ended the song. Her expression was one of complete and innocent joy.

"Oh, what a sweet Christ, what a precious Christ," she recited, as in a trance. "What fullness and beauty I see in Him."

Juba looked at the rapturous faces in the crowd.

"I believed in Him and He was so willing to save me. It was like in a dream, you know, when you're seeing things that you can't understand. I was so overwhelmed by the vision that when I looked at the cow, it had turned its head toward Jesus and was down on its knees, cowering on the ground."

Several women in the crowd stood up and brought their hands to their faces in shocked recognition. They had seen cows do that, but they had never been in the presence of Jesus.

"I ain't never seen nothin' like that," she told them. "It was happenin' to me and the cow right there in the shed while I was doing the milking. It was no daydream, it was real."

Juba swayed unsteadily on her feet and looked exhausted, close to collapse. Clara quickly came forward and put an arm around her for support. They began to sing a familiar hymn, accompanied by voices in the crowd.

> *"Whenever you meet with troubles*
> *And trials on your way,*
> *Then cast your care on Jesus,*
> *And don't forget to pray:*
> *Gird on the gospel armour*
> *Of faith, and hope, and love;*
> *And when the combat's ended,*
> *He'll carry you above."*

Ninety-six

As Emily stepped out of the viewing room, she heard the door open and in came Mr Jennings, the bookkeeper.

"Ah, Miss Emily. I saw your calash out front. I just came by to collect a few things. Have you come from the camp meeting?"

"Yes, I have, Mr Jennings."

"They say it is a wonderful thing."

"Yes, they do."

"You've heard that Mr Maloney is dead and Constable Riley arrested Mr Biggs."

"I hadn't heard," said Emily.

"It's been a terrible week."

Emily nodded.

"How can I help you, miss?"

"I'm looking for someone and thought you might have some information."

"Let's go upstairs to the office."

Emily followed the bookkeeper up the stairs to the staff office. Jennings sat down behind his desk and waved to Emily to take a chair.

"I came by because I'm looking for Paolo Morelli. He's disappeared."

"You don't mean the criminal who escaped from jail?"

"Yes, the same man. The constable thinks he's innocent."

"We haven't seen him, miss."

Emily remained silent, trying to figure out what to do.

"Is there anything else, miss? I have a few things to do before I go back."

"Just one more question. Where were your crews working on Friday and Saturday?"

Jennings looked surprised by the question.

"Well, we had several men working in the cemetery, but we're short-handed. The cholera men have refused to work until they get their pay."

"Are you still getting a lot of bodies out on the road?"

"No, not so many."

Emily stood up to look at the map of the cemetery taped to the wall.

"Can you show me," she turned to Jennings, "where you are digging the new graves?"

"Of course, miss." Jennings stood up and came over. "We're opening new graves here."

He pointed to the eastern side of the cemetery, which spilled over onto public land. Emily looked at him, dismayed.

"That seems like a very large area."

"It is, miss," he conceded solicitously, "but I hardly need to remind you how many tragic deaths we have experienced in the last few months."

Emily lowered her head sadly while Jennings waited in respectful silence.

"Mr Jennings," she said, looking at the map. "Can you show me which of these new graves are the most recent?"

Ninety-seven

In the woods away from the crowd, Reverend Wigan was feeling euphoric and light-headed due to the heavenly presence inhabiting his being. He always felt elated and powerfully invigorated after delivering his sermons at camp meetings, even though he might have looked a mess. He was shirtless, his hair was unkempt, and he didn't have a hat. He was returning to the manor house to get cleaned up and change his clothes when he noticed young Betty, the pretty blonde, coming his way in the wagon with the lunch for the crowd.

"Betty, my dear, I need your help. Get down off that wagon right now."

Betty stopped the wagon, startled by the Reverend's dishevelled appearance.

"But, Reverend," she said timidly. "I'm gonna be late with the lunch."

"Come with me, girl," he gestured impatiently.

Betty was in awe of the man and agreed to his demand. She obediently stepped down from the wagon.

"What is it, Reverend?"

"This won't take long, my dear," he said, taking her hand. "Come along now."

The reverend led her toward a copse of trees a hundred yards off the track.

They had just entered the cover of the trees when Wigan grabbed her by the throat and forced her down on a bed of dead leaves. She tried to cry out, but Wigan squeezed her larynx so hard, she couldn't get a word out and was having trouble breathing. He worked fast, ripping her underclothes away with his other hand. There was nothing she could do to stop him. Betty was no match for the wiry reverend with his hard-muscled arms.

It was hot and dark when Paolo woke up in the tight space. At first, he wasn't sure if he was alive or dead. His initial confusion turned to panic in a matter of seconds. He tried to call out, but the gag in his mouth transformed his shout into a strangled groan. He tried to move his arms and legs, but any movement was impossible. The space was so tight that the slightest movement came up against a hard surface. He could move his head a bit so he tried to bang it against the top of the restricted space.

Finally, he lay back, exhausted and lost consciousness. After a time, he became aware of the familiar, bumpy movement of a wagon and the sound of muffled voices. He thought he heard a man laughing. Now he knew where he was, although his mind had resisted the horror of it. He was in a coffin on the way to his final destination.

Ninety-eight

Lunch arrived late that day and was served on long tables by the sisters with the help of the farmers' wives. Abigail, embarrassed by Betty's tardiness, had had a few harsh words with her daughter who now sat alone away from the crowd. Abigail wondered what was going on with Betty, who was always so cheerful and happy, but she had no time to find out when she was called on by Clara to help serve the food. Eleanor stood next to Clara and Abigail in the line of women serving the families, while Virgil sat in the shade behind them playing with his arrowheads.

After the lunch break, the reverend reappeared in a clean white shirt, a frock coat and a top hat. He looked like any other distinguished member of the Adventist church as he climbed back on the wagon and waited for the crowd to become silent once again. The mourner's bench was empty and people were fanning themselves in the afternoon's heat. They were wary of the reverend and feared him. He was a man close to God and a gatekeeper on the road to hell, but now his tone had changed. He was all sweetness and love as he spoke to them.

"Brothers and sisters, there are days in our lives when the Lord visits us. One of the earliest of those blessed days for me was when I first had a sense of sin. I had no thought how black my heart was until that day. I never dreamed how corrupt I was, how vile my nature was, how desperate was my condition, how near the borders of hell I stood till then. That day the light of God shone into my soul and I saw the evil of my state, the danger of my condition, and the horrible rottenness of my whole nature. Do you remember such a day in your experience, beloved brethren? I know you do."

"Hallelujah," cried several people, nodding their heads in agreement.

"Before that day, you thought yourself to be very fine, few were more respectable or honourable than you. If you did not have many glittering virtues, you felt you had no degrading vices. There was much about you that others might imitate and respect. But when that day came, you were ashamed of your self-righteousness and wanted to disown it. If they had begun to preach the amazing mercy and the love of God in Christ, your heart would have leaped to hear the very sound of it, for there are no two things that ever so sweetly meet together like an empty sinner and a full Christ. When a person can look into himself, that person is ready to see Jesus. He that can see his own deformities, shall not be long before he sees the Lord's unspeakable perfections. In that day of self-humbling, and cutting away, and casting down, I knew that sin was gone from my life, gone forever."

There were more cries of 'Hallelujah' from the crowd as Clara and Juba joined the reverend on the wagon.

"Let us sing *A Closer Walk with God*," said Wigan and they started to sing the old song by William Cowper.

> *"Oh, for a closer walk with God,*
> *a calm and heavenly frame,*
> *a light to shine upon the road*
> *that leads me to the Lamb!"*

Ninety-nine

Constable Riley drove the wagon with Biggs in shackles along a rutted track for a mile or two before he parked it under a huge oak tree with spreading boughs. He pulled a coil of rope out from behind the seat and tossed one end to Fuller, who had been following the wagon on horseback. Fuller trotted his horse toward the tree, throwing the rope over an overhanging bough and collecting it on the other side.

"Hey!" Biggs yelled, his eyes wide with fear. "Whaddya doin'?"

Riley took the coiled rope and climbed down into the wagon bed. He unlocked Biggs' shackles from the wagon upright and dragged him in handcuffs to the back.

"My deputy here," Riley said, slipping the noose over Biggs' head, "has told me many times I'm too old-fashioned. He says that we need to use modern law enforcement methods. Ain't that right, Deputy?"

"Sure is," Fuller said with a grin as he finished tying his end of the rope to the saddle horn and pulled back on the horse.

Biggs groaned in terror as the slack came out of the rope and the noose tightened.

"You see this tree here, Biggs? This tree is a hanging tree," said Riley. "It's been used for some fifty years for all sorts of hangings. Innocent men, guilty men, thieves, murderers, pickpockets, Negro slaves escaping from across the border. You can see the rope burns on that bough over your head. A lot of men have cried for their mothers before they were hanged from this tree."

Biggs gazed up at the rope burns on the bough of the magnificent oak.

"Of course, all that was before my time as a constable in these parts, but I have always admired the way they did things back then."

"Ain't that the truth," Fuller said, nodding.

"I got you down for grave-robbing and murder, Biggs. Anything else I should know about?" asked Riley.

"You can't do this, sir. I'm an innocent man. I never killed nobody."

"Fuller here thinks not, and I have to agree with him."

"You ready, sir?" asked Fuller.

"Don't be in such a hurry, Fuller. We're civilized people. Now, Biggs, did you kill your boss, Mr Maloney?"

"'Course not, sir. I had no reason to want him dead."

"And what were you doing in his hotel room?"

"I needed to pay the men at the quarry, sir."

"But you were searching his room before the body was even discovered."

"Miss Daphne told me she killed him, sir. She came by the office with those two eejits, Reuben and Thaddeus, looking for his money."

"So after you got rid of them, you went to the hotel to look for his stash?"

"Yes, sir, but I didn't find it."

"Well, that's a start. You've met the remembrance man, Paolo Morelli. He's disappeared too. Did you kill him?"

"No, sir, that's a bleedin' lie. Did Miss Emily tell you that?"

"Where is he, Biggs?"

"Probably in Detroit, sir. That's what I've been hearing."

Riley nodded at Fuller, and the deputy backed the horse up another step. The noose tightened around Biggs' neck.

"I beg of you, Constable, don't do this."

"Any last requests, Biggs?"

"You got some tobaccy, sir?"

Riley knew the man was just trying to buy time, but he shrugged and looked over at Fuller.

"Fuller, you got a smoke for our man here?"

The deputy pulled a hand-rolled cigarette from his shirt pocket and tossed it to Riley, who caught it. He lit it with a wooden match before sticking it between Biggs' lips. He watched as Biggs puffed nervously on the cigarette, trying to make it last as long as possible. Riley wondered if there was anything more they could get out of him.

"Okay, Biggs, that's enough," said Riley as he yanked the cigarette out of his mouth and threw it aside. "It's time to meet your maker."

Riley looked over at Fuller holding the horse.

"Please, Constable," Biggs pleaded. "You wanna hear a story before you do something you'll regret?"

"What is it, Biggs?"

"See with the blue death in St. Francis these last few months, there are lots of people whose lives that have been turned upside down, know what I mean."

"Go on."

"A person can go through a real bad patch. A man dies and the in-laws inherit, so wifey has to put up with the mother or cousin who hates her guts. Or wifey has a husband who beats her and she wonders why can't the blue death take her man.

Or a man wants to be rid of wifey 'cause he fancies the woman next door, who juss lost her husband. See what I'm saying, sir."

"Yeah, I do."

"Mr Maloney was a man who talked to everyone. If you needed money, you could ask him for a loan. He had a fearsome reputation. I've seen grown men shit their pants when Maloney came after them for payment. If you couldn't pay him back, he'd seize your home and any land attached. Then he'd kill you and your family if he could get away with it."

"I'm not surprised, Biggs. I've heard a few things about the man."

"But the folks around here, they would still come to him and ask for advice or a helping hand. Now with the blue death, people were coming to him - him being in the funeral business - to ask him to disappear a person, you understand."

"No, I'm afraid I don't."

"See, Maloney figured it was a good business. He didn't care how the person died, it was all the same to him. He got paid a hefty fee to collect the body and double for the casket, to put some innocent person in a pine box and dispose of the body in the cemetery. Then the family could announce that old Joe or Maggie had the blue death and went wandering on the road."

"I don't believe it."

"Constable, it's true. It was easy money. Maloney fixed an appointment with the family late at night. When we got there with the casket and wagon, we'd take the box into the house and put the dead victim in it. Then no one would be the wiser when we came out."

"Did Maloney order you to do this?"

"'Course, he did, sir. Most of the time, it was just me and another fellah he hired to help. We didn't know nothin'. All we did was put the dead person in the box and haul it out to the wagon. We reckoned the person was dead and needed to be buried. Mind you, some of the victims were still bleeding, but dead is dead, right? We didn't ask questions."

Riley raised his eyebrows and looked at Fuller.

"The families were happy to see the last of the nasty old skinflint or the wrinkled old biddy. Know what I mean?"

"What kind of people are we talkin' about, Biggs?"

"All kinds, sir. Men, women, the old, the not-so-old."

"How many are buried in the cemetery?"

"Maybe twenty since the cholera started in June."

"When was the last?"

"A couple of weeks ago, sir."

"You're sayin' that Maloney was behind all of this."

"Constable, if you look in the cholera pit, you'll find not all the victims died of the blue death. Some had their throats cut. A lot of grudges got settled this summer."

"Let's hang this man, Mr Fuller," Riley said, disgusted. "Ready to put some weight into it when I give the word?"

"Yes, sir."

"Please, sir," Biggs said in desperation. "I bet it was Daphne and Reuben, who did it."

"Did what, Biggs?"

"Well, after they came to me, they went to the cemetery. I know that for a fact. They probably ran into young Morelli and shot him. Have you checked the fresh graves?"

Riley thought about how he had been ready to hang the bastard less than a minute ago. In the old days, he wouldn't have hesitated. He'd killed dozens of men like Biggs when he was a bounty hunter. Now, he needed Biggs to find Morelli.

"Deputy Fuller, we're gonna go for a ride," Riley said, as he quickly removed the noose from Biggs' neck.

Riley pushed him down in the wagon and shackled him to the wagon upright.

"Thank you, sir," Biggs whimpered as Riley climbed up on the seat and took the reins. He whipped the horse into a fast trot and they returned to town along the rough track.

One-hundred

"What am I to do? I'm a fallen woman!" Betty sobbed.

Her mother, Abigail, and the sisters exchanged worried looks. They had gathered in the darkened kitchen in an attempt to comfort Betty, who sat on a stool near the stove.

"You must calm down for now, Betty," said Clara. "There's nothing we can do at the moment."

"But surely it's time to stop him," said Abigail, who was furious at the reverend for deflowering her daughter. Betty was the joy of her life after she had sacrificed everything to get away from an abusive husband.

"No one will marry me now," Betty wailed. She wondered whether it was her own fault. Had she been reckless flirting with this man or careless where modesty was concerned?

"It's not your fault, my dear," said Abigail. "Wigan is a beast. I hate him."

"You know men, Abigail. If you go at him, he'll just use it against us," Juba said, looking around nervously to see whether Martha was in the room.

"Don't worry," said Lucy. "Martha's not here. She's outside in the garden."

Martha was not to be trusted. She had been seen sneaking upstairs at night to sleep with Wigan.

"Well, you know what will happen. He'll twist the truth with Martha and she'll stand by him," said Juba. "Then he'll tell lies about us when we get back to New York."

"We have two more camp meetings to go," Clara reminded them. "We can't do them without the reverend."

"What about Betty?" asked Abigail indignantly.

"We need the money from the collections, Abigail," said Clara.

"Is that all you're worried about, Clara?" Lucy asked, pouring the tea. "The money?"

"Of course not, Lucy, but we need a plan," said Clara. "We must keep Betty away from him so he doesn't try again. That's all we can do for the moment. Never leave her alone in his company."

"Clara's right," said Juba. "We must wait."

"The Lord is good to those who wait for him," said Clara.

"Ecclesiastes 7:9 says: 'Do not be quickly provoked in your spirit, for anger resides in the lap of fools'," said Teresa with a knowing smile.

"Amen," said the sisters.

There was a heavy mist in the night air as Emily rode into the cemetery on her white gelding. The dew was heavy on the grass and gravestones in the new part of the cemetery. She tied her horse to a tree and removed a shovel and an oil lamp from her bag. She lit the lamp and carried it with her, starting at one end of the row of fresh graves described by Jennings. She surmised that the three-digit numbers, written in charcoal on pieces of cardboard pinned to the ground, must refer to the names of the victims on the chart in the office.

When Emily got to the sixth grave, she stopped for a moment. The other graves all had numbers identifying them, but not this one. There was no piece of cardboard to identify the victim. She asked herself why someone would be buried in a grave with no number?

It was a slim hope, but what else did she have? Could someone have buried Paolo here? She made her decision. She put down the lamp and ran back to collect the shovel. When she returned, she dug furiously in the soft earth. The tip of her shovel struck something hard sooner than she had expected. She quickly removed the soil from around the coffin and dropped exhausted to her knees. She removed the remaining traces with her bare hands.

"Paolo, please don't give up," Emily whispered to herself.

She picked up the shovel again and used it to pry off a corner of the cover. The cover was made of soft pine planks and the nails holding the top in place pulled away easily. Dreading what she might discover, she reached for the lamp and held it over the casket. It was Paolo, his face grey and immobile. She had come too late.

"I'm sorry, Paolo," Emily sobbed, touching his face with both hands. "It's all my fault."

At first, she thought she was imagining things. She could feel some warmth coming off the body. She moved her hand over his chest, feeling for a heartbeat. She couldn't detect one, but she felt his chest rise ever so slightly.

"Don't die on me, Paolo," she pleaded, beating on his chest. "Wake up, Paolo, please wake up."

She waited, watching for even the slightest response, but there was nothing.

"My, my. What's going on here?" said a familiar voice from the trees.

One-hundred-one

Constable Riley drove the wagon in the dark as fast as he could along the rough track to the cemetery. Biggs was still in shackles in the back of the wagon while Fuller followed on horseback.

"Tell me about the last one," Riley ordered Biggs.

"She was an old woman," said Biggs with a shrug. "She wasn't one of mine. Maloney had two cholera men bring her in."

"How we gonna find the bodies?" Fuller shouted.

"That's easy. The special clients are all buried in a reserved section of the cemetery. That's how Maloney charged the maximum rate for his services."

They drove on in the moonlight.

Reuben, in a filthy coat, emerged from behind a tree and stood above the grave, looking down at Emily. Thaddeus and another man approached, passing a bottle of whisky between them.

"Leave the dead alone, young lady," said Reuben. "Gimme your hand."

The two men had parked their wagon near the Maloney family plot on the other side of the cemetery. They had hoped

337

to catch Biggs or someone else looking for Maloney's hoard in the cemetery. They had heard the sound of someone digging in the new part of the cemetery, so they had come to have a look.

Emily was stunned by their arrival. She stood up and started to climb out when the third man jumped her from behind, throwing her into the bushes. He grabbed her hair and started to kiss her. Thaddeus kicked his friend off Emily and pulled her upright. He tried to embrace her, but Emily fought back, clawing at his face.

Meanwhile, Reuben had jumped into the grave and grabbed the shovel, pushing it down on Paolo's neck.

"You want to keep his head, do you miss?"

"Please don't touch him," said Emily, frozen with fear.

From the grave, Reuben grabbed her legs and pulled at her clothes while the other man put his boot on her arm, pinning her to the ground.

Suddenly, Reuben screamed in pain for no apparent reason. Paolo was sitting up in the coffin. He was alive. He had grabbed Reuben by the testicles, squeezing with all his force. Paolo had been digging graves for weeks, and his hands and arms were very strong. Reuben was in a state of shock as Paolo let him go and he collapsed in pain in the dirt. Paolo used the shovel to whack him over the head.

Thaddeus grabbed a pistol from under his coat and fired blindly at Paolo, who had ducked down in the casket. The third man released Emily and ran off into the woods as two shots rang out, coming from the trees.

Constable Riley's head popped up as he fired his Nock six-barrel musket at the escaping cholera man who returned fire with a pistol. Thaddeus tried to use Emily as a shield, but Riley shot him before he could make a move. As Fuller and the third man exchanged fire, Riley pulled Emily away, out of danger.

"Keep your heads down," said Riley as he helped Emily pull Paolo out of the casket and set him down on his shaky legs.

"Keep out of sight. There may be more of them."

"I think I got him, sir," said Fuller, off in the trees.

"Stay where you are, Fuller. I'll come in from this side."

The constable ran off into the trees with his musket.

One-hundred-two

The constable left Emily and Paolo, disappearing into the trees. Paolo was immensely tired and dehydrated. It had taken all his energy to fight off Reuben. Emily held him up and gave him water from a leather flask.

"They found Maloney's body in the quarry," said Emily.

Several gunshots were heard in the background.

"I checked with Jennings and he gave me the location of the new graves. I took a chance. They could have put you in the pit with the no names."

Emily and Paolo stumbled away from the grave and immediately ran into Daphne in her hooded cape behind a tree. She smiled with a menacing air.

"Damn you, Emily," Daphne said. "I had Reuben and Thaddeus go to a lot of trouble digging out that grave so you would never find him."

"Daphne!"

"We buried him alive and you go and dig him up."

"What did he ever do to you?" Emily asked, astonished to learn that Daphne had done such a deed.

"You think you're so smart," said Daphne, drawing her pocket pepperbox and pointing it at Paolo. "Well, you can't have him, Emily. His time is up. He's a dead man."

Emily stepped in front of Paolo just as Daphne fired. The ball's impact knocked Emily to the ground. Daphne, horrified that she had just killed her only sister, dropped the gun and ran off into the trees as Paolo rushed to Emily's side.

"It hurts, Paolo," she murmured weakly. "She shot me, my own sister shot me."

"Where are you hit?"

"I don't know. Am I bleeding?"

Paolo tore at her clothing in search of the wound. Emily winced as his fingers found a bruise on the top of her breast.

"You're not bleeding?" he looked down at her, astonished.

Emily stared back at him, her eyes wide with disbelief. She fumbled in the breast pocket of her coat and retrieved a Spanish silver dollar. The piece of eight was bent out of shape by the impact of the bullet.

"*Grazie al cielo*," Paolo marvelled. "You are one lucky lady."

He took the silver dollar and ran his finger over the head of the Spanish sovereign. It was a solid piece of silver, about an inch and a half in diameter.

"This is Lionel's silver dollar. The ball struck it dead centre."

Emily touched the bruised skin on her breast.

"You'll have a nasty bruise. You shouldn't have taken the risk."

"I never thought she'd shoot me."

Paolo could only shake his head in wonder. He took her into his arms as gently as he could and held her.

"She's mad, that woman. She almost killed you."

Nearby, they heard the sound of horses as one of the cholera men made his escape.

"Daphne will go to jail," he said finally. "You'll be in charge of the estate now. You can sell it, if you want."

"Will you stay in St. Francis?"

"No, I don't think so," Paolo said, stepping back. His expression was serious, but there was a mischievous glint in his eyes. "I'm going home to Detroit."

"No, you won't."

"No one will be shooting at me in Detroit, Emily."

"Yes, that's true."

"No one will be trying to drown me or bury me alive."

"I have to admit that's true."

"I'll be much happier in Detroit."

"No, you won't."

"I won't?"

"You'll be safer in Detroit, but you won't be happy."

One-hundred-three

Three weeks later, the summer cholera outbreak had almost died away. The cooler weather had arrived, and the harvest was in full swing. Since so many men and women had succumbed to the blue death, there were not enough people to work in the fields. Many families had to enlist the help of their neighbours to get the crops in.

Constable Riley arrived at the Smythe Manor in a calash in the early morning to collect Eleanor and Virgil, who were moving back to town. He had found Eleanor a job in the hotel kitchen, one that offered free room and board, and Virgil would soon be starting school.

There were boxes packed up outside the summer kitchen, so Riley walked down to get them. Virgil was outside, playing with a wooden ball.

"Hey, Virgil. Where's your mum?"

"She's up at the house, sir."

Riley picked up several wooden boxes with cooking utensils, clothes, and things, and started up the path. Virgil fell in beside him.

"I found another arrowhead, John."

"You did?" Riley said, smiling at the boy. "Well, you better show it to me. I like arrowheads."

"You do?"

"Sure do. Arrowheads don't fall out of the sky, Virgil. They all have a story to tell."

"What kinda story?"

"A story about the people who lived here way before we arrived."

"A story about cowboys and Indians?"

"Sure, cowboys and Indians, trading posts..."

"What's a trading post?"

"It's a place where Indians traded with white men. They traded furs for guns and ammo, trinkets and food."

Virgil looked up at Riley, impressed.

Arriving at the house, Riley put the boxes in the calash as Eleanor was coming out the front door.

"Hello, John. So you found Virgil?"

"Yep, he was guarding the ranch with his arrowheads."

"I bet he was."

"When are the sisters leaving?"

"Today. Reverend Wigan left already."

Clara and Juba came out of the house with boxes of hand-written Methodist pamphlets and loaded them in their wagon, which was backed up to the porch.

"Good day, Constable, Virgil," Clara said. "How are you?"

"Fine, can I help you carry some of that stuff?"

"No, we'll be fine," Juba said, chucking Virgil under the chin.

"I heard the camp meetings were a big success."

"They were," Clara said. "Thank you, Constable. And thank you, Eleanor, for all the cooking."

"We better get a move on, Eleanor," Riley said as he picked Virgil up and set him down in the calash.

Eleanor turned to Clara and Juba.

"We'll miss you," Eleanor said, hugging the sisters in turn. "Maybe we'll see you again next year."

"We'll see, can't promise you anything," said Clara. "There's a big demand for camp meetings."

Juba gave Virgil a hug as Eleanor climbed on board and sat next to her son. Riley drove off, and they waved goodbye to the sisters.

One-hundred-four

The morning shift was almost over in the hotel kitchen. Eleanor had been cooking eggs, bacon, grits and buckwheat pancakes for dining room customers for over two hours. Hot and sweaty, she finally found a moment to sit down with a cup of tea after serving Riley and Virgil at the kitchen table. They were eating hotcakes with corn syrup and licking their fingers.

"You've got quite an appetite, young man," said Riley, smiling at the boy.

"He's gonna be busy today showing off his arrowheads, aren't you, my dear? Mr Wilson over at the dry goods store was curious about them."

"Mr Wilson is a geologist," said Virgil.

"He's a nice man," said Riley. "Geologists like to collect fossils, Virgil. So I'm sure he'll want to see your arrowheads."

"Any news about the Grenville woman?" Eleanor asked.

"We caught Daphne last night along with her accomplice. Fuller is going to accompany them to Hamilton on the coach today. They'll be picked up by the York police tomorrow."

"Is that safe?"

"They'll be in shackles, Eleanor."

"Yeah, well, he ain't the sharpest knife in the drawer, John. I'm just thinking she's a cold-blooded killer."

"I'm sure Fuller will be okay. He was keen to offer his services after that fiasco with Morelli in the river."

As Riley finished his plate and drank his tea, Paolo stepped into the kitchen and nodded at Eleanor. He looked in better health and wore a new frock coat and a white shirt.

"Well, look who we have here," said Riley. "Eleanor Ross, this is Paolo Morelli. And this is her boy, Virgil."

"Hello," said Paolo nervously, shaking hands before sitting down.

"How is Miss Emily?" asked Riley.

"She's fine, sir. We're very busy with the harvest at the moment."

"I'm sure you are. Emily is a fine young woman, Mr Morelli. She has been under tremendous stress with that sister of hers."

"Yes, she has."

"Have you asked her to marry you?" inquired Eleanor, smiling at Paolo as the constable raised an eyebrow. "John, I'm sure he doesn't mind telling us. Everybody knows he's in love with her."

"I'm sorry, Morelli. Eleanor doesn't like to beat around the bush."

"No, I haven't asked her yet."

"I suggest you make your move soon," said Eleanor. "It won't be long before a lot of handsome young men will be knocking on her door."

"Thanks for coming, Morelli. Have you ever seen a deathbed will?"

The question surprised Paolo. He had always felt hopelessly ignorant of the law when he lived in Detroit. Italian and Irish immigrants in the city were often arrested for crimes they didn't commit and they weren't able to defend themselves because they had no idea of how the law worked. So Paolo had taken an early interest in legal issues.

"A deathbed will is a will that is made when a person is sick and expected to die, sir."

"What happens if the person survives the illness?"

"It is automatically null and void."

"Null and void," repeated Riley, who had taken a liking to young Morelli.

"Yes, sir."

"What if the person who is dying is under pressure to sign the will?"

"The will can be challenged in court, sir. It might not be valid."

"You're very knowledgeable, Morelli. You're cut out to be a lawyer. I can see you love this stuff."

"Well, sir. I would like to study the law."

"What about *Donatio Mortis Causa*, do you know what that means?"

"Yes, sir. It's a deathbed gift. Same principle, the gift becomes yours when the person dies, not before."

"Good, we need people like you in this town," said Riley. The constable figured that it was Morelli, who had found Maloney's treasure trove and turned it over to him. The message about Daphne had given him away.

"I have a job for you, Morelli."

"A job for me, sir?"

"Yes. Let's go over to the office and discuss it."

Riley and Paolo stood up.

"Bye, Eleanor. If I have time later, I'll take Virgil over to the store to see Mr Wilson."

One-hundred-five

Paolo appeared at the door to Wilbur Barnes's rundown shack. It was an old sharecropper's house with weathered wooden planks for walls and rotting wooden stairs leading up to it. The house was nothing to look at, but it sat on a large piece of farmland. When Wilbur came to the door, he instantly shrank back in fear.

"Hello, Mr Barnes. You remember me. I almost shot you at the Grenville manor when you were running around with those cholera boys."

Wilbur was not alone. Two young children were watching from the confines of the kitchen.

"I have some business to discuss with you."

"What business?" said Wilbur, still fearing the worst.

"My name is Paolo Morell. I work for Constable Riley. Can I come in? I need to show you something."

Wilbur opened the door and Paolo stepped inside. The parlour had a large, soot-blackened fireplace and walls covered in old newsprint. There were buckets here and there to catch rainwater from the leaky roof. The children remained in the kitchen, watching Paolo's every move.

"Can we sit down somewhere, Mr Barnes?" said Paolo, moving to the kitchen.

"Yes, of course," said Wilbur. "Theresa, wipe down the table and Julian, get a chair for Mr Morelli."

The wisp of a girl fished a rag out of the sink before giving the table a quick wipe down. Julian brought over a clean chair for the stranger. The kitchen was filthy, but the kids didn't seem to mind the dirt.

"Would you like a cup of tea, sir?" asked Theresa politely as her brother Julian stood close behind his big brother.

"Yes, please," said Paolo, smiling at her.

Paolo took a seat and pulled some papers from his coat pocket as Wilbur sat down.

"I heard your father, Darius Barnes, died of cholera in the summer."

"Yep, the blue death got him."

"What happened to your mother?"

"She died in childbirth five years ago, sir."

"So you, Theresa and Julian are the only surviving family members?"

"Yes, we are."

"You ever hear of a deathbed will, Mr Barnes?"

"Nope."

Theresa was all smiles as she brought Paolo his tea in a chipped china cup with a brown stain on the rim.

"Thank you," he said to the girl, as he looked suspiciously at the brown stain.

"Did your dad owe money to Mr Maloney?" Paolo asked.

"Sure, everybody hereabouts owed money to that man," said Wilbur.

"Did you know that your dad signed a deathbed will with Maloney?"

"What's that supposed to mean?"

"It means that after your dad passed away, the property went to Maloney and his family. They own the house and the land."

"That's not possible. My dad would never do that to us. Where are we gonna live without the house and land?"

Paolo removed the will from his pocket and opened it on the kitchen table.

"Maybe Maloney put pressure on your dad to reimburse the loan?"

"He never told me."

"This is the will that gives the house and land to Maloney. See, your dad signed it back in July. That's his signature."

Wilbur looked at his father's initials on the bottom of the document.

"I can't believe this, Mr Morelli. He had the cholera and knew he was gonna die."

"This deed is perfectly legal. Maloney owns your house and land."

"What can we do, Mr Morelli?"

"This is the original deed. There is no other copy. When I walk out of here, I am going to forget it and leave it on the table."

"You're givin' it back to us?" asked Wilbur, stunned.

"I didn't say that, Mr Barnes," said Paolo, giving him a conspiratorial wink. "I said I would forget it. I never came here, and I never brought any paper with me. You never saw me. You understand?"

"I never saw you," said Wilbur, suddenly catching on. "You never came here."

"That's very good. If I were you, I would burn the document and forget it ever existed."

"I never saw you," said Wilbur with a laugh.

Paolo smiled at the children and stood up. He left the will on the table with the untouched cup of tea, and nodded at Wilbur before walking out of the house. He mounted his horse and rode off.

One-hundred-six

At the hotel bar, Constable Riley was drinking whisky and talking to Eddy, the bartender, when Paolo entered and sat down opposite him.

"So how'd it go, partner?" Riley asked.

"It's done, sir."

"Okay, Morelli, I've got five or six more to go before Judge Waters arrives on Thursday. Let's have some lunch, then I'll drive you out to the Carson family farm."

"Wilbur Barnes got it, sir. That's one happy family. The will is burning as we speak."

"Good, not all of them will be that easy. They've got to forget that their ma or pa ever signed such a document."

"I understand, sir, but couldn't you do the families a favour and simply destroy the wills yourself?"

"It's against the law to destroy a legally binding contract, Morelli. Only the signatories can. That's why I'm sending you out to meet with each of the families."

The constable looked up to see Deputy Fuller approaching his table.

"Constable, I've got Biggs over at the jail. He's found a body."

"A body? Whose body?"

"He won't say, sir."

Riley stood up.

"Look, Morelli. I've got to go. Can you find your way out there this afternoon?"

"Yes, sir. I'll be fine."

Biggs had been humbled by his scare at the hanging tree and had decided to go straight in the future. There was no proof he had murdered anyone, so Riley had to let him go. He had returned to his job at the quarry while a new funeral director was appointed by the Maloney family.

Riley followed Biggs's wagon along the main road out of St. Francis. After a couple of miles, they approached two men waiting in a cholera wagon on the side of the muddy track.

"Well, Biggs, why don't you tell me who it is?" asked Riley as he dismounted.

"You need to see it for yourself, Constable," Biggs said as he stepped down and followed Riley over to a body, lying face down in the ditch, surrounded by a swarm of flies. Whoever he was, he had been dead for a while.

"Is that who I think it is?" asked Riley.

"It's that fella, the reverend, sir. That's what my boys are saying. They were at the camp meetings."

Riley pulled his bandana over his nose to keep the flies out of his face as he turned the body over. The eyes were gone and the bearded face had been horribly mutilated by small animals and rodents.

"I'll be damned," Riley said. "Reverend Wigan."

Riley looked for marks on the body that might explain his death, but found nothing significant.

"What did he die of?" asked a young man.

"I don't know. Maybe a heart attack," said Riley, puzzled.

It didn't seem likely. Wigan was in the prime of life. Riley walked around, looking for tracks of horses or a wagon.

"He could have fallen off his horse," said Riley. "You see a loose horse around here?"

"No, sir. Ain't seen no horse," replied a young man.

Riley did a quick search of Wigan's trouser pockets. Just odds and ends, no money. The reverend was a Methodist minister and should have had a good deal of cash on him for his journey east, thought Riley. He looked up at the young men standing over the ditch.

"You boys didn't take anything from the body?"

"No, sir," said the young men in unison.

"These are good boys, Constable," Biggs said. "They wouldn't do nothin' like that."

"Well, we better haul the body back to town and have it examined now that Doc Walker is back. Maybe he can tell me what happened."

Riley had just about given up on finding anything when his fingers found something in a small inside pocket of the reverend's frock coat. He fished out an elegant, trumpet-shaped purple flower with a cream interior. It must have been slipped into the pocket with some care, because it appeared undamaged. There was something familiar about the flower.

"What's that?" asked Biggs.

"Looks like a devil's trumpet," said Riley, holding the flower to his nose. "It smells like one, too. We call it jimson weed down south. It's a nasty plant to have around."

"What's the reverend doing with a flower in his pocket?" asked Biggs.

"Maybe he likes flowers," said a young man.

"That ain't no flower you'd put in your pocket, son," Riley said. "It smells bad, and it's poisonous."

Riley stepped back from the body and looked out over the nearby field. There was a large expanse of grassland, but no jimson weed was visible in the area.

"I ain't never seen jimson weed out here," said Biggs.

"Neither have I," said Riley. "Okay, boys, let's put him in the wagon."

The cholera men covered their faces and put on gloves before starting down into the ditch. Riley had never seen jimson weed around St. Francis, except perhaps at the Smythe Manor house. He remembered the lush gardens, all in a state of abandonment. Clara and the Methodist sisters had shown an interest in the plants and flowers. Eleanor had told him they could even name most of them.

Riley allowed himself a grim smile as the boys lifted the reverend onto the wagon.

"What's so funny, Constable?" asked Biggs, giving him a strange look.

"You ever hear of a man getting religion?"

"Sure."

"Well, it looks to me like someone held a grudge against the reverend, Biggs. You don't put a poisonous flower in a man's pocket because you like him."

"Revenge, sir?"

"Sure, it's possible. Maybe his past finally caught up with him."

One-hundred-seven

After the harvest was in and the worst of the cholera epidemic was over, Paulo and Emily decided to take a holiday together. They took the mail coach to Hamilton and then continued on to Niagara Falls, which Paolo had always dreamed of visiting. Niagara Falls was one of the seven natural wonders of the world and a huge attraction among Americans, Canadians and European visitors. Horseshoe Falls on the British side was the most powerful waterfall in North America with a drop of 187 feet while American Falls and Bridal Veil on the American side had a drop of half that height. Over several days, Paolo and Emily drenched themselves in spray as they clambered down to observe the cataracts from below and then climbed back up to observe the thunderous falls from above. They enjoyed every minute of it.

After a few wonderful days at the Falls, the couple took a four-hour boat trip on a steamer from Niagara across Lake Ontario to York before returning to St. Francis. On their last day in York, they left their hotel and took a hansom cab to a doctor's office. They made an attractive young couple, Emily in her new summer outfit on the arm of Paulo in his frock coat and top hat. The cab dropped them at the Adelaide Street address of Dr Jakob Becker, a famous Austrian psychologist in the city. The bronze plaque on the wall told them that the illustrious doctor had an office on the second floor.

Emily had written to the doctor when Paolo had started to suffer from night terrors due to his extreme claustrophobia. At first, Paolo had refused to admit that there was anything abnormal about his panic attacks and had dismissed Emily's offer to consult. She wasn't sure how forthcoming he would be in the presence of a doctor, so she had demanded to accompany him. They sat in the waiting room holding hands until they were called by a matronly woman with a German accent.

"Dr Becker will see you now, Mr Morelli."

Paolo and Emily stood up together and followed the woman into Becker's office. It was a large room with an enormous desk covered in patient files, floor-to-ceiling bookcases and oak panelling on the walls.

"Hello, Mr Morelli," beamed the good doctor, who looked like the proverbial absent-minded professor as he sat at the desk filling his clay pipe.

"Dr Becker, this is Emily Grenville," said Paolo. "She's my fiancée."

"It's a pleasure to meet you," said Becker as he indicated two leather armchairs in front of his desk. "Please sit down. I believe it was Miss Grenville, who contacted me."

"Yes, sir," said Emily.

"I hear that you are suffering from some kind of claustrophobia, Mr Morelli."

"Yes, sir."

"Why don't you tell me how you came by it?" Becker asked, fussing with his pipe. "When did it start and how have you been coping?"

"Well, sir, I don't remember ever having a fear of confined spaces when I was younger," said Paolo.

He glanced at Emily who gave him a reassuring look.

"Where are you from, Mr Morelli?"

"I'm Italian, sir. I grew up in Genoa and joined my parents in Detroit a year ago."

"Ah, Genoa," said the doctor as he lit his pipe. "I believe the famous navigator, Christopher Columbus,was born there."

"Yes, sir."

"Dr Becker," Emily said, trying to hide her impatience, "Paolo gets panic attacks when he sleeps in a room with a closed door and no windows."

"Please describe the attack, Mr Morelli?"

"I feel lightheaded and dizzy," said Paolo. "I sweat a lot and have a dry mouth. It's gotten worse over the last month."

"Did something happen to you, Mr Morelli, to bring on these attacks?"

"Well, yes, they started after I was buried alive."

I died in that coffin. I had struggled to breathe for so long. I think my heart gave out, and I was delivered into the next world. I suppose I've always been claustrophobic to some degree, but after the panic attack in the coffin, I lost consciousness and died. Then, later, I was yanked back into a world of pain and suffering when my Emily was in danger. Dr Becker says I have an anxiety disorder of the mind. There is no cure and I may never get over it.

END

HISTORICAL NOTES

Cholera arrived in Canada in the summer of 1832 in overcrowded ships where poor immigrants were forced to live in dreadful filth and squalor. The response to the onslaught of immigrants was to establish a quarantine station on Grosse Isle, thirty miles below Quebec City. It became the first landfall in Canada for numerous immigrants. Ships that had cases of cholera on board were quarantined for fifteen days. Passengers were taken ashore and were required to clean themselves and their belongings by health officers on the lookout for infection.

In 1831, some 50,000 immigrants had arrived by way of the St. Lawrence River and many more were expected the following year. By June 1832, more than 10,000 immigrants had landed in Quebec City and they jammed the houses and filled the sheds that had been built to lodge them. They spilled out over the beaches, the streets, and into the fields where they camped. The onslaught of sick immigrants strained the resources of Lower Canada almost to the breaking point. The explosive nature of the cholera epidemic stunned the citizens of both Quebec and Montreal (population 28,000 and 27,000 respectively). In Quebec City, the death toll mounted rapidly and, after June 15, it was well over one hundred a day where it remained before starting to decline. In Montreal during the week of June 19, the death toll reached over one hundred and forty-nine per day and began to drop over the summer, ranging from ten to forty a day.

It is hard to imagine today the gravity of the cholera epidemic back in those days. In Quebec and Montreal, a total of some 5,300 people died from cholera out of a population of 55,000. In New York City, there were 3,500 deaths from cholera during July and August out of a population of 250,000. So around 10% of the population of Lower Canada succumbed to the disease while only about 1.5% of New Yorkers did. Lord Aylmer wrote that the city had been hit "with a degree of violence far surpassing anything that has occurred in Europe and officers, now serving here, assert that even in India the disease was never so rapidly fatal or so universal in its seizures as during the first few days of its prevalence in this place."

Initially, it was thought that cholera was a disease of the lower classes since they were the ones who were hardest hit. Society soon discovered that the disease was also common among the upper classes. Health boards sprang up to provide advice to people who were cautioned to avoid over-exertion, anxiety and sudden changes in diet and to keep out of the night air. They were told to keep clean, wear flannel and have plenty of anti-cholera medicine on hand. The latter was a homemade brew of laudanum (opium) and brandy. Neither the message nor the medicine was of any help.

Schools and shops were closed while smoke from the smudge pots cast an ominous pall over every neighbourhood. Because cholera was contracted by ingesting water or food contaminated by cholera victims, quarantine alone could not hope to contain the disease. As it struck towns across Quebec, people fled up the St. Lawrence River carrying the disease with them into Upper Canada. Towns like Kingston, York Township (Toronto), and Hamilton were soon under attack. It is estimated that cholera claimed the lives of 5-10% of the population in towns around Lake Ontario. Hamilton, like many small towns, was unprepared to defend itself against the cholera epidemic. It was little more than a hamlet on the western shore of Lake Ontario, with eight hundred citizens surrounded by farms. During the summer of 1832, the port received large waves of immigrants. The first case of cholera was a German immigrant who died on June 26. By August, the epidemic was killing up to sixteen people a day in the small community. Water sources became contaminated with the cholera bacteria, which would get into clothing and find its way into drinking water. Whole families were wiped out in one day from the disease, so people fled the towns going out into the countryside and taking the cholera bacteria with them.

The fear was so great that family members turned against family members, friends against friends, and soon everyone was out for themselves. Cholera victims were simply abandoned on the roads by their families, and wagons were sent around to collect the bodies and bury them in cholera pits.

ACKNOWLEDGEMENTS

I would like to thank my editor Doug Sutherland, my wife Andrée Tousignant, readers Clare Dyer and Carole Beauchamp, my son Thomas and daughters Eve and Josée, and everyone else who believed in this adventure and provided assistance.

THE AUTHOR

Nicholas Kinsey is a Canadian / British writer and director of feature films and television dramas. He has been a successful director, scriptwriter, director of photography, film editor, and producer over a long career. He is the bestselling author of five historical novels and twenty feature and television drama screenplays. He is owner and producer at Cinegrafica Films since 2014 and writes a history blog. He lives in Quebec City, Canada.

His novels include:

Playing Rudolf Hess
An Absolute Secret
Shipwrecked Lives
Remembrance Man
White Slave: 15 Years a Barbary Slave

www.nicholaskinsey.com/
facebook @NicholasKinseyAuthor
twitter@KinseyAuthor

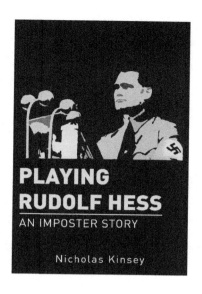

PLAYING RUDOLF HESS

One of the greatest mysteries of WWII

After parachuting into Scotland in 1941, the German Reichsminister Rudolf Hess is revealed to be an imposter. MI5 puts together a team of intelligence officers led by Paul Cummings and his German wife Claudia to investigate the Hess double. They are sent to Camp Z where Hess is being held in relative comfort following Churchill's orders. The team soon starts to uncover the imposter's secrets involving the shadowy Herr Oberst and his secret training by the SS. But the British government decides to bury the truth and it is only in 1973 that a British doctor confronts the imposter during a medical examination in Berlin and discovers the truth.

"Makes history come alive like a thriller"

"Must read, forgotten WWII story"

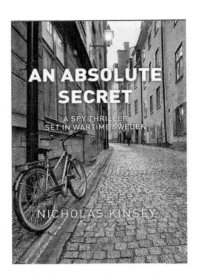

AN ABSOLUTE SECRET

A spy thriller based on real wartime intelligence operations in Sweden.

On his first assignment for MI6, British agent Peter Faye is sent to Stockholm to spy on German intelligence officer Karl-Heinz Kramer. At the British legation, he meets his new boss Bridget, a very proper, smart-as-a-whip, diplomat's daughter and immediately falls in love with her. They struggle to work together as they recruit an Austrian maid, Hanne, who works in the Kramer household. Hanne makes a copy of the key to Kramer's desk drawer and delivers secret documents to Peter and his driver Bernie who photograph them in a shed nearby. The documents are so sensitive they cause a huge commotion in London. With the help of a Swedish journalist, Peter discovers a network of Soviet moles working in British Intelligence and becomes the target of Soviet NKVD terror tactics.

"Kinsey has written a book that will comfortably sit along with the best writers of this genre. I thoroughly enjoyed this book and can wholeheartedly recommend." BookSirens

SHIPWRECKED LIVES

LIVES

A NOVEL ABOUT
THE GOVERNMENT INQUIRY INTO
THE DISASTROUS SINKING OF
THE *EMPRESS OF IRELAND*

NICHOLAS KINSEY

SHIPWRECKED LIVES

The *Empress of Ireland* disaster and the cover-up.

The *Empress of Ireland* passenger liner collided with the Norwegian collier *Storstad* in the St. Lawrence River on a foggy night in May 1914, sinking in 14 minutes and claimed the lives of 1,012 people. This is the story of the survivors and the government inquiry presided over by Lord Mersey, the gruff and opinionated British jurist and politician. He had led the investigation into the *Titanic* and the later *Lusitania* disasters but was sorely tested by the *Empress* Inquiry. It tells the story of the ruined captain of the passenger liner, the woman who survived the disaster and tried unsuccessfully to claim the body of her disfigured son, the Rimouski fisherman whose job was to search the debris field for the bodies of the victims, the Norwegians who were quickly condemned by the press, the shysters and wagon-chasers who fraudulently claimed insurance policies on next of kin, and the inquiry which pitted a multinational transport industry giant against a tiny Norwegian coal-hauling firm.

"Kinsey has written a historical novel that is impossible to put down," Rosalie Grosch, www.norwegianamerican.com

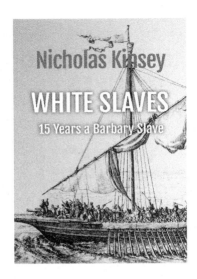

WHITE SLAVES: 15 YEARS A BARBARY SLAVE
The tragic story of the Baltimore captives

This brilliantly imagined novel tells the true story of the enslavement of the Baltimore captives and the horror of the Barbary slave trade. In the summer of 1631, the famous corsair and pirate Murad Reis attacked the peaceful fishing village of Baltimore, Ireland and seized 109 men, women and children subjecting them to a thirty-eight-day voyage down the coast of France and Spain to a life of slavery in Algiers. This is the story of that horrendous voyage and their new lives as slaves in North Africa before they were ransomed fifteen years later by the English Parliament.

"Raw, emotional and gripping are the best words for me to describe it. It was one of those "just one more chapter" scenarios at two o'clock in the morning." BookSirens

"A wonderful read!" Shonna Froebel, Canadian Bookworm

"A skillfully rendered fictional account of an obscure but fascinating slice of history." Kirkus Reviews

Printed in Great Britain
by Amazon

44057864R00219